"I meant no offense, Lola."

Bridger stepped closer but refrained from reaching out. Instead, he dipped his head to catch her gaze.

She brushed a tear from her cheek. "I'm sorry, too. I wasn't fair to accuse you so quickly, either. We've had more than our share of grief and sadness in Quiver Creek these past few months. I'm praying for a better season ahead."

Bridger nodded. "I hope for your sake that's the case." He turned to the tray, his appetite dulled. "I'm especially sorry to upset you after you went to the trouble of this fine lunch."

Lola managed a shaky smile. "I'm sorry I allowed my lack of sleep and temper to get the best of me so that you're forced to eat it cooled."

"Let's say we're sort of even, then, and start where we were a half hour ago," he said.

"Who's to say I trusted you half an hour ago?" Her eyes lit with humor, but he recognized the truth in her jest.

His breathing eased as he focused on her guarded expression. "You offered me lunch and gave me the key to your father's woodshop. At least I'm on the right track."

Books by Kerri Mountain

Love Inspired Historical

The Parson's Christmas Gift
Wyoming Promises

KERRI MOUNTAIN

grew up surrounded by books and storytellers, writing stories of her own since elementary school. But she never thought of writing books until searching for a degree in children's literature. What she found instead was a master's degree program in writing popular fiction. With strong support of family and faculty, she learned to develop the seed of a story into a novel.

Kerri lives in rural western Pennsylvania with her parents on their small family farm, but enjoys traveling at every opportunity. She especially enjoys the mountains of Wyoming and visiting the National Parks. She is blessed by the quiet lifestyle of country living, and by spending time spoiling her nieces and nephews on a regular basis.

Wyoming Promises

KERRI MOUNTAIN

HARLEQUIN® LOVE INSPIRED® HISTORICAL

Recycling programs
for this product may
not exist in your area.

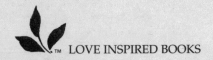 LOVE INSPIRED BOOKS

ISBN-13: 978-0-373-28261-6

WYOMING PROMISES

Copyright © 2014 by Kerri Mountain

www.Harlequin.com

Printed in U.S.A.

You need to persevere so that when you have done
the will of God, you will receive what
He has promised.
—*Hebrews* 10:36

In honor of my grandparents,
Gilbert and Mae Good,
and their legacy of faith, love and stories….

I can't say thank you enough to my family
and friends, who encourage me in so many ways.
With special gratitude for the Whitlock family, who
so graciously reacquainted me with Wyoming's
beauty when I needed it most. And thank you to
Cindy Elliott, critique partner extraordinaire!

Praise the Lord for His many blessings!

Chapter One

Wyoming, 1870

Lola Martin opened her door and raised a lantern, its flame flickering in the cool night air.

"I'm looking for the undertaker, ma'am. Got a body for him." The man's voice was worn and gritty like an old straw tick, but his tone gave nothing away.

He glanced over her shoulder, as if the undertaker would appear from the shadows behind. Light reflected off his brown eyes as if off an empty store window. Desperation lurked in the hard lines of his face, making it difficult to guess his age. A deep scar cut across his cheek to the edge of his crooked lip, just escaping the whiskers that wouldn't hide his stubborn jaw.

"I'm the undertaker. What can I do for you?"

His spurs rattled as he shifted, but if she surprised him, his face didn't show it. He rocked his hat on his head and heaved a raw sigh. "I found a man dead out on the trail, not far from here. Head busted on a big rock. Looks like his horse threw him."

Lola's heart tripped. She wished the sheriff hadn't been called out. Pete McKenna always kept an eye on her place, out on the edge of Quiver Creek. Grace, his wife, Lola's dearest friend, insisted on it.

She'd have to find a way to notify the man's family, and hoped he turned out to be some drifter. But her conscience pricked her. She should be praying the man died ready to meet his Maker. She hung the lantern outside the door and grabbed her shawl. "Let's see him."

The man's jaw twitched. He stepped back to make way for her. "If it's all right by you, ma'am, I'll bring him inside. You tell me where you want him."

The idea of a stranger bringing a "guest" into her home after dark gave her pause, but she couldn't carry the body herself. No one else would be around at this hour. She looked into the man's eyes, seeing the exhaustion shining from their dark depths. She didn't recognize him, probably wouldn't even without the pounds of trail dust he carried. He stood taller than her, though that didn't say much for his height, and a worn hat sat low over his forehead. *Lord, keep me safe,* she prayed. She swallowed hard and nodded. "I'll get the table ready."

Lola swung the door wide, its knob bouncing against the inside wall. She pulled a fresh sheet from the corner cupboard and draped it over a long table in the middle of the room. Her stiff muscles and sleepy eyes protested the work ahead, but she couldn't let it wait until morning. She'd at least clean him up before turning in. And she'd have to talk to Ike about a carpenter. Business had picked up in the months since her father's death. Supplies she could order, but this "guest" would use the last remaining coffin he had made. She'd learned all aspects of the business from her father—except that one. She'd need to find a woodworker who could build a few to have on hand.

A blanket-wrapped body heaved over his shoulder dwarfed the stranger easing through the door. He walked with firm steps, spurs ringing as he trod across the wooden floorboards.

Lola closed the door and followed, lighting more lanterns. She pumped water into a kettle to heat. "Will you be around a few days, Mr.—?"

"Jamison. Bridger Jamison," the man supplied. "Depends on whether or not I find work. Why?"

Lola rolled her sleeves, determined to prepare her guest with care. The slack body swayed as Mr. Jamison carried him, proof he'd lain on the trail long enough for rigor to pass. The head bobbed a little too freely. She suspected a broken neck had ended the man's life in an instant. She donned a fresh apron. "Well, Mr. Jamison, I'm sure the sheriff will have questions, so he can investigate the death. He's been called to help track a cougar that's been aggravating the local ranchers."

Mr. Jamison tensed as he bent over the body, laying it across the table with careful ease. He straightened with slow stiffness and then faced her. "I expected there'd be a man here, ma'am, no offense. I hoped to talk to him and explain what I could right off." He drew a step closer, hand digging into the breast pocket of his long duster.

Lola drew back, hands frozen around the knob of her hair she'd twisted in preparation for the job ahead. The man held out a battered tin star that gleamed in the lantern light. "When I found him, this was pinned behind his lapel."

Time froze as her gaze met his. Her hair fell down her shoulders, unsecured. Lola took the unmistakable medal from the man's rough fingers. She stumbled to the table and jerked the blanket down. Pete McKenna's rowdy red curls fell away from a gash and slight indent near the temple. His normally sun-darkened skin carried the pale grayish cast of death.

A sharp, cold pain sliced through her. "Precious Lord!" she cried, grabbing Pete's collar and burying her face against his chest. "What will I tell Grace?" How could she tell the woman she loved like a sister the baby she carried would never know his pa?

Lola pressed the tin star into his vest. Tears blurred the letters proclaiming the job he held with such pride.

She'd tended bodies at her father's side since her mother died, and on her own in the months since his death, but she'd never mastered the mechanical nature he always possessed when preparing guests for burial. Her empathy made her good with grieving families, Papa always said. Now compassion betrayed her as she sobbed, unable to think beyond the pain of this moment.

Calloused fingers brushed against her hair as Mr. Jamison patted her head. Lola didn't face him, couldn't hear any words said beyond the pounding in her ears and the ache in her heart.

When her sobs slowed to quiet tears, she draped the sheet back over Pete's body. The soft jangle of spurs faded out the door that latched softly behind her.

Bridger trod the grit beneath his boots. He never could abide a woman's tears. And the good Lord knew he'd seen more than his fair share in his twenty-seven years.

He led his horse along the bend into the main thoroughfare of the town, too tired to mount. No street fires lit the road this far out, but he heard lively music pouring from the saloon at the end of the street already.

Bridger didn't feel very lively at the moment and had seen firsthand all the trouble liquor could bring to a man, but he'd also seen enough of Quiver Creek to know this was the only place he'd get a hot meal and a soft bed to-night.

He thought of his brother, Frank, still back at camp rumbling around on rocky ground. Guilt flared, but it couldn't be helped. Hadn't Frank caused the mess that pushed them out on the trail in the first place?

Bridger shook his head and gave the horse's reins a jerk. He knew Frank bore no fault, not really. Frank wouldn't hurt a fly if he could help it. Other folks with their fear and judgment were to blame. If they knew—

He pushed those thoughts away. Things would look better after a good night's sleep, even if he had to go into a saloon to get them. The town sported few busi-nesses, but several buildings looked to be new construc-tion. Maybe a small town would make it easier to hide Frank. Maybe after they settled in awhile, he could con-vince people to see Frank's true self: harmless, kind, hardworking.

First things first. No sense in staying if he couldn't find work, and he couldn't find work looking like he did. He wondered at the undertaker-woman letting him in the door at all. She really should be more careful, especially now with no sheriff. He'd never heard tell of a woman in that line of work, but the strange tone in the liveryman's voice when he directed Bridger to find the undertaker made sense after seeing her at the door.

He stopped at the dingy window of the saloon, hearing the wild noises from inside vibrating against the glass. A plain brown paper with crooked black letters caught his attention—HELP WANTED: Inquire Within. A sa-loon would be the last place on earth he chose to work, but finding a job hadn't been an easy thing. The Lord worked in mysterious ways, though, and he wasn't about to pass the chance by without at least checking it out.

He tethered his horse to the post and stroked the white blaze across its forehead with a silent promise to untack him soon. Bridger walked through swinging doors into a well-lit room.

A bottle smashed at his feet. He stepped back as a well-dressed man tossed a grubby drunk out the doors. The man dusted his hands together and smiled broadly. "Welcome to Ike's Tavern. You look like you just crawled from under a stampede, if you don't mind my saying so, stranger. Plenty here to ease your troubles."

Plenty to cause them, too, Bridger thought. "If you serve food and have an empty room, it would go a long way. And who do I see about the help-wanted sign out there?"

"That'd be me," the man said, his voice rising above the crowd and music. He motioned Bridger to a small table in a back corner. "Let's start with a name, stranger. I'm Ike Tyler."

"Bridger Jamison." He took a seat by the wall, keeping a clear view of the door and the rest of the room. "What kind of help are you looking for?"

Tyler pushed his hat back on his head and smoothed his string tie and loose suit coat before taking the seat opposite him. "I like that, a man who keeps his eyes and options open, prepared. Right to the point, too." Ike motioned a blonde woman with plenty to entice a man over to their table. "Get my friend here a drink."

"Looks to me like he could use more than just a whiskey, Ike." The woman trailed long red fingernails over his shoulder in a way that suggested everything she intended.

"Food, ma'am. I'm hungry enough I could eat a bear down to the bone." He pushed a grin to his face, feeling the pull of his scar. "Course, I'd settle for a good steak and a baked potato."

The woman looked at Ike, who nodded. She trailed her painted nail over his lip, along his scar and around his ear into the hair against his neck. "My, you are a handsome one. I suppose that's a good place to start, but you need anything else, sugar, you come see Mattie first, won't you?" She adjusted her corset in front of Ike and turned with a wink. "One steak and potato, coming up."

Ike watched her work through the crowd with a wolfish smile. "Lots of benefits, working in a place like this."

Bridger adjusted his hat and leaned forward, hoping the man didn't hear his stomach rumbling. But the tinny piano and boisterous patrons drowned most of a man's thoughts, along with everything else. "I'm more interested in the kind of work I'd be doing, Mr. Tyler."

"Hmm…respectful, too," Ike said, almost to himself. "Nice town, here, Quiver Creek. Quiet, growing…new businesses coming in. I have several interests. I'm looking for someone strong, not afraid of hard work, willing to do what needs done, loyal…"

"If you're hiring for personality, sir, I'd fit that bill. But what skills are you looking for?" Bridger stifled the urge to yawn, even in the hubbub of the room.

Ike lit a long, thin cigar and added his own puff of smoke to the already cloudy air. "What skills do you have to offer, Mr. Jamison?"

"I've done a lot of different jobs. But I suppose you could say my pick is woodwork, construction, building things."

"Well, now, it just so happens I'm planning to build a hotel right here in town. Quiver Creek finds itself between the main railroad line and a hot-springs resort being built further up the pass. We're getting a lot of visitors in town. Not all of them are suitably impressed with our present accommodations, you see. We need some-

thing grand, a hotel reminiscent of those back East. I'm
the man with the vision—and financial wherewithal—
to build it." He looked around the room with its ma-
roon wallpaper and barely faded gilding and then back to
Bridger with a grin around his cigar. "I need more than
someone who's good with a hammer, though. I need a
man willing to do all kinds of odd jobs, run some errands, some out-of-town deliveries, whatever comes up."

"What's the job pay?" It sounded crass, even to his
own ears, but his plans required more than a dollar a day
and all you could eat. Bridger rubbed his fingers against
the smooth wood of the table, wondering if the hunger
would hold off his exhaustion.

If the question offended Ike Tyler, nary a blink told it.
"I treat my men well. Room at the boardinghouse next
door, meals here, good wages—" his voice trailed as
Mattie came up behind him, rubbing her free hand across
his back "—and plenty of added benefits."

Bridger thanked the woman for the plate and she sauntered off with a wink as Ike swatted her bottom. He
didn't bother with niceties but dug into the thick steak
and steamy potato. "Don't get me wrong, I'll be grateful for the soft bed tonight, but it doesn't seem like a
real restful spot."

Ike smiled. "Might be a room in the new hotel once
it's completed." He puffed on his cigar, eyes glittering. "I
like the looks of you, Bridger Jamison. It's not bragging
to tell you, you'll not find a better boss in town, maybe
not in the territory. Ask my men. You do well with the
jobs I give you, and I'll see about throwing more work
your way. Ones with greater pay more befitting a man
with your needs."

Bridger focused on his plate—one cleaner than he'd
have expected in such a place—and worked a bluff.

"Don't need anything but a quiet place to stay and work to earn my keep, Mr. Tyler." He chewed another tender bite of meat. "When can I start?"

"Supplies for the hotel are to arrive by end of the week, but there's no reason I can't call on you for some odd jobs before that, right? Why don't you get settled in next door and I'll see what comes up over the next day or so to keep you occupied in the meanwhile."

Bridger pushed his chair away and stood, shaking Ike's outstretched hand. "Sounds good. I reckon anyone looking for a stranger in town might check with you, then?" He tossed coins from his pocket to pay for the meal onto the table.

"That a problem for you?" Ike asked with more interest than concern.

"No, sir. But I found a body out on the trail—turned out to be your sheriff. I would suppose someone will have questions for me sooner or later. I want them to know I didn't run out."

The glitter of coins on the table reflected in Ike's eyes. "What happened?" He pulled the stub of cigar from his lips and leaned forward.

"Looks like his horse threw him and he hit his head on a rock. The undertaker lady, she seemed plenty shook and not of a mind to discuss much when I delivered him." Bridger blinked his tired eyes.

"Lola will handle it. You'll not find many women with her strength. I'll see to it she knows where to find you, but it doesn't sound like there's much to tell."

"Not so far as I could see, but that doesn't stop the need to ask the questions." Bridger smirked. Lying low never came easy to him.

"You think people should be worried about your answers?" Ike grinned.

"I didn't do anything but find the poor guy. But the way I look right now, I don't reckon it'll stop any wagging tongues. If you're worried about the answers I'll give, I may not be your man for the job."

Ike waved him off, his easy smile tight and the gleam in his eye sharp. "Don't bother me none, either way. Sometimes a man with secrets makes him the best asset of a business."

Bridger ran a hand over his scrubby whiskers. "Strange thing, finding a woman undertaker."

Ike Tyler leaned back in his seat, one leg crossed over the other, and twirled the stub of cigar between his fingers. "Well, I think mainly Lola doesn't know what else to do with herself yet. Her father died a few months back, murdered by some drifter coming through town. First hanging we've had in these parts that I recall." He snuffed his cigar on the edge of Bridger's empty plate. "Lola worked with him since she was real young. I suppose folks around here are giving her a chance to mourn and sort through everything before she figures out what to do next. Besides, there's no one else in town. Doc Kendall travels between Quiver Creek and four other towns, so we only see him once every couple months."

Bridger stacked this information against the small woman he'd met. Tough thing for any woman alone in Wyoming Territory. But she hadn't exactly acted unsure of herself. And knowing her pa had died recently, it made more sense that she'd been driven to tears when the sheriff turned up dead.

"You can let her know I'm bunked here. I'd like to get the matter settled quick as I can. A man never knows when he might need to move on. I'd as soon not let that kind of tale follow me, if you know what I mean."

"I understand you, friend. Room's second door on the

left at the top of the stairs. I'd be glad to send Mattie over to air it out for you." He watched Ike follow the woman's form as she laughed and chatted with some of the other cowboys but tossed a wink his way as she downed a shot. "Looks to me like she wouldn't mind so much, either."

Bridger shook his head. "I need to untack my horse, get settled in. I'll be ready to start day after tomorrow, if that's all right by you. I appreciate the work."

"Sounds fine, Bridger. I know where to find you when I'm ready. You do what I say and mind your own secrets, you and I will get along just fine." Ike stood and shook his hand, nearly crushing it. Bridger felt his dark gaze bore into him. Ike jerked him close enough to choke him with his smoky breath. "You do as you're told, and don't ever cross me, you got that? Loyalty is rewarded handsomely among my men. But your life won't be worth a plug nickel if you ever go against me."

Bridger stepped back, a cold grin pulling at his lips. "Mister, all I need is a job in a town big enough to not attract attention to myself. No man has been able to intimidate me since I left home to join the War Between the States when I was eighteen, so you're wasting your time trying. Now, if you want a hard worker who knows how to mind his own business, you got it. But no one owns me, and you best understand that from the start if you're looking to hire me."

He pulled his hand out of Ike's loosened fist. For a moment, the man's eyes flashed hot, but it passed in an instant and he threw his head back with a hearty laugh. "Now I like that—a man who won't let himself be pushed. Yes, sir, Bridger, you're exactly the man I've been looking for. I just wanted to be sure we had an understanding."

Bridger nodded and kicked his chair under the table

without breaking his gaze. "I've understood men like you since I wore short pants, sir. You got no worries from me. I only mean to do the job, collect my pay and live quiet."

He stepped around Ike, tipping his hat to Mattie and another friend of hers as he stomped out the doors. Her coy wave lacked the warmth of Miss Martin's determined green eyes.

The sign in the window caught his eye again as he untied his horse. This was the first notice of work he'd seen in almost a month. The town and Ike's saloon had all the up-and-coming signs that would help him save what he needed to start his own business. Ike's tone set him off, but experience taught him big talk often came from lesser men. Ike relied on others to do the real work for him. He probably pulled that tone with every new hire. With the lack of sleep and food he'd had over the past two weeks, he might have misunderstood Ike's intent, anyway.

He hoped the lady undertaker made no mistake about his. Bringing the sheriff into town on the back of a horse had to raise questions, but his conscience prevented anything less. He hoped Miss Martin found rest tonight, in spite of the trouble he'd brought to her door.

All he knew now was he needed to get his horse to the livery and get a couple hours of sleep. He had to get back to camp and move Frank into town before sunup. He'd learned the hard way, keeping Frank away from other folks—especially beautiful, refined ladies such as Miss Martin—saved a lot of trouble in the end.

Chapter Two

Dawn slipped over the sharp ridges to the east of town as Bridger rode the slopes north of Quiver Creek. His brother, Frank, rode beside him, half-asleep. The few hours in a real bed had done wonders, but Frank hadn't had that luxury. Thankful for the moonlight, Bridger had headed back up the trail to wake Frank and clean up the meager camp they'd set the night before, not far from where they'd found the sheriff's body. He needed to get Frank into town before folks started stirring. It would be much easier to get Frank into their room undetected.

"Frank? You with me?" Bridger asked, his whisper echoing in the silence of the morning.

Frank shifted in the saddle, rubbing beefy fists into his eyes. He blinked dully and breathed deep, drawing himself awake, then turned his ruddy face to Bridger with a wide smile. "Good morning."

Bridger couldn't help but smile back. "Morning, Frank. We're almost there."

"Good. I like town, seeing all the people."

"Shh!" Bridger warned. "Remember what happened in that last town? We need to stay put for a while this time, Frank. We can't do that if you get too nosy again—"

"I didn't do nothing!" Frank protested. "I didn't do what that lady said, Bridge—"

"I know. I know you didn't. But sometimes…well, people don't understand what a great brother you are. They think—"

"I know, Bridger. We're a scary-looking pair, right?"

"Right. Me with the scar, you all big and strong… We have to be…careful, that's all. I have the promise of a good job here, a chance to make enough money so we can afford a place of our own like we've been talking about."

"With horses?" Frank asked.

"With horses," Bridger conceded. He knew enough about farming and ranching to hold an odd job now and then and enough to know he wanted something different. But all Frank wanted was horses to care for. He'd never seen a man who knew the beasts better. "But to do that, I need you to help me. You have to do as I say."

"I always try, Bridger. You're smart. I know that."

Bridger winced. Frank did know that, just as well as those folks who saw fit to judge him. Frank's brain worked slower, and his speech was thicker and simpler, but not enough to make him unaware of his own deficiency. Then, too, Frank's looks didn't help him—tall, broad, rawboned—everything like their father. Before Frank's… before his brother lost that part of himself, a keen, teasing wit and sharp mind had kept the young ladies back home plenty impressed with Frank Jamison. The familiar knot twisted in Bridger's chest.

"I'm just saying I need you to do your job. It won't be forever, Frank. Just until we save enough for a little spread. Nothing fancy—a few horses for you, a woodshop for me. Away from town, but close enough I can sell my furniture to those fancy outfits back East…"

"And some chickens and a dog."

Bridger looked at his brother, smiling at the dream they'd been talking about ever since he'd made it back home from the war. "The way you keep adding animals to the list, we're going to need a bigger barn."

Frank grinned and rubbed his sleepy eyes again. "I'm tired."

"I know you are. We're almost there, and then you can sleep in a real bed and get a good rest."

"Real beds cost lots of money," Frank said, eyes closed again.

"Not this time. It's part of the pay for the job I found. Meals, too, I think."

"You don't have to cook no more?"

"Nope. They have a cook."

"Better than you, right?"

Bridger glanced from the trail to his brother's dozing form. Every so often, hints of Frank's old, teasing self would slip out. But never at his whim. Still, sometimes it was hard to tell.

"Not just better than me—good."

They wandered onto the main thoroughfare in silence, Bridger thankful for the quiet that greeted them. The town felt deserted.

"We're here," he said, sliding down and tying his mount. Frank did the same. "We have a room upstairs here." Bridger nodded toward the dilapidated boarding-house. It had to have been one of the town's original structures. But it seemed sparsely used, if not quiet. A saloon next door made for a rowdy neighbor, but it beat the hard ground and would have to do. He only needed to convince Frank. "You can get a good sleep, in a real bed. How's that sound?"

Frank nodded, eyes still heavy from his early-morning wake-up call.

Bridger motioned him to follow as they walked toward the rear entrance, which lay in shadows from a few spindly aspens. Between the trees and the distractions of a lively saloon next door, Frank would be relatively free to come and go. The notion of this dingy building and the tiny room they'd share being Frank's new prison gnawed on him. *But only for now, just until he settles in—*

"What's this place? People drink here!"

Bridger pivoted, hand on the doorknob. He had hoped the dimness would disguise the nature of the establishment next door. It would be easier to have this debate once they were tucked away in the room upstairs.

"Listen, Frank," he said, moving to his brother's side. He raised his hands to his brother's shoulders and tried to draw him away from the narrow alley between the boardinghouse and the saloon, filled with broken amber bottles and litter.

"I'm not working there," he said. It wasn't exactly a lie. "But the man who gave me the job, he owns this place. He's building a hotel, Frank, and I'm going to help him with that."

"Saloons make people mad, Bridger. Folks drink too much and get loud and fight, and—"

"The owner, he keeps it from getting to that. I watched him throw a man out last night for causing trouble. It gets loud, maybe, but with music and people, Frank."

"God doesn't like people drinking and fighting. I don't want to stay here."

Frank's voice grew louder. His eyes darted while his breath heaved. Bridger knew he had to calm him before he bolted.

He pressed his hands on either side of his brother's head, acting as blinders to everything except his own face. "Listen! Calm down and listen to me, all right?"

Frank's breathing eased as Bridger spoke in low tones. "It's going to be all right, you hear me? We'll be together, and it's only for a little while. We'll sock away every penny and get those horses. I don't like living here any more than you do, pard, but it's the first sign of work I've seen in weeks."

"Mama wouldn't like it, Bridge," Frank said, his voice soft, quiet, still tinged with fear.

Bridger sighed. Frank was right, but she hadn't exactly stopped Pa from spending the majority of his time in such a place, either. No sense in bringing that up to Frank, though. "She'd be sad to know if we were going the way Pa did, but we're not. This is only a place to rest up, lie low awhile, until we can afford our own place."

His brother's dull eyes shifted, trying to see beyond Bridger's hands, but he held firm. "With horses?" he finally asked, his voice softer and not so panicked.

"With horses."

Frank shook his head, pulling away. "No drinking, either, Bridge."

"Nothing Mama wouldn't approve of," he promised. He hadn't ever been a drinker. But Frank had reason to be suspicious, given what they'd grown up with.

"I miss her," he whispered. "Can we go to church?"

Bridger lowered his arms, taking a step toward the stairway. "You know we can't. Folks don't—"

"You can. You can go and tell me about it."

Bridger took his hat off and raked his hands across matted hair. "I can't promise, Frank. But, well…I'll try, all right?"

Frank beamed. "Thanks."

"So you'll stay here?"

"I have to stay with you, Bridge. We're a scary-looking pair, remember?"

"I remember." He grabbed his brother's thick arm and led him up the dark stairs to their room. Frank had sacrificed his independence for Bridger's life. He never mentioned it, and maybe the fact was lost in his muddled thinking. Or maybe he chose not to remind his little brother of it. But Bridger could never forget.

"We often ask the Lord 'why' in cases such as this," Pastor Evans said. "And the simple answer is 'because it's the Lord's Will.' When our pain is fresh, that answer leaves us hollow. It's only with time and faith that we can come away from grief stronger and, at the same time, with greater reliance on God."

Lola shivered in the morning mountain shadows as Pastor Evans gave the eulogy for Pete McKenna. She stretched her arm around Grace, who stood shrouded in black with a heavy veil to hide her tears. Had it been only six months ago their positions had been reversed when Papa died?

Lola squeezed Grace's shoulders in support as a soft wail broke from under the black veil, and she scanned the crowd standing silently around the gaping hole in the ground. The Rigger family looked almost as sorrowful as Grace. They lived farther up the pass and had asked for Sheriff McKenna's help in tracking the mountain lion bent on killing off their herd. Mrs. Rigger squeezed her husband's hand and gathered their two little girls close, no doubt thinking how easily it could have been her husband's body that man had found.

Lola rocked Grace as Pastor Evans guided those in attendance in the 23rd Psalm. Her eyes settled on that same man in question. He stood behind Ike, shovel in hand and hat pulled low. But she recognized the deep, angry scar that crossed his face.

Her heart jumped as his gaze locked on her, surprising her with a warmth she'd missed at their first meeting. But she didn't turn away. Let him know she recognized him. She hadn't expected him to still be in town, let alone be here as they buried Pete, but she was glad to see him. It would make the U.S. marshal's job that much easier when he arrived.

She had sent a request early the very next morning after Pete had been brought to her door. She was sure the marshal would have questions for him when he arrived. She'd like to ask a few of her own, but patience reigned. The law would prevail.

Lola gave Grace a parting hug and kissed her cheek with a promise to visit soon. Her heart ached to watch her friend leave with Pastor Evans to deliver her home.

She waited for the crowd to clear before turning to Ike and his men. Ike Tyler had been especially helpful in the months since her father's death. For as much as Papa had disapproved of their courtship, Ike had proved himself a good friend even after she ended that part of their relationship over a year ago. Papa didn't trust him but hadn't refused her from seeing him. He didn't push the cut deeper by reminding her of his reservations when she'd found Ike kissing Mattie, either. After she broke their engagement, Ike had bought the saloon, and she realized how very wrong she had been about him.

Ike had assured her it all meant nothing, insisting it was "only part of business." While wisdom prevailed, it didn't help that Ike Tyler was a handsome cut of a man and had done everything in his power to help her in her grief.

She tilted her head to see his hazel eyes peering at her. His long fingers stretched out as if to grasp her arm, but he caught himself and held back with a soft smile. "Anything more you need?"

"No, thanks, Ike. I'll gather up the flowers to lay across the grave when you're finished and place the cross." She wiped a tear that rolled unbidden down her cheek. "I wish there were more I could do for Grace, that's all."

Ike took her hand with a gentle squeeze. "I know you do. You will, in time. Why don't you let my men tidy up when they're finished so you can join her now at the church?"

She caught his hopeful smile. He always found a way to give her what he thought she needed most. "You've done so much already, Ike. I don't want to take advantage."

"Nonsense." A smile touched his narrow lips before he set his men to task with a nod. "I've hired an extra man. They'll have things finished in no time."

She watched the men shovel dirt back into the hole they'd dug earlier that morning. The man with the scar was lean and about a head shorter than the men he worked with, but he carried himself with a strength his size belied. Dark sinewy arms poked out from long sleeves he had rolled to his elbows. "What do you know about your new hire?"

"Not all that much—you know how it is. His name's Bridger Jamison. He's new in town and needed work. That's about it."

A breeze caught spring leaves on the trees nearby, brushing her ears with their gentle music. "He's the one that brought Pete in," she said. Her voice sounded hard and flat, revealing more than she'd intended.

"He did mention something about that. I'll keep an eye on him, Lola. You don't have anything to worry about."

Ike smiled, drawing her from the shadows and into the sunlight closer to the church.

"I'm not worried." Well, she didn't want to be worried, anyway. "The U.S. Marshals Office will be sending someone to check his story very soon."

Ike stopped. "Why is that?"

"Because I sent a telegraph. We have no sheriff now, and with the trouble we've been having here, I thought someone ought to check into it." *Into the stranger with the scar.*

A long huff of air came from Ike's tight lips. "I wish you'd asked me first, Lola. We don't need any trouble stirred up with a stranger nosing around town."

Fire rose in her chest. "A man *died,* Ike. The sheriff. We can't handle this ourselves."

"Do you really reckon the man would have gone to the trouble of bringing him in and getting the body to an undertaker if he'd had anything to do with his death?"

Lola glanced sideways at the men working. It did sound a little far-fetched, she supposed.

"But what if he did?" She pulled away and crossed her arms around her waist.

Ike stepped away, taking a look at his workers. He clenched and unclenched his fingers, a long habit she recognized. "Then it's good I hired him. A job will hold him in town." He faced her with a smile. "But you need to check before you go off trying to handle these things on your own. That's what I'm here for."

She sighed. Maybe it was foolish to wire for a U.S. marshal to come all the way out here to investigate without consulting anyone first. Maybe the hour and the man's appearance and the memory of her father's death had made her too skittish. "Well, it's done now. I guess I wanted to make sure there was someone looking out for this town. Especially now that Pete's gone."

Silence surrounded them as the last of the mourners left the cemetery. "My men and I can do that, like we helped Sheriff McKenna before. Once that U.S. marshal clears out, they'll hold an election. Maybe I'll run for sheriff myself. Something nice and respectable like your pa would have liked from the start."

Lola winced. Papa wouldn't have approved of Ike even if he'd been governor of the territory.

"I'll talk to the marshal when he arrives in town. Maybe if I explain things, he won't need to waste any more time than getting here will cost him."

Ike drew closer, his head bowed toward her. "You always were overcautious, Lola. But your beauty made up for it."

She stepped away, staring him in the eye. "It's good you realized my downfalls before we made it to the altar, then." Her voice rose, clipped and sharp.

She caught Bridger Jamison's form in the corner of her eye. He punched his shovel into the dirt, arms crossed loosely over the end of the handle, brown eyes glittering in the moving shadows caused by the waving tree limbs over his head. His scar looked deeper when his jaw tightened.

Ike started. "Lola, I didn't mean—"

"Never mind, Ike. It's just been a hard few days. Forgive my sharpness. I have a lot on my mind."

"Any help I can offer? Say the word," Ike said, his voice soft and over-warm.

Lola squared her shoulders. "Not unless you know a good woodworker. I used the last coffin Papa...Papa made, for Pete."

"You know, it just so happens, I do know a man. I

can't vouch for his skill, but he says he does like to build things with wood."

Lola returned his smile. If anyone would know the skills of a new man in town, it would be Ike. She warmed. "That would be wonderful! If you introduce us, I could make the arrangements."

"Whenever you like, Lola. I know where he lives. You can stop by anytime and I'll be glad to make the acquaintances."

"Stop by? Where?"

Ike gave the grin he used when he thought he had the upper hand. The one she hadn't recognized as a little frightening until after they'd parted company. "In a room at my boardinghouse. It's Bridger Jamison, my new man."

Chapter Three

Frank was due back any moment. Overdue. Bridger didn't like the idea of his brother being confined upstairs, but he'd have to restrict his roaming to those early-morning hours before the town started to stir after this.

Bridger stood at the door of Ike's private quarters. Evening sun crept low through the far windows, but the saloon itself sat empty. He peered into the tree line behind the boardinghouse, praying for a shadow.

With folks attending the funeral today, Frank had waited until midmorning to make his escape. The risk he'd be caught rambling around town increased each time he wandered the back alleys. Bridger hoped Frank paid attention to their grandfather's watch. It ought to be good for something. He'd been sorely tempted to sell it several times over the years, but he couldn't do that to Frank. Something about the soft whir spoke of both sturdiness and elegance, and brought comfort to his brother. Not to mention the fact that even when Pa came in liquored and mean and turned the house inside out for funds to buy more, Mama had managed to hang on to it. That should count for something.

Bridger knocked on the open door of Ike's office.

"Mattie said you wanted to see me, Mr. Tyler. What can I do for you?"

"Come in, Bridger." Ike motioned him to a curved-back chair. Even in the confines of this small room, his boss managed to convey a sense of wealth and splendor in the green velvet chairs and tiny mahogany table. He might live behind a saloon, but Ike Tyler had a taste for fine things and apparently had the means and eye to acquire them. A painting Bridger could tell would not come cheap hung on the wall over the fireplace.

"I have a job for you," his boss said once he settled into the plush chair. "Supplies for the hotel have come in, and I want you to pick them up. I'll have a wagon ready tomorrow, and I'll send Toby along to help load. Think you can handle that?"

Bridger nodded, slowly removing his hat. He brushed his hair back and forward again. "Where we headed?"

"Wilder Springs, next town up the pass. Railroad runs through it, delivered the boards yesterday." Bridger watched him pull an envelope from his suit coat and feather the bills inside.

"I'll give you the payment tonight so you can get an early start. I tend to rise later in the day due to the nature of my business." Ike grinned.

Bridger twirled his hat by its brim. "Toby knows how to get there?"

"Sure. But listen," Ike said, sliding to the edge of his seat. "The mill owner there, he's got himself a poor reputation. If he wasn't the only big-outfit lumberman in the area, he'd be run out of business, I'm sure."

Bridger adjusted his hat before taking the wadded envelope. He tucked it inside the hidden pocket of his duster. He'd never been one for theatrics. But he could see in Ike Tyler's eyes how he thrived on it. "So you're expecting trouble?"

Ike stood and smiled. "Right to the point, that's it," he said, almost to himself. "It's likely he'll dispute the payment, you being a new face and all. You be sure to get everything on the list in that envelope with the money you've been given."

"You want me to notify their lawman when we arrive, ask him to tag along?"

"No sense in that. He's just an old man looking to live out his days in a quiet town, and mostly it stays that way. My men give him a hand with that sometimes, so having Toby with you should help. You make certain the man satisfies our agreement. If he complains too much, remind him that his own wife and their pretty young daughter witnessed the deal, you got that?"

"Sure thing, boss." Bridger watched through the window as a lumbering form that could only be Frank skulked into the boardinghouse. He coughed to cover his distraction. "Anything else?"

"Actually, I have another job for you, if you're interested. You said you like carpentry, right? Woodwork?"

Bridger nodded. "Yes, sir."

"Miss Martin needs some coffins. She told me yesterday she used the last her pa had made before he passed. She needs a few on hand, you see." Ike pulled a cigar from the box on the stand next to him, offering one.

Bridger shook his head. "Coffins, Mr. Tyler?"

"Right. Her pa handled all aspects of the business, you know? Lola helped prepare the bodies and made it nice for the families and such, but..."

"But she can't build the caskets," Bridger supplied.

"Yes. She wants to speak with you herself—independent

woman that way. I told her I'd introduce you, but I wanted to ask you myself, as well."

"Why's that?"

"Some men wouldn't take kindly to working for a woman."

"If the pay is fair, I have no problem with that. Her money will spend as well as a man's, I reckon."

"I hoped you'd think that way. You can work out the particulars with her, but I still want you working for me, you understand. This would be extra, on your own time."

Bridger rubbed his chin and smiled. "I appreciate that. No reason why I can't handle both. I need the money." He glanced around the sitting area. His feet sank into the plush carpet, its rich colors in stark contrast to his worn boots.

"So I gathered," Ike said. His eyes took on an almost predatory gleam for an instant, and Bridger felt the man's gaze pass through him.

He hoped Frank had tucked himself in their room without anyone the wiser.

Ike took a long draw on his cigar, puffing rings of smoke into the air. "One other thing—"

Bridger jerked to his feet. "Yes, sir?"

Ike took another drag on his cigar. "I'd consider it a personal favor if you'd keep an eye on Miss Martin— Lola. I'd feel better knowing someone's looking out for her."

He'd wondered about the two of them as he watched them talking at the cemetery earlier. No surprise a businessman with an eye for fine things would be taken with a smart, beautiful woman like Miss Martin. Still, she hadn't seemed any shrinking violet that needed looking after by Ike. "Why is that?"

"Because someone should. Woman alone out here,

even in a town as dull and quiet as Quiver Creek, she needs looking after. I trust you—and it wouldn't be wise to break that trust."

Bridger shifted his stance and narrowed his gaze. "Trust goes both ways, sir…but you can count on me. If you don't mind my saying so, though, I'd have thought you might want to handle that yourself, after I saw you talking with her this morning."

Ike twisted in his seat to snub out his cigar, his thin lips pulling to a sharp grin. "I had my chance. And it wouldn't be a lie to say I hope to have another. But for now, she'd not stand for it. I figure if you work for her, you'll have opportunity to keep an eye on her for me."

"She might not even hire me, Mr. Tyler. I didn't exactly make my finest impression, bringing the sheriff's body to her door like I did."

"She'll come around to you sooner than she will me. I wanted to be sure we had an understanding about Miss Martin, before you had reason to spend time around her." Ike stood, almost a head above Bridger. "Most men in town realize how things lie and stay away from her. But you're new here, so I thought you might like the information up front."

Bridger squared his shoulders. Ike had nothing to fear from him. Fine, independent women like Lola Martin wanted nothing to do with his kind. Besides, he had no time for sparking a lady. Not until he had a place of his own, something to offer…but it didn't mean he appreciated being warned off like a rabid dog. His jaw clenched. "I understand you fine, boss."

Ike stepped back. "I'm glad to hear that, Bridger. You remember that, and you and I will get along fine."

Bridger walked to the door, pausing with his hand on the knob. "I understand all right, sir," he said, "and you'll have no problem with me. I got enough troubles of my own without adding a woman to the mix."

Under the overhang, Lola smoothed long wisps of hair behind her ears. She placed her hand at her waist and breathed, slow and deep. Just outside the swinging doors, warm dry scents of sage blowing off the bluff mixed with lingering smells of oversweet liquor and cigar smoke from the previous night.

Lola hated this place. Hated the fact it represented the biggest gathering place Quiver Creek could offer and the only restaurant in town. But mostly, she hated that her father had been killed here.

Lola ran a hand over her eyes and drew herself up, refusing to give in to the memories of her father's body lying on the dingy bed, the drunken drifter denying his involvement with adamant pleas.

It didn't sit well that she'd once considered the owner her beau, either. What had she been thinking? She huffed and stepped through the doors, almost crashing into Ike.

"Lola! I expected you earlier. Mr. Jamison should be over soon, unless you'd like me to call him."

Lola shook her head. "I can wait."

Ike swept a chair out with a grand flourish. "I'll be glad to wait with you, make the proper introductions if you like."

She didn't like, not at all. She and Ike had been friends before their courtship and continued to be afterward, but today it only added to the heavy press she felt over the past few days.

She sat and chucked the seat closer to the table. She tapped her foot, trying to think of something to say. Silence stretched, empty and hollow.

"You're looking as lovely as ever, Lola, if I may say so."

She smiled. Ike had said so—often. And to many other women during their courtship, leading to their broken engagement. But it didn't change her reaction to his smile. They'd made a handsome pair....

Light footsteps came from the stairway and they both turned. "I need to step out for some errands before the crowd shows, Ike." Mattie? Not the person she wanted to cross paths with today. Lola tried hard to be pleasant to the woman, thankful—truly—that she'd opened her eyes to the kind of man Ike was. Mattie's personality sparkled. She knew Mattie was more than just a good-time girl who urged the men into buying more drinks, and she didn't envy her the life she'd chosen. But she was beautiful, with well-pinked cheeks, bright blue eyes and a dimpled smile, full of curves and fun.

Lola glanced down at her second-best dress. Faded, flat, dim—like the last rose of summer compared to a spring daisy. She adjusted her skirt and forced a smile.

"How have you been, Mattie?"

"Just fine, sweetie. Business is good and keeps me busy."

I'm sure of that. She shook herself, irritated at her unkind thoughts. Mattie's answer wasn't intended to bring the blush that Lola felt warm her face. But Mattie was just…Mattie.

"See you later, sugar." The woman's long fingers trailed across Ike's shoulders and Lola felt another pang of unpleasantness sweep through her.

Lola watched her sashay out the swinging doors with a wave.

"Mr. Tyler?"

The voice, soft and low, drew her attention. Mr. Jamison stood in the entry, buttoning the top buttons on his shirt, unable to resist a glance at Mattie's departure. No doubt working around Mattie would be one of the fringe benefits of employment with Ike. Well, it made no matter what he did with his time, so long as he would build the coffins.

"Lola, let me introduce you to Mr. Bridger Jamison. Bridger, I'd like to introduce you to Miss Lola Martin, the undertaker of our fine town." He paused dramatically. "I understand you two already met, but for gentility's sake, I thought I'd make it formal."

"Miss Martin." The man nodded politely, a soft smile easing the harshness of his scar.

"Mr. Jamison." She nodded just as politely.

"Bridger, ma'am," he said, voice warm and quiet.

"Then you must call me Lola."

"I'd be happy to, Lola. Mr. Tyler said you wanted to talk with me about a job."

She motioned him into the seat across from hers at the small table. "That's right. I understand you have carpentry skills."

"I'll leave the two of you to discuss business," Ike said, with emphasis on "business." He smiled and left them with a bow and a mock salute.

Lola faced Bridger, feeling awkward being alone with this stranger, Ike's formal introduction notwithstanding. She couldn't keep her eyes from tracing the path of the scar as it slashed his high-boned cheek and grazed the corner of his lip, appearing white against his tan skin in the midday lighting of the saloon.

"I got cut, ma'am. When I was a boy. I didn't mean to frighten you the other night. I expected you'd want to speak with me about that sheriff."

Lola swallowed, feeling heat nip her ears. "I beg your pardon. How terribly rude of me to stare. My mind wandered a bit." She paused, breathing deep. "But it's not me you'll answer to about the sheriff's body. A U.S. marshal has been assigned to the case and should be here any day to investigate the matter."

Bridger nodded. "Like I said before, I'm glad to answer any questions that will put your suspicions to rest."

"*Suspicion* isn't really the word. If that were the case, I wouldn't be here to ask for your help." She didn't add that now, in the daytime, his warm brown eyes hardly looked as dangerous and frightening as they had that night. Still, she hadn't been the best judge with Ike, either.

"Fair enough. What can I do to help you?" He held his hands together, calluses lining his long fingers in contrast to the softness of the felt table cover. Hands used to hard work. They also held a precision, a sense of strength she recognized in her father's hands from the woodwork he had done, as well as the same types of cuts and scrapes.

She looked him in the eye. "I need someone to build coffins for me. A few now to have on hand, and then replacements as needed. Ike says you work with wood."

"That I do. But I've never built a coffin."

"Fortunately for you, no one else in town has, either. Do you think you could do it?"

"I'd need details." He rubbed his lip, without a mustache but in need of a shave. "If you can get me some measurements, I'd be willing to try."

Papa kept drawings and lists and such in a folder of papers at the back of his ledger. "I can get those for you. My father had tools, too, in case they require some you don't have."

Bridger smiled, leaning back in his seat. "That's real good, because I'm down to a hammer and a boring tool."

Lola noticed how the smile brightened his face and hid most of the scar in the happy lines created. "What is your fee?" she asked.

"Until I've built one, that's hard to say. Are you supplying the materials?"

Lola bit her lip. How would Papa have done this? He wouldn't have had to, she reminded herself. He'd seen to all aspects of the business, including this one.

"Generally, I'd get the materials and figure it into the cost. But right now I don't have means to do that." The tight set of his jaw testified how deep the admission rankled within.

She huffed and looked at her clamped fingers, thinking hard. "Suppose you check my father's shed, find out what you need. I'll open a line of credit at Anthony's General Store for you, under my name. You get what you need, and if it works out, you figure the bill into the cost. If you aren't able to do the job, I'll pay off the bill and we'll leave it at that."

Bridger scraped his whiskered jaw. "Sounds fair enough, ma'am—"

"Lola."

He smiled, eyes lighting. "Fair enough, Lola." He stared at her a moment, and she resisted the urge to push loose flimsy strands of hair back into their proper place. "How do you know I won't stock up on your bill and head out of town?"

She leaned back, sensing his curiosity. "If you were of a mind to run, you would've done so as soon as you dropped off the body—if not before."

His smile dimmed. "I am sorry about our first meeting, the way it happened. I hear your sheriff was a good man, and that ain't always the case." He tipped his head, and she found her gaze drawn to his. "But I'm grateful you're giving me the benefit of the doubt."

Lola stood and smoothed her shirtwaist and skirt. She held her hands together, fingers pointed at the man as he slid his chair away from the table. "This job isn't about trusting you, Mr. Jamison. If the U.S. marshal's investigation proves you had more to do with Pete McKenna's death than bringing the body into town, I'll be the first to testify against you at your trial."

Bridger stood, too. "Fair enough, Lola Martin. As I said before, I have nothing to hide."

"Time will tell," she said. A cool breeze wavered the swinging doors. "In the meantime, I need your services. And at the rate of business lately, the sooner the better."

Chapter Four

Bridger's footsteps echoed across the planks as he walked past the empty saloon. Hard to believe this place had been roaring into the wee hours of the morning. Every chair sat on a tabletop, legs pointed upward like a beetle on its back, blacker than the dark gray of morning. Without question, Ike hired diligent workers. And Mr. Tyler paid well, if talk could be trusted. So long as Frank had a bed and a roof over his head, and didn't cause a fuss in town, Bridger planned to work until he saved up for a little spread of their own.

Building coffins in his spare time would hasten that dream. He wasn't sure exactly how things stood between his boss and Lola, but he had to admit, spending time in a woodshop, in close proximity to a woman of Miss Martin's caliber, held high appeal. Even if he built something as mundane as a coffin.

Lola certainly could capture a man's attention. Bridger hadn't spent much time around women of her status, especially of late, but there was no denying her strength, taking on her father's business as she had. Not to mention the fact her black hair glistened like a moonlit river.

Bridger planned to arrive at the livery in time to have

the horses tacked and ready, but Toby surprised him, having the job already started when he pulled the livery door open with a rumbling screech.

"Morning," he greeted. "I meant to beat you here."

Toby yawned, ending in a scowl under his long mustache as prickly as the man's personality. "When you're new, Boss won't let you do anything without one of us watching."

Bridger stepped into the lantern's glow and took up a harness for the second horse. "That go for when I'm on the job or for everything?"

Toby's frown deepened, clearly not happy to be awake this early in the day. "When you work for Mr. Tyler, boy, the job *is* everything."

Bridger focused on the lines, refusing to be baited. "You make it sound like a death sentence."

Toby lifted his head, his heavy eyes piercing through the dimness. "Only for the man who doesn't live up to Ike's expectations." He turned his gaze to the horse and seemed to ease back. "Boss has high hopes for you. You do what you're told, he'll soon have you working on your own. But for now, you're stuck with me at this forsaken hour of the day."

"Not a morning person, I take it."

Toby climbed the wagon, handing him a crumpled paper. "Don't be funny. I suppose you can follow directions, so shut up and drive. Wake me if you get lost."

Toby was not happy about his early-morning assignment, no bones about it. Bridger couldn't help but hide a smile. Toby's head start meant they'd get back to Quiver Creek sooner than he'd expected, and maybe he could stop and check out Lola's woodshed and tools. He wasn't one to chalk up everything that happened to divine providence like Frank did and like Ma had. But thinking of how things had changed in just a few days' time, he'd be a fool to not consider the Lord might be looking out for them after all.

Bridger prayed he could save the money they needed for that ranch they'd been dreaming of before the Lord took a notion to slap him back to where he'd been.

Bridger dragged his hand along the taut skin of his scar. He'd chalked up Ike's warning about this particular businessman to the boss's flair for drama. Unfortunately...

"You listen here, mister. I don't know what game you think you're playing, but there's no way you're getting all those boards for what you brought in that envelope. So you either take what's been loaded or head back for the rest of the money you owe."

Bridger slid his hat back on his head. He hadn't even bothered to count the money in the envelope Ike had given him the night before. This was Mr. Tyler's deal, after all, and delivery was his end of the job. "All I know, sir, is that I'm to deliver this list of supplies to my boss for the money you agreed upon, and that's in the envelope I handed you." He looked back at Toby, who leaned against the side of the wagon with a raw smirk splitting the bushy space between his mustache and beard. No help there. Apparently, results of this test would be part of Toby's report to Ike.

"I'm new in these parts, but I've already heard tell about the way you conduct business, sir. I'm not about to lose my job by not bringing back everything my boss paid for. So you let us load the rest of this now, and we'll be on our way."

Earl Johnston's face turned a fine shade of purple. His lips scrunched in fury, and his shoulders fairly shook with anger. Bridger rolled to the balls of his feet, ready to duck the swing he felt coming.

Instead, the man spun on his heel and headed into the mill's office. Bridger turned to Toby, who eased off the wagon to help load the second half of the supplies they'd been sent to pick up.

Bridger stooped to gather his end of a thick stack of boards. A sudden shot kicked dirt at his feet, and he dropped his end and grabbed the edge of the wagon box to keep from kissing dust.

Mr. Johnston stood in the doorway with a revolver. "I'll not stand by and watch you rob me blind. I don't care if you're working for Ike Tyler or the president of the United States!"

Bridger pivoted on his boot heels and stood, hands raised. By the look on his face, the shot surprised Johnston about as much as it had him. But his aim showed it wasn't the first time he'd used a gun to intimidate his way through a corrupt business deal.

Bridger slid toward him. "Listen, mister, there's no need for that. Mr. Tyler paid your asking price for all the items on this list." He took another step, slow and steady, as Johnston's revolver wavered. "I'm just a man looking to do the job he's been sent to do."

He struck out to grab the man's gun hand and dropped, pulling Johnston's arm until his body twisted and slammed into the rough board side of the mill. The gun slipped and Bridger held it in his left hand. He pinned the man against the wall, using his knees to prevent the man from kicking. Johnston's ragged breath echoed in harsh pants. "And I ain't about to fail because you plan to back out of your contract."

He leaned close to the man's ear and growled. "Especially when it's my understanding that your own wife and daughter stood as witness to the deal."

He felt it then, a sharp tenseness in the muscles, followed by a rigid slackness. He shoved harder. "You have any problems with that, you talk them over with Mr. Tyler. You understand me?"

The man nodded, face still scraped against the jamb. "I understand." His voice shook. "I understand you just fine."

Bridger eased off the man's back. Johnston twisted and pointed the revolver toward the clouds. "Next time Mr. Tyler has business with you, I'll forget his idea and bring the law with me anyway."

Johnston released the trigger with a laugh that sounded more like a bark. "If we had any law to speak of around here, mister, I'd have invited him myself." He slumped, revolver hanging loose at his side. "You tell Mr. Tyler this was all a misunderstanding, you hear? There's no need to involve my family."

Bridger backed away. "So long as we get what we came for, Mr. Johnston, I see no reason to mention our misunderstanding to anyone."

A twinge of relief crossed the man's haggard features. "I'd appreciate that, sir," he ground out.

Toby sauntered forward to help load the remainder of the supplies onto the wagon. "You surprise me, Jamison." The hair around his lips split to allow a toothy grin through. "Never expected you to move that fast. Ike'll be happy to hear how well you handled yourself."

Bridger looked across to Earl Johnston, slightly stooped and rubbing his neck where he'd pressed the man into the wall. Something strange about that man, for certain. It was a wonder he did any business with the temper he held. "Ah, he was fired up, but he didn't want to hurt us.

We got what we came for, anyway, and we had the original agreement on our side. Good thing Mr. Tyler warned me about him, though. It could have turned out a lot more painful for us."

Toby's eyes took on a peculiar gleam and he stared at Bridger a moment. "I'm catching on to what the boss sees in you, Jamison. I understand what he's found. You do as you're told, there's no telling where you'll end up." He laughed out loud, tossing the last small stack of lumber on the wagon bed and clambering to the high seat. "No telling at all."

Grace's pale, drawn appearance broke Lola's heart. She hadn't been to town since the funeral a few days ago. With her usually vibrant blond hair and sparkling blue eyes looking faded and dim, Grace seemed a washed-out version of her former self. Lola pushed a plate of freshly baked cookies closer to her friend.

"When are your parents due to arrive?" Lola asked, pouring some steaming tea.

Grace took the cup and wrapped her slender fingers around it, seeking greater warmth. "They should be here early next week."

"And they'll stay until the baby is born?" Lola took a seat opposite her friend at the small table near the window. Glimmers of sunshine dappled the tablecloth through the lace curtain.

"Ma says they'll stay until they can convince me to come back home." Grace took a sip, then set the cup against the delicate saucer with a rattle, her eyes focused on some distant point beyond the windowpane.

Lola bit her lip. "Do you suppose they'll have a hard time of it? Convincing you, I mean?"

A tremor passed through Grace, as if she awakened

from a trance. "I haven't thought of much beyond the fact that Pete's really gone and not coming home."

Lola leaned back and sighed. It was selfish to want Grace to stay. She'd been told often enough in the months since Papa died that Quiver Creek was no place for a woman alone. But at least she had the business. Grace had a ranch to run and a baby on the way.

"How are you managing out there in the meantime?"

Grace rimmed the gilding on the cup with her finger. "One day at a time. Pete's parents have been wonderful, of course. His brother comes out each evening to check the animals and see that I want for nothing. He's only fourteen, but a very sweet and capable young man. Just too young to tend to all the details of the ranch, and with spring roundup coming, he can't manage alone. My pa plans to take care of that, hire wranglers to brand the calves and move the herd out for summer grazing."

"Your father's a shopkeeper, Grace. How does he feel about taking this on?"

Grace broke a crumb off her cookie and nipped it into her mouth, swallowing before the sweetness could barely register on her tongue. "From Ma's letter, I think he's honestly excited about getting into the saddle again. He grew up on a ranch in Texas and spent some time cowboying before he met Ma."

"So, do you think you'll stay on until the baby is born, or are you planning to be back East before that?" Lola asked, fighting the tears in her voice.

Grace's eyes darted, a spark of surprise lighting them briefly. "I'm not leaving."

"But you said your parents were only staying until—"

"They're determined to take me home with them. But I can't leave here, not now."

"But then—"

Grace sighed and leaned back in her seat, rubbing a hand over her growing stomach. Afternoon sunlight slanted through the window, making her appear even more wan and washed-out than before but giving her eyes a light of determination. "I'm not sure exactly what I will do, but I can't just walk away from all Pete and I have. McKennas have ranched this area from way back. A boy deserves the chance to claim that inheritance."

Tears washed over Lola's vision. Pete had been so sure Grace carried a son. "But what if the baby is a girl? And what about you?"

Grace shook her head, as if tossing away any threat to her determination. "I'm trusting the Lord to give me wisdom. But I don't want to leave. The mountains around here…there's something about them that settles in your soul. I couldn't live without them, I don't think."

Lola nodded. Leaving Wyoming had never occurred to her as an option, either. "You'd be welcome to stay with me, for as long as you need. There's plenty of room. You could—"

Grace's lips pulled in a shadow of her usual smile. "I appreciate that, and I know you mean it with all your heart. But I'm staying in our house. Pete built it for me, and we've filled it with so many memories in such a brief time. I feel close to him here. I want that for our baby. I'll sell off the land and keep the house if it comes to that, but Lord help me, I'll raise this child in the home we built together."

Lola glanced around her own house. What would it be like to build a life with someone you loved the way Pete had loved Grace? Suddenly her own house felt a little empty, even with her dearest friend sitting beside her.

"Talk to me about something else. I want to think about something other than being sad."

Lola stood to refill her cup and warmed Grace's by filling hers to the brim. Topics from town whirled through her mind, but all connected in some way to Pete, his job, how he died and her part in it. Silence grew awkward, but no words came. She faced her friend but avoided her gaze.

"I know." Grace's whisper rasped with sorrow. "But I want to know what's happening, what people are doing in town. It hurts, but in some ways, I like hearing that Pete was so respected, so vital to this town, that he's still connected with it, even after his death. Right now it hurts so bad that not much helps, except to know that. Am I making any sense?"

Lola nodded. Tears slipped from her eyes and she grasped Grace's hand with a fierce squeeze. "I'm just so sorry I couldn't do something for him."

"Oh, Lola!" Grace slid to her feet and came around the table to embrace Lola in her tired arms. "Even if you had been the greatest doctor in the world, he was gone by the time you saw him. Trust me, I thank God you could do what you did. You spared me from seeing the tragedy of his death. Instead he looked restful, at peace, the way his spirit looks before the Lord."

Grace's warm tears mixed with hers against Lola's cheek. She squeezed her friend's arm. "This isn't how it's to be, you comforting me. What kind of friend am I?"

Grace slid back into her chair and took a sip of tea. "The kind who wants to spare me and everyone else around any hurt. You do that very well. But I want to know what you've been doing. I'm not ready to join into the lively rush of town yet, but I can't shut myself off from living. I want to, but Pete wouldn't want that for me." She smoothed her dress over their growing baby. "He wouldn't want that for us."

Lola patted the ruffled edge of a doily lying in the

center of the table. "A U.S. marshal should arrive early next week to talk with the man who brought Pete to me." She sipped her cooling tea without looking at her friend.

"U.S. marshal?" Grace's eyes were wide, and her face grew a shade paler if that were possible. "What's going on, Lola?"

Lola abandoned her teacup with a wave of her hand and grasped Grace's wrist with the other. "Nothing, Grace. I panicked. Papa's gone, it was late, a frightful-looking stranger brings the sheriff to my door... I sent a telegraph first thing the next morning."

Grace slumped in her seat, taking a deep, calming breath. "I can understand that. But you don't really think...?"

What did she think? Did she believe Bridger Jamison to be a murderer? Not really. But she wasn't always the best judge of a man, either. And some of Pete's bruises seemed...odd, not quite consistent for a man thrown from a horse. Not unusual enough to point any fingers, but something definitely felt out of place. Without facts, though, she didn't dare share those concerns with Grace.

"I acted without thinking things completely through. It won't hurt to have a U.S. marshal investigate what happened, though." She took another drink of her tea and looked Grace squarely in the eye. "But, no, in talking more with Mr. Jamison, I can't find anything overly suspicious about him regarding Pete's death. And the fact that he's sticking around town, I suppose, holds greater weight for his innocence than anything else."

Grace held a hand to her mouth and breathed deep, eyes closed. "Good—that's good. It was hard enough losing your father that way. I wouldn't want..."

Lola let the words fade. "I hired Mr. Jamison. Papa never taught me the woodworking aspect of... I never learned how..." Everything about her business sounded cold and crass in her thoughts. Why hadn't she chosen weather as the topic of conversation?

"Your father never taught you how to build the coffins," Grace supplied. She smiled again, briefly, a narrow moon of teeth peeking through this time. "He always said you'd nail your own thumb to the casket."

Lola smiled, too. "He was probably right. He just always figured he'd be around to do the job, I guess."

"He knew you'd be able to find someone to do that. The part you do takes something that not everyone has." Grace stretched across the table to squeeze her hand, looking her in the eye. "I'm glad it was you, Lola. I know it wasn't easy for you, but I'm glad that man found a way to bring Pete to you."

An odd scrape from outside jolted them. Lola started to her feet and made short, clipped steps to the rear door. She glanced at her friend, standing by the table with hands twisted in front of her, and motioned for Grace to stay quiet. Slowly she lifted the latch, then jerked the door wide. "Who's there?"

Magpies chatting on the fence were the only sound to greet her. She poked her head out and searched the shadows around the lone shed where her father had his woodshop. After a few moments she returned to the cozy room and shut the door.

"Whew!" Grace let loose a nervous giggle, fingers laid against her long throat, her other hand resting on her stomach. "Do you feel as silly as I do?"

Lola brushed long, loose hair behind her ears. "I'm not so sure it's only silliness."

Grace gripped the table and sat down. "What are you saying?"

"Nothing," Lola said, shaking her head. "Just my overactive imagination, I suppose. I've been more nervous than I ought to be lately—"

"Thinking you're here on the end of a town that no longer has a sheriff to keep his eye on you. Is that it?"

Grace always could make the right conclusions about her, before she said a word about the problem. She laughed. "Probably the neighbor's cat I never paid any mind to before, that's all." Lola peered at the lengthening shadows as afternoon slipped away. "God will be my protection now, same as always. I'm in His hands."

Grace took in the lowering sun outside the window, too, and stood again to gather her things. "That's all that can be said for any of us." Grace's cool kiss pressed against her cheek. "This visit has done more for me than you know, my friend. But if I want to be home before dark, I need to head out now."

"The Lord has comfort and wisdom for you, Grace. Hold on to that."

"I will. Please say you'll come out for a visit next week," Grace said, pulling a shawl over her shoulders.

"Your folks will be there. I don't want to intrude," Lola said.

"You're the sister I never had, Lola. You're my family, too, and I'm inviting you for lunch next Thursday. How's that?"

Grace's determination to stay cheerful and strong couldn't be denied, and Lola wouldn't do anything to take that from her. She couldn't promise what next week would hold, but she couldn't bear to bring up her work again. "I'll try."

Grace focused on the door leading to the mortuary for an instant, then forced her gaze away. "I know you will. I'll be waiting for you."

Lola walked her to the side door and watched her rumble into the cart, hefting the reins in her gentle hands. "See you next week, then."

"I'll expect you unless you send word, all right?" Grace called.

Lola nodded.

Grace moved to slap the reins, then pulled them taut. "I'm glad you'll have a man working around here. If he's a trustworthy man, he may scare off any who aren't, make you feel safer."

Lola smiled, thinking of Bridger's strength in helping her that night and the gentleness he had shown both to Pete and to her. Yet her wariness also raised caution. "And what if he's not the trustworthy sort?"

Grace grinned, a hint of her old teasing self peeking through the grief that shrouded her. "Then it may be just as well you have him where you can keep an eye on him."

Lola laughed and waved her off. She moved back into the house, leaning against the door and saying a swift and silent prayer for her friend.

She added one for herself, then bolted all the doors.

Chapter Five

Bridger pulled the horses to a halt as the sun dipped below the mountains to the west, peeking between snowcaps. He spotted the large lot in the center of town where Ike planned to build his fancy hotel, with supplies guarded by his men. Bridger's jawbone ached, riding all the way from Wilder Springs with Toby's cantankerous load growling in the seat beside him.

He set the brake and hopped from the seat. "This is the rest of them, fellows."

Toby scowled and shifted his bulky frame to the ground.

"Get on. Tell Ike I'll be along shortly to give *my* report of the day."

Toby stalked down the dusty street, the sharp rays of sunset hiding his heavy tread. No matter how it came about, a break from Toby merited every particle of gratitude Bridger could muster.

Bridger washed his dusty hands in the trough and slicked limp hair back under his hat. He'd done what he'd been asked to do, and done it well, which only added to Toby's ire. The man probably thrived on delivering less-than-stellar reports on every new man.

It made no matter to him. All he wanted was a hot meal. Frank would be starving about now.

Lola's home sat out of sight of the hotel lot, around the bend leading away from town. Awful strange vocation for a woman. Bridger felt a certain uneasiness to wonder how she could sleep in that house alone with a dead person in the next room. He shook his head. He had no call to judge. The idea of home depended on what a body grew used to, he supposed.

Many times a dead man would've been preferable to sharing a home with his father growing up.

Dusk settled over the town. The sky above still held the brilliance of a clear day, but the mountains already blocked the sun's long rays. No street fires had been lit yet, but Ike would probably set his men on it before long.

Bridger nodded to Mattie as he ducked into the slow-filling saloon. "Hey, sugar, Ike's in his office. He told me to send you in straightaway."

"Sure thing, ma'am. That's where I'm headed."

"'Ma'am'? I sure ain't no friend of your ma, darlin'. You'd best call me Mattie, same as everyone else." She stepped around the counter and grabbed his arm in one hand while her other slid across his chest, her eyes gleaming. "Most fellows around here are happy to be on a first-name basis with me," she said with a wink.

He couldn't help but smile at her. Mattie had spark. Add to the fact she knew how to dress her beauty to her own advantage, and it wasn't hard to see why Ike's tavern packed folks in until the wee hours. But he had more on his mind than playing her games, tempting as they were.

He hoped this meeting with Ike didn't last long. It wouldn't do for Frank to wander in search of his own meal. It wasn't fair to keep him confined there for so many hours. But in Frank's case, not much was fair. *It's only for a time,* he reminded himself.

Bridger knocked on the door to Ike's office and opened it at his muffled invitation.

Tyler waited behind his desk, reading some kind of ledger by lantern light. "I'm on my way out to greet the crowd. How'd it go today? Any trouble?"

"No more than what you expected. We brought back all you ordered, sir. That's the main thing." Bridger removed his hat and stood, feeling drops of water from his still-damp hair sinking into his dusty collar.

"So Johnston gave you trouble?" Ike asked, and the eagerness of his tone grated on Bridger's frustration.

"I handled it, sir. And I appreciate the warning." He smacked his hat against his leg to air it out. "Toby and the others are unloading supplies now, but you said you wanted to see me as soon as we made it back."

Ike grinned and stood. "I wanted to hear how things went and to give you this for today."

Bridger opened the envelope Tyler handed him. Five dollars? "What's this for?"

"Today's pay. Starting tomorrow, you'll be on the roster, get paid regular every Friday. Today was the start of those extra jobs I mentioned. Thought it might help if you had a little cash in your pocket."

Bridger slipped his hat back on his head. "Five dollars for one trip?"

"I told you, I treat my men well. If you brought back everything on that list, it's nothing compared to what you saved if Mr. Johnston had decided not to honor our agreement. Regular wages are a dollar a day, plus room and board, but you show me you can handle it, I'll have plenty extra jobs to pass along."

"I'd appreciate that, sir." Bridger stretched his arm

over the desk to shake Mr. Tyler's hand. Ike's grasp crushed, but not a callus to be found on those long, pale fingers. The overall effect lacked strength but not force. "It means a lot to me to have the opportunity."

"I hope so." Ike slid a cigar out of a large wooden box on his desk.

"Well, sir, unless you have something more for me, I plan to grab some supper and head to my room. I'll be ready for an early start tomorrow morning."

Ike's smile pulled to one corner as he lit the cigar. "Come on back over later. The night's young and you've earned yourself a good time this evening."

Bridger shifted as Ike shook out the match and took a long draw. "Unless you need me, I plan to see Miss Martin about those coffins before I turn in. I'd like to check out the tools and materials I'll need so I can start early next week."

Ike glanced out the window by his desk. "Not quite dusk yet—you ought to have time. You're in a lot of hurry, though, son. All work and no play—"

"All due respect, Mr. Tyler, you ain't near old enough to be my pa, so I'll thank you to not call me 'son.'"

Fire blazed across Ike's face, but he ground out his cigar with deliberate slowness, snuffing his anger out with it. "Merely a manner of speaking, and I apologize." Ike's stare penetrated in a way that made Bridger's anger build. "You seem in an awful big hurry to make money. How much do you owe?"

Bridger stepped closer, tilting his chin to meet Tyler's snide glare. "I told you, I don't owe any man. But I do have plans for that money, and the sooner I can earn my way out of here, the happier I'll be."

Ike moved to the edge of his desk and leaned against it. "You're planning on leaving already?"

"Not exactly." Bridger stepped back, pulling his shoulders straight. "But there's nothing wrong with a man having plans for something more, and I have some of my own."

Ike crossed his arms and stared at his feet a moment, as if considering. "I understand that drive myself, Bridger, and I like to hire men who have ambitions. Keeps them focused. But hold those aspirations in check. Nothing interferes with my plans."

"You won't have any complaints about my work, Mr. Tyler. I guarantee you that. But you also won't stop me when I'm ready to move on."

Ike stood and smiled, giving Bridger a hearty pound to the shoulder. "Well, then, I guess it's my job to be sure you're in a position you can't walk away from." He smiled in a way that didn't connect with his tightly controlled anger of moments before. "I can do that, Bridger. I can. And I have a whole crew out there to prove it."

Bridger trudged up the stairway and creaked open the door of the room he shared with Frank. It wasn't large by any standard, but it held a bed, a battered desk and a dry sink with a mirror, along with the two of them, without anything getting knocked over every time one of them turned around. The cleanliness of the room surprised him, even if the walls sorely needed to be planed and painted, and stood paper-thin. All told, they hadn't had a nicer place to stay since they'd left home—and maybe before then.

Frank sat at the desk near the window, scratching pictures of horses into the old copybook he'd carried with him all the way West. Bridger peered over his shoulder, admiring the graceful lines of ink seeping into the thick pages. "For such a big guy, you sure can hold that tiny pen well."

Frank wiped the nib and carefully stopped the ink bottle before turning. "I was just here waiting on you, Bridge. I sat by the window so I wouldn't need to light no lanterns."

"All right," Bridger said. He set the covered plate he carried onto the desk next to Frank and turned to the dry sink. Frank never lit the lantern. He'd been afraid of fire ever since the night of the accident. Bridger shook his head as he washed. He'd tried to get his brother to strike a match once he'd…recovered, but after a while, Frank's continued fear made him give up.

"That's okay. I shouldn't be this late most nights. I can light it before I head over to Miss Martin's place. You want supper? Might as well eat while it's still hot."

Frank beamed and peeked under the cloth covering the plate. Bridger watched his face light, then fall as he flipped the cloth back.

Shaking his hands and wiping them dry, Bridger pulled the napkin away. "What's the matter? There's plenty here. Pull out the camp plate and we'll split it."

Frank sighed and moved for the plate and utensils they kept on the tiny shelf over the bed. "Steak and baked potato again?"

"Yep, and what's wrong with that?"

"Nothin'."

"I like steak. I'd eat it every day if I could." Bridger cut the steak and potato and slid half onto the spare plate. "You don't like it?"

"Sure."

Frank sat on the bed and took his plate, staring at it with resignation. "I like fried chicken and mashed potatoes, too, Bridge."

Bridger cut into the steak and sampled a bite, cooked through and fairly tender. He cut another bite before answering. "I'm sure the menu changes. I'll ask Mattie, okay? Now eat before it gets cold."

"Wait! We have to say grace first." Frank laid his plate to the side and bowed his head. Bridger wiped his mouth with a guilty nod. Frank never forgot to say grace—even for a meal he wasn't particularly fond of.

"Jesus, thanks for this food, and for my brother, Bridger, who doesn't get mad when I do dumb things and who got this food for us. Amen."

Hair prickled down Bridger's neck. "What 'dumb thing' did you do, Frank?"

His brother, suddenly interested in the meal, avoided his glare. "Nothin' special."

"How about you tell me and I'll decide." He felt frustration wave up. After spending the day with Toby, trouble was the last thing he needed.

"You said I could go for a walk during the day." Frank didn't go so far as to point at him, but Bridger heard it in his tone.

Bridger pushed his plate aside and drew a deep breath. He'd long learned that getting angry with Frank only made the problem worse. "That's right—I did. So where did you go?"

"Around the field by the church…"

"And?"

"And back through the town, the way we rode in…past that lady's house." Frank's voice dropped to a whisper.

"What lady?"

"The lady with the pretty black hair, who lives in that house around the bend." It came out in a whoosh of soft breath.

"Miss Martin?" Bridger looked out the window and

across the roofs of the businesses next door. "What happened?"

"Nothin', I promise! She didn't even see me." Frank always managed to tell the story through his protests.

"Why would she? You weren't anywhere near her, right?"

"But I had to help the cat and that's all, Bridger. I didn't mean to fall and crash her door." His brother looked at him with a curious mix of determination, fear and truth.

"'Crash her door'? Hard? Did she hear you?"

"She didn't leave the porch or nothin'. I ran away quick. I know you said—"

"Calm down, Frank." He stood and settled his brother with a hand to his shoulder, his thoughts flying like a racehorse. "She probably didn't even hear you."

"Yes, she did! I heard her tell the other pretty lady."

Bridger groaned. "If you're close enough to hear, you're too close, Frank!" His anger echoed against the bare walls, and he forced his tone to ease.

"I'm sorry, Bridger. Don't be mad. I know what you said. It was dumb. Dumb, dumb, dumb."

Bridger slumped to the bed next to his brother and wrapped an arm around his broad shoulders, swaying a little until his mind cleared and Frank's breathing returned to normal.

"I'm sorry, too, Frank. I didn't mean to yell. It's been kind of a long day for me. I'm not really mad." He stood, looked at his brother's repentant face and grinned. Frank would never intentionally frighten anyone or cause trouble. "Listen, I'm making a mountain out of a molehill. Miss Martin didn't see you, right?"

Frank nodded. Bridger breathed a sigh of relief.

"Good. And I'm to go and talk with her this evening, anyway. I'll see if she says anything about today. It's probably slipped her mind already. In any case, she wouldn't know it was you. But you have to promise me, Frank. You have to promise you'll stay away from the busy part of town. And no going near people's houses, all right?"

"All right." Frank nodded with vigor, eyes gleaming with promise.

Bridger sat down again and bumped shoulders with Frank. "It will be all right. We scary-looking guys have to watch out for each other, that's all."

Lola started at the faint knock outside her front door. Another late-night guest? She marked the book she read, smoothed her hair into place and wound her way through the empty preparation room. Blue sky peeked through the window, but muted gray crept over the buildings as the sun sank below the mountains.

With a deep breath, she opened the door. "Mr. Jamison?"

"Bridger, ma'am." Though his stance took full advantage of what height he had, his eyes drooped with fatigue. "I hoped it wouldn't be too late to take a look at your father's workshop. I'd like to find plans and see what supplies are on hand. Then, if I think I can do the job, I'll start next week, if that's agreeable to you."

Tension across her shoulders eased at his business-like tone. "That sounds fair…Bridger. Come in and I'll get the key."

His weary eyes scanned the room over her shoulder, then glanced along the street behind him. "With all due respect, ma'am, I think it's best I meet you around back at the shed."

Whether the nature of the room behind her or concern for her reputation prompted him, Lola appreciated his propriety.

Bridger's shadowed form rounded the corner as she stepped onto the narrow porch. The brilliant sunset of a clear day lent a golden glow to the last rays that clung in spots around them, reluctant to make a complete escape. It burnished the rim of his hat, highlighted the angry scar across his face, lit his eyes with a warm glow.

Lola forced her attention to her trembling hand. She jammed the key into the lock. Bridger Jamison brought far more questions than she had answers.

"The U.S. marshal should arrive in a few days." The lock sprang open and heat rushed to her cheeks as she faced the man.

Bridger dipped his head with a quirked smile. "Be glad to see him myself, ma'am. I'm anxious to clear any poor notions of my character."

How many times had her father cautioned her about thinking out loud? "I apologize for the insinuation. You did a good thing, finding Pete and bringing him in like you did. I've just learned to be leery of strangers."

His head tipped back, eyes blending with the growing darkness. "Mr. Tyler told me some of what you've been through this past while, and I'm sorry for your loss. It behooves you to be wary of scary-looking fellows like me." He smiled and reached for the latch.

Lola bit her lip. She'd judged this man on circumstance and outward appearance, and her conscience pricked her. Yet not enough to prompt a full change of heart. Who was this man and what brought him to Quiver Creek? Maybe Grace was right. Having him in her employ would give her the opportunity to learn more about him—for better or for worse.

His voice interrupted her thoughts. "Mind if I light the lantern, ma'am?"

"Go ahead. The one Papa used should be inside the door." She watched him trim the wick by feel alone and light it to a comforting glow within minutes.

"Anything you prefer I not touch in here?" he asked, keeping his lean back to her. He held the lantern at shoulder height and peered around the long room.

She wrapped her shawl tighter, looking to the gold-tinged peaks and stars winking in the darkening sky. The view failed to lure away memories brought on by the musty warm scent of wood shavings trickling through the doorway. Blinking tears from her eyes, she shook her head. "To tell you the truth, I haven't a clue what's in there. I haven't opened the door since my father died." She drew a snuffled breath. "You're welcome to use whatever you find. I appreciate you considering the job."

His warm hand grasped her forearm as she turned to go. The warmth of his calloused fingers clashed with the cool, damp night, and she shivered. Or perhaps the tenderness in his gaze caused the tremor. She bit the inside of her cheek to forge away fresh tears.

"I can do this another time, ma'am. I forget how quickly darkness settles here in the mountains. This might be easier by daylight."

She knew by his tone he spoke to her emotions, not to what suited him. "No, you should have time for a quick look around before the lantern won't be enough. Papa kept his notes in a box at the far end." She gestured to the narrow door. "You're welcome to take those along to study. They should give you the details you need as far as supplies and such. I'll leave you to your search."

Bridger held the lantern high, its light wobbling against dusty tan walls and glimmering tools. Even in the dimness, he saw two things: Lola's father kept his work space neat, and he'd done more than fashion coffins. There were a large variety of tools, some old but well cared for, others with hardly a scratch to them.

His hands itched to think of the fine tables and cabinets he could make when he had his own woodshop someday. The main material lacking seemed to be proper lengths of wood, which he could order. He made a mental note to check with the general-store owner to see where a smaller order could be placed, hoping to avoid another visit with Mr. Johnston.

A row of windows lined the western wall, allowing the last remnants of sunlight to mix with the lantern's flickering glow. A similar row on the opposite wall would allow a good work space to take advantage of morning light, should he have opportunity to use it. It also gave a direct view of Lola's back door. If Mr. Tyler was serious about him keeping an eye on his former sweetheart, he wouldn't have to feel quite like a spy.

What did Ike expect him to see? Being alone, even in town, couldn't be easy for her. Raw grief still clouded her clear green eyes when she spoke of her father. Maybe a little fear, too.

His thoughts turned to Frank. A man his size falling into her door had to make a commotion, and Frank knew she'd heard him. Was it still wearing on her mind as she turned in for the night? Dare he ask?

Every great once in a while, the thought struck through him that his life would be simpler had Frank not stepped in that night to his defense. Their father might well have killed him, but then Frank would have a mind to make his own way. Now it rested on Bridger to care for the brother he'd lived his childhood looking up to.

Picking up a mallet, Bridger pounded against the

anvil, comforted somehow by its hollow echo. Being in this place as darkness took over wasn't doing him any more good than it had Lola. He needed to grab the box and get back to Frank.

The Lord knew the mess they were in, all the hows and whys. Frank continually reminded him it was enough to trust He'd clear the way for them. But so far, that way seemed filled with bad roads and crooked paths.

Bridger found the box Miss Martin had mentioned, though smaller than what he'd imagined. He'd study her father's notes in the evenings and be ready to work as soon as he secured the supplies. The more he had to keep his hands busy, the better off he'd be.

He grasped the box by the handles. If he could be certain Frank hadn't been spotted yet, this would all be a little simpler.

Lola wiped the dishes, set the kettle to heat and swept the floor before giving up the pretense to wait by the kitchen window for the lantern light to go out in Papa's woodshed. It brought a curious freshness to her loss to have someone root through his tools, through the place where he'd spent so many hours—so many happy hours they'd spent together.

"Lord, give me wisdom. I need someone to build these if I'm going to stay in business. Help me know the right direction to go," she prayed.

Finally the light moved from the door. Bridger fastened the lock before snuffing the lantern and hanging it on the hook outside. She opened the door at the first soft knock. Surprise widened his eyes. The minimal lighting hid her blush at being caught spying, her response coming too quick for anything else.

The man fairly disappeared under the overhang of the

porch, which blocked the moonlight. Still, the rustling told her he'd removed his hat as she opened the door.

"I found the box. Looks to me like he was quite a wood smith, ma'am."

She sucked in a delighted breath, somehow warmed at the observation. "You're right. And please, call me Lola, remember?"

"All right…Lola. If you're willing to take a chance on me, I'm more than happy to have the opportunity." His voice carried whisper-soft on the dry evening wind.

"I'll expect you next week, then, whenever Ike can spare you. Good night, Bridger."

"Lola?"

His voice caught her ear before the door closed. "Yes?"

A long pause greeted her, as if he'd tried to word his next comment several ways before speaking it aloud. "I don't suppose you get many visitors to this door. Will it be all right if I knock here to get the key for the shed?"

She hesitated. "Yes."

She heard an anxious shuffle of feet. "I just thought hearing, uh, unexpected noises back here…even during the day, it might…"

Her mind returned to the strange thud today during Grace's visit. "It might if I weren't accustomed to staying here alone." She hoped her voice hid her lack of bravado. "Most folks aren't anxious to snoop around this type of business establishment, I suppose." She managed a ripple of laughter, suddenly realizing the truth of the statement. "Besides, Ike's men will patrol the town until a suitable sheriff can be elected."

"I reckon you're right." She heard the smile in his voice and an awkward sense of relief. "Just, if there were something…anything that…disturbed you in some way… well, I hope you'll grow familiar enough with me being around to let me know. Working for Ike, I'd be glad to keep an eye on the place."

Lola nodded, unsure how she felt about having this man "keeping an eye" on her place. "I appreciate the offer," she told him, strangely pleased by it in spite of herself. "But I assure you, I know how to handle things, Bridger." She prayed for truth in that claim.

He stepped forward and leaned toward the door. His eyes glittered in the kitchen light, and the jagged edge of his scar rippled and pulled at the edge of his lip as he spoke. "From the little I've seen, Lola, I have no doubt that's so."

With that he slid from the porch with a light step. She heard his soft "Good night" as the door creaked closed.

Chapter Six

Bridger surveyed the lot where Tyler's Hotel would stand in a few weeks. Various sizes of river rock wedged into tight stacks created an impressive foundation. Toby's precise instruction and knowledge on how to build it surprised him. Despite an overbearing tone in directing the men, Bridger recognized the skill behind it. They would be ready to construct the walls by the middle of next week.

Bridger covered the last of the supplies with heavy canvas before meeting his boss at the front of the worksite. "Looks like you're making progress." Ike waved his cigar hand and smacked Bridger's shoulder with a hearty thud using the other. "I have an errand for you, and a favor to ask."

Bridger stepped from under his bony fingers. "What's that?"

"First, I need you to pick up supplies at Anthony's store. Tell Cecil you're the new man for the weekly pickup. Got that?"

Bridger squinted into the sun, rubbing dust from his hands onto an old blue handkerchief. "Sure thing. I can see about supplies for Lola's job while I'm there."

He followed as Ike nodded him into a walk. "I also wondered if you'd be interested in working the saloon tomorrow evening. Lots of cowhands rumble into town with money burning a hole in their pockets. Things get busy, might get a little rowdy. It'd be good to have you on hand."

Bridger adjusted his hat and tucked the handkerchief into his back pocket. "I prefer not to work in any saloon, Mr. Tyler. Besides, I hoped to do some work at Lola's."

"I'll give you tomorrow afternoon off for that." Tyler drew the promise out like a bone waved before a hungry dog, totally ignoring any preference Bridger might have. "Pay's good."

Ire brewed in Bridger's chest. No good ever came from having a greater interest in money than you ought to. And outright trouble came when someone else discovered the weakness. Still…he thought of Frank holed up in that hotel room, of the fine tools Lola's father had, of his promise to take care of his brother and his dreams for his own business. "I said I don't much cotton to working in a saloon, Mr. Tyler. That's not what I signed on for."

"Agreements can be adjusted, right? I'm talking this one time. If I don't get more men somewhere, you won't have much chance at a restful evening, anyhow."

Bridger stopped, his boots kicking dusty rock ahead. "What about the others?"

"Ah, they're only muscle." Ike's voice grew as slick as the mustache wax he used. "You have something they'll never have—intellect. They can handle situations that get out of hand, true. But you, sir, can prevent the problem in the first place. Besides, I'm shorthanded without you."

Back home, old Reverend Harvey read warnings about idle flattery, and Bridger wasn't fool enough to believe this was any more than that. He scanned the street, watching wagons rumbling around the bend that led to Lola's place. Frank would hate it if—

"I'll pay you double what the other men get, if you keep quiet about it." Tyler grinned, leaning back with his hands clasped before him and a too-wide smile. "And Sunday off."

He'd be free to go to church. Bridger rubbed a hand along his scar. Frank would pitch a fit about him working in the saloon, but keeping his promise to attend church might smooth things over. Besides, Frank would never settle to sleep if things got wild next door. His conscience seared him. But double the pay?

"I'll do it." Bridger stopped and faced Ike's knowing smirk. "Like you said, it's one night. But no more."

"That's the spirit. I believe it's always wise to keep an open contract. It's good to see you're a flexible sort, Bridger." Ike clapped him on the shoulder. "Don't forget my order from Mr. Anthony, now. You can drop it in the saloon kitchen with Mattie if I'm not in my office. Then you're on your own until tomorrow night."

Bridger nodded him off, stopping by the water trough while Ike sauntered down the street.

Bridger wet his handkerchief at the pump and washed over his face and hands. Did Toby know of Ike's offer? Somehow, Bridger didn't imagine he'd be pleased if he did. Then again, Toby wasn't easy to figure.

Bridger had little time to wonder. If he didn't stop woolgathering, he'd never make it to Anthony's store before it closed.

But he felt no hurry to return and tell Frank about the change in his working arrangements, either.

A tiny bell chimed as Bridger stepped through the door into Anthony's General Store. Cecil Anthony, a tiny man with olive skin and a thick gray mustache, greeted him from behind the counter with a cheery hello. "What can I do for you today, sir?" he asked. Bridger couldn't place the bold accent, but he smiled at the brightness of it. Mr. Anthony tapped the worn counter with thick fingers, his apron still crisp and white as the day wound down. Sunlight slipped through the front windows and gleamed across his smooth head, glistening along his spectacle frames. He stood straight and firm, though he barely rose above Bridger's chin. His square shoulders matched his jawline, and Bridger knew in an instant he liked the man.

"I'm here to place an order for some wood lengths, if you can get them." He sidled against the counter. "Pine boards."

"Sure-a thing, sir. Let me get an order slip." Mr. Anthony reached under the counter and pulled a pencil from behind his ear. "What sizes you need?"

"I hoped you could help me with that. Do you have records of what you ordered for Mr. Martin in the past? I'm to make coffins for his daughter, and—"

"You're the man a-helping Lola?"

"I guess so, sir. She hired me to build them, providing my work meets her approval."

Anthony slapped his pencil next to the tablet on the counter and nudged glasses down his Roman nose. His bushy eyebrows drew together and the man's stare pinned Bridger in place. Though his head tilted down to meet the old man's gaze, he dared not break from it.

After a long moment, the shopkeeper leaned away and picked up the pencil again. "Humph! You're a-going to do a fine job for Lola, or you'll find a new place to do your business, you hear? Don't you be bothering that fine girl, either. You understand-a me?"

Bridger bit back a smile. He had youth and strength on his side, but somehow, he didn't doubt if he bothered Lola in any way, this man would dole out justice. "Yes, sir. I only aim to do a good job for her. Strictly business."

Mr. Anthony harrumphed again, pushed his glasses into place and pulled out a ledger from behind his counter. He made little musical clicks of his tongue as he searched through the pages. "Here we are, sir. I can duplicate the last order I placed for Mr. Martin, God rest his soul. It's about-a time—he gave me an order every six months."

The shopkeeper shuffled to a supply room behind shelves at the back. "I understand her business has been better than she'd like of late," Bridger said, by way of conversation.

Mr. Anthony swung around with a fiery glare. "And what would you know about-a that, sir? Who are you?"

Bridger gulped, sticking his hand in the pocket of his slicker. "Bridger Jamison, sir. I meant no disrespect. I heard it from my boss, Mr. Tyler. See, I'm new in town and I—"

"Then you had-a better speak more carefully about things you're only learning about, Mr. Jamison. You're one of Ike's boys, is that it?" His tone made Bridger thankful for the empty shop. He felt as if he'd been caught with his hand in the candy jar.

"I suppose that's right, sir. As a matter of fact, Mr. Tyler asked me to pick up his weekly order. I'm the new man," he offered weakly.

"Has you out handling business for him already? He must see something special in you that my old eyes are missing." Anthony's scowl deepened and his fists grew stiff at his sides. Then he spun on his heel and disappeared in the back room a moment before returning with his notepad and a thin envelope.

Bridger stood silent, confused about the sudden cold fury bursting from the man. Mr. Anthony came to the front of the counter, shoving the envelope under his nose. "Here's Tyler's 'order.' Burt Sampson didn't have everything, but he's expecting to make up for it next week."

Bridger stared at the envelope, slowly reaching to pull it away from the end of his nose.

"If that's a problem, you tell Ike he can come and talk with me himself. You got-a that?"

Bridger shook his head. "I'll tell him. I supposed his order would come in a box or a crate, something for the hotel he's building, that's all."

Mr. Anthony stared at him a moment, then shook his head, tramping to his place behind the counter again. "Oh, that-a be something for his hotel, all right." He stretched his arms along the counter, knobby hands grasping at the smooth, weathered wood.

Bridger held his breath in pause, not sure what Mr. Anthony might be doing. He tried to think of what he'd said to offend the man and wondered if it were age or temperament that affected his change of tone. Bridger shifted his feet, dusty boards squeaking around his boots.

The older man blew a long, forced breath. "I'll place the order you need, for Lola's sake," he said, his voice low and graveled. He looked up, fire shooting from his eyes. "I suppose I ought to be glad you can do what she needs you to do. Ike, he'll make sure you treat-a her right."

"You have my word, Mr. Anthony. The last thing I'd do is hurt any woman." If Mr. Anthony detected something in him to be wary of and talked to Lola about it, he could lose the job before he even tried.

The man flapped his hand as if swatting at a fly. "Beh! So you say."

"Yes, sir." Bridger rubbed a hand along his face, feeling the rough need of a shave and every moment of the long day. He adjusted his hat and took another step away from the counter. "If you could let Lola know when the supplies are in, sir, I'd appreciate it. I'm anxious to get started. You'll have to trust me on this, but I'm the last thing you need to worry about."

Mr. Anthony slammed the ledger closed and returned it to a shelf under the counter. "And you trust-a me, Mr. Jamison. Should you do anything to harm that girl, you'll have more than-a Mr. Tyler to look over your shoulder for, and that's a promise."

Lola rinsed a lone plate and set it to dry. The sun grew brilliant and warm through the windowpane, but this morning had started late. A scratching sound at her back door had startled her as she drifted off last night, leaving her restless far into the wee hours of the morning. Now, in the bright daylight, she felt silly for the way she'd allowed her imagination to run wild. But her thoughts slogged through fog, and her steps lacked the vigor sunlight usually brought.

A knock at the house door interrupted her thoughts. Lola hastily dried her hands and smoothed her hair before answering.

"Good morning!" Grace's soft voice greeted her. She smiled as Grace waddled through the door. "I got word early this morning that my parents are arriving on the first stage. I know it's a little early, but I thought— Lola, are you ill? You look exhausted."

"No, nothing like that." Lola greeted her friend with a hug and motioned her into a chair in the front room.

"I didn't sleep well, that's all. Then I overslept. I've only been up a short while, I'm embarrassed to say."

Grace paused at the chair. "I don't want to steal your time if you're busy. I only thought I'd take the chance to visit you a bit while I wait."

"Of course. Don't be silly," Lola assured her. "I have all afternoon for chores. Work is the one thing guaranteed to wait without complaint. Besides, I haven't had my morning tea, and it will be nice to share it with you."

A knock sounded at the front door—a business call. She snapped to her feet, nearly upsetting the teapot. Grace's cup rattled in the saucer and she looked ready to bolt. "Please wait, Grace. No sense in rushing off to sit at the depot alone. I'll be back soon as I can."

Lola took pains to close the partition door with a solid latch before donning her special apron by the second knock. A tall man with brilliant blue eyes swept off his hat as she swung the door open. A quick flip of his lapel revealed a burnished badge.

"Jake Anderson, U.S. federal marshal, ma'am. We received a report from the undertaker of Quiver Creek about a suspicious death. I was told I could find him here."

"You can. I'm the undertaker. Won't you come in?"

The man adjusted his hat and pulled a telegraph from his front pocket. "I'm sorry. I'm looking for a gentleman, surname Martin."

"Would that be 'L. Martin'?"

The man peered at the paper closely, as if convincing himself. "Yes, ma'am."

"That's me, Lola Martin. I sent the telegram last week."

The marshal stepped back with a gentle grin. "Well, I'll be. Begging your pardon, ma'am, but I wasn't exactly expecting…"

Lola smiled. "People usually don't." The man glanced up and down the street, where wagons bounced around the curve and into the thickest part of town. Indecision flashed across his face, and Lola found herself with similar pause.

A man coming into her home without a body might not bode well for her reputation if the wrong sets of eyes witnessed it. Grace made a perfectly suitable chaperone, but to hold this discussion in her presence...would be awkward, to say the least. On the other hand, Mr. Anderson might have questions for Grace. And wouldn't she want to know what transpired with the investigation?

"Please, come in. Mrs. McKenna, the sheriff's widow, happens to be visiting. You might as well meet with her. She'll be sufficient to stop any wagging tongues."

Jake Anderson rubbed dark fingers over his scruffy jaw. "If you're certain it suits you, ma'am, that will be fine with me."

Lola led him through to the parlor, praying his arrival wouldn't upset her dearest friend. "Let me introduce you to Mrs. Grace McKenna," she said. His towering form bowed slightly, hat held across his chest. His eyes lit up as Grace held her hand out with a wan smile. Even draped in black, sallow with grief and well along in her pregnancy, Grace McKenna was a beautiful woman.

"Grace, this is U.S. marshal Jake Anderson."

"Pleasure to meet you, ma'am, although I'm sorry for the circumstances. From all I've gathered, few men lived up to the honor of the badge like Pete McKenna. You have my sincerest condolences."

Grace nodded as the marshal took the offered seat. His large frame looked almost comical folded into the flowered chair with gilded edges.

"I beg your pardon for my appearance, ladies. Had I

known I would be meeting with such fine company so soon, I would've taken greater pains to clean up before coming. I like to talk to the source of the initial complaint before I make my presence in town known, if possible, and I came off the trail just this morning."

"No matter, Marshal. Would you care for some coffee?"

He waved her off. "No, thank you. I won't stay long. I only need to get some preliminary information for my inquiry."

Lola sat and leaned forward. "I hadn't expected you so soon, sir. Law enforcement isn't usually high priority in the little towns around here."

He grimaced as he pulled out a small pad of paper and a pencil from an inside coat pocket. "To tell you the truth, I was already headed this direction on another investigation. But my superiors passed your telegram along to me, so I wanted to start with your case."

Lola swallowed the knot of unnamed fear in her throat. "Do you think they're connected?"

The marshal's smile calmed her. "That's what I'm here to find out, ma'am. I'm sure hoping they aren't."

Lola studied Grace, rigid in her chair, teacup frozen at her lips. Did she also suspect something?

"From the telegram, I gather the body was discovered on the evening of April 17. Is that right?"

Lola nodded. "That's when the—Pete—was brought to me. The man found him out on the trail late that afternoon, from my understanding."

Marshal Anderson nodded, glancing at Grace. "Did you know the man who discovered the body?"

"No." Lola shook her head.

"Not a local? Did you get his name?"

Lola scooted to the edge of her seat, pinching her fingers together. "Bridger Jamison."

The man jotted some notes. "Can you describe him for me?"

"Dark…brown hair in need of a trim, brown eyes… a scar that cuts across his face. Slight to medium build, but strong—he carried Pete in over one shoulder without trouble."

"Scar, you said?"

"Yes, old, but very distinct. Runs from his temple to his lip." Lola traced the path on her own face to demonstrate. The memory of his stance in the dimly lit doorway brought a shiver.

Jake Anderson paused in his writing to stare at her. "Any chance you know where he went from here? It would be helpful to talk to him and learn the details of how and where he found the sheriff."

"He's still in town," Grace said, finding her voice. "He's working for Ike Tyler."

"Tyler?" The marshal flipped farther back in his notebook and tapped his pencil against some notes. "He's the saloonkeeper, right?"

Lola looked at Grace, her eyes reflecting the same curiosity she felt. She nodded slowly. "That's right."

Jake made further notes and then turned to Grace. "I know it's not easy to answer questions like this when grief is so fresh, Mrs. McKenna. But do you know of anything in particular your husband was working on in regard to his position as sheriff? Did he mention any cases he had conducted, or particular trouble with anyone in town?"

Grace took a sip of tea, then settled the trembling cup in her other hand, as if trying to draw warmth. "No, he hadn't. He rarely discussed his job with me. He thought

I'd worry too much." She glanced out the window. "He was right, but I worried anyway." Her voice ended in a whisper-soft break.

"I reckon that would've been the case regardless of his job title, ma'am," the marshal said kindly. He stood abruptly, tucking his notepad back into his coat. "I may have questions for you later on, as the investigation progresses. Again, my sympathies for your tragic loss." The warmth in his eyes conveyed a depth of sincerity that seemed to bolster Grace.

Lola smiled at her and faced the lawman. "I may have been premature in bringing this matter to your attention, Marshal Anderson. Mr. Jamison's sudden arrival late in the evening, along with his appearance at the time…"

"Never hurts to be cautious, ma'am. I have to testify for a case in Billings next week, but I plan to return and continue looking into other matters. It won't hurt to have a talk with Mr. Jamison and have him take me to the place where he found Sheriff McKenna, make sure his story checks out."

Lola stood to see him out. Grace also rose, teacup clattering to the saucer on the table at her side. "I really must be going, if you'll pardon my hasty departure, sir. My parents are arriving with the stage, and it's due anytime now."

The marshal took her hand and bowed slightly over it. "Of course, ma'am. I'd see you to your destination, but for now, it's best folks don't know who I am or what I'm doing here. It's easier to get the truth if people believe I'm a drifter passing through." Lola felt the quick grasp of his hand around hers as she held it out. "To that end, I'd appreciate if the two of you didn't mention our visit to anyone for now. Rest assured, I'll inform you of anything I learn about your case when I'm certain the matter is closed."

Lola walked her guests to the back entry. Grace reminded her to come for lunch next week as she left.

Grace tugged into the wagon and gathered the reins. Holding them taut in her inexperienced hands, she gave a tremulous smile and a tiny wave before slapping the horse's rump into motion. They watched her continue around the bend deeper into town.

Marshal Anderson followed her with his gaze from the bottom step. "Strong woman. She seems to have the determination it will take to survive, though it won't be easy."

Lola nodded her agreement. "I hope I haven't waylaid you, sir. This is probably a goose chase I've set you on, being too hasty and allowing my imagination to carry me to the telegraph station before good sense could catch up."

"Please don't concern yourself with that. It only makes sense to look into the sheriff's death while I'm here. But please, call me Jake. I don't want to tip my hand too early. I'm asking you to not betray this trust until the time is right."

Lola tucked a hair behind her ear, pulled loose by the breeze wafting from the cool peaks. "You have my word, Jake. Believe me, I'm anxious to have this matter settled." The memory of Bridger's gentle voice and kind brown eyes sent a warm ripple across her shoulders. "Because it gets more complicated by the day."

Chapter Seven

Bridger slipped into the end of the row, third from the rear. Sometimes sitting in the farthest pew made a man as conspicuous as the man seated on the front bench. He placed his hat next to him on the seat and brushed dust from the brim. Given the length of time since he'd sat in a sanctuary, he felt a mite dusty himself. A tiny woman with snow-white hair nodded and smiled as she passed along to a pew nearer the front. The music had started, and Bridger smiled at his fortunate timing as the minister came in through a door behind the pulpit.

He studied the church, grand in its simplicity. Cedar lent its red-gold luster to the walls and exposed rafters, giving the meeting room a rich hue. A pine altar made with simply designed spindles spanned the front. Directly behind that, a narrow pulpit with a beveled front stood before the pastor. A small cross made of dark mahogany hung above. Tiny panes of real glass blocked together to allow a view of the sunrise sweeping over the mountains. It couldn't be easy for a minister to compete with that kind of distraction.

The sheriff's widow, dressed in black, played a tiny organ off to the side. A slight pause in the music brought everyone to their feet, and Bridger grasped the smooth wood of the pew ahead as he joined them.

"Welcome to the Lord's house this glorious day!" The reverend smiled over the crowd, his head and shoulders barely seen behind the pulpit. His thinning gray hair was carefully groomed, and kind brown eyes peered over small spectacles situated at the end of his nose. "I'm Pastor Rhett Evans, and whether you greeted me on the street yesterday or I've never had the pleasure of seeing your face before this moment, I hope you'll feel at home here and that you'll return often, as the Lord allows."

Bridger would've been tempted to chalk such cheery talk up to a clever method of filling the offering plates later, if he were more cynical. He glanced away. It had been too long since he'd been in a church service, among other believers. Besides, strength radiated from this man—his hands, his stance, his gaze. His demeanor spoke of integrity and peace. Bridger ducked his head in shame, shifted his feet and added his voice to the others singing "Joyful, Joyful, We Adore Thee."

A sweet, lilting soprano drew his attention to the other side of the sanctuary. Lola Martin stood, hair delicately rolled along the side of her face, ending in that long, black cascade at her back, her slender neck graced by a high lace collar. Directly behind her stood Ike, hymnal opened in one hand, more show than song.

His boss took a longer-than-gentlemanly gaze at Lola, then met his stare with a smirk.

Bridger tightened his grip on the smooth rolled back of the pew before him, seething. Lola was too fine a woman—a lady—to have any man look her over that way.

He bit the inside of his cheek in frustration. Frank waited, holed up in their little room at the boardinghouse, barely able to sleep with excitement of hearing about church service secondhand, all because a woman mistook his attentions in that last town. And this man, leering at women from the pew!

The song ended and Bridger fell to his seat a half beat behind everyone else, fighting his ire with Ike.

The pastor returned to the pulpit and leaned over it. "I don't trust folks too well," he said in a conspiratorial tone.

A low murmur of laughter floated over the crowd, and Bridger found himself leaning closer. "Not that this is a confession. Folks who've known me longest and best aren't at all surprised to hear it, I'm certain. But I have struggled with it. I mean, I'm a 'man of the cloth,' called by God, after all. How can I be so skeptical of other people?"

The man paused, returned to a full stand behind the pulpit and flipped open his Bible. His heavy brows bobbed over the rim of his glasses as he searched out the page. "I want to start this morning with the reading of Romans, twelve-nine."

The congregation stood, Bridger with them. He crossed his arms over his chest. His mind lacked as much practice in attending to a speaker as his spirit at attending to God. But the pastor certainly had caught his interest.

Lola greeted familiar faces with a smile, hiding her consternation—she hoped. She hadn't been able to put aside the distractions of the past week well enough to attend to Pastor Evans's fine sermon. Especially after seeing Bridger Jamison slip in just before service started. Could he be one of the good guys after all?

She staggered, jolted to attention as she flowed into the vestibule with the rest of the congregation. "Excuse me—"

"Pardon me—"

Instant warmth flushed her cheeks as Bridger steadied her with a careful grasp of strong fingers. "Welcome to Quiver Creek Church. It's good to see you."

Bridger grinned, a half smile that tugged against his scar. "Surprising to see me, you mean."

That truth brought a prickle of embarrassment, and denial was useless. Ike always told her she'd make a poor poker player. "Well, I hope you were blessed just the same."

He followed close through the doorway, brown eyes alight. "A fine sermon—reminded me of my grandfather's preaching when I was a boy. I admire your sanctuary, too. Someone took a lot of care in building it."

Pride filled her heart. "My papa did much of it, the pulpit and altar and such."

Bridger glanced around, and his attention returned to her in a way that brought peculiar comfort. "No great surprise to me. I've found the care a woodworker takes with his tools tends to reflect his craftsmanship. I also appreciated the singing, thanks to a particularly strong soprano—"

"Miss Martin is a woman of many talents."

Ike. Her smile tightened, suddenly forced. While Bridger's conversation brought warm joy to her chest, the disappointment of Ike's rude interruption doused the feeling.

"Most fine ladies are," Bridger said. His jaw rippled and boots shifted as he widened his stance. He nudged closer, but not improperly so. He turned toward Ike as if he sensed her irritation and wanted to shield her. She shook her head. Enough romantic notions—Ike's dalliance had taught her better.

"I appreciate your compliments, gentlemen," she said,

"but if you'll excuse me, I want to catch up with Grace."
She extended a gloved hand toward Bridger, feeling a
tingle as he clasped her fingers. "I trust I'll see you this
week. And here for service next week?" Lola glanced
away from Bridger, lest the hope she heard in her own
voice shone too prominent on her face. Her fingers lingered a moment longer in his rugged hand. Wasn't it right
she should be eager for this man to show reverence for
God if he were going to work for her?

"Lord willing, I surely hope so." A fine row of white
split his lips, even if it puckered his scarred cheek all the
more. With a nod toward Ike, he crossed the churchyard
toward the boardinghouse.

Ike cleared his throat, drawing her attention from
Bridger's easy stride. "Makes me uneasy, that one." His
lips drew a sneer. "Never hired a drifter who'd darken
a church door. Could be he'd do anything to get in your
good graces."

"Why, Ike Tyler, isn't that a bit cynical?" Lola protested, but her heart tripped at the thought he could be
right.

He drew to her side as Bridger crossed the road and
became lost among the buildings of town. "I only think
of your safety, Lola. Are you certain you don't want me
to send Toby along, keep an eye on that one?"

She drew her arms around her waist. "No, I impose
too much already. Besides," she said, a light shudder
passing through her as the cool spring air blew across
the still-bare trees overhead, "I have to start trusting a
little more." She only prayed Bridger deserved it.

Chapter Eight

Bridger glanced around before cutting alongside Lola's place to reach the woodshop behind. He bypassed her front door like a thief, but she kept the key at the back, and the less he disturbed her, the better.

He didn't pine for a return through that front door, anyway. The gleam of fear across Lola's face the night he'd brought the sheriff's body to her haunted his memory. Bold as she had been, he recognized it. He hoped seeing him at church this past Sunday had eased her mind about him.

Maybe her wariness gave Ike Tyler the notion to watch out for her. Strange for Tyler to trust him for the job so early on, but then, the thought of any others in the crew being charged with her care made his skin crawl. And that included Ike.

He shook his head. Was it any concern of his, the company she kept? Ike had made it clear his hat was still in the ring, but Lola gave no impression she felt the same. A successful—not to mention beautiful—businesswoman had no reason to give one whit about a seedy saloon owner...or the rough-looking characters he hired.

Lola's lilting soprano carried across the breeze in a

tune he faintly recognized. He slowed his steps, hesitant to interrupt. She sang as pretty as she looked. He adjusted his hat. No time to dally with such thoughts. He whistled "Battle Cry of Freedom" as he rounded the corner, announcing his presence.

Lola twirled with a gasp, fingers trailing across her mouth. A pink flush graced her cheeks. "You startled me."

"I apologize, ma'am. I've come to start on those coffins, if that's all right."

"I didn't expect to see you so soon. Your show of industry is admirable, Bridger." She grasped the rail with one hand and slipped a loose wave of hair behind her ear with the other. She wore a simple white shirtwaist with sleeves that rustled gracefully in the soft morning breeze and her blue-gray skirt lacked fancy, but everything about this woman spoke of gentleness and refinement, a true lady. Even with a basket of laundry in her hands.

"I won't be able to do much until more supplies arrive," he said. "I came to take a closer look at the tools, find out exactly what I have to work with, now that I have daylight. I haven't had a chance to study your father's notes yet, but I'll see everything is in good working order." He paused, reluctant to end the conversation. "Can I, uh, get the key?"

"Sure." She stretched inside to grab it, never leaving the back porch. Her warm, smooth fingers brushed his calloused ones as she handed the key over the rail to him. "I was about to have some lunch. Are you hungry?"

Bridger glanced at the sun, nearly overhead, and tried not to think of the hearty lunch he'd sneaked over to their room for Frank. "Don't bother on my account, ma'am. I didn't come to disturb you."

She leaned away, but a wide smile lit her face. "But I

didn't hear you say you aren't hungry. It's no bother, trust me. It's also not a grand offer. Just a cheese sandwich and a little vegetable soup. You go on and get started. I'll bring it out to you when it's ready."

"I shouldn't be long. I don't expect you to—"

"If you did, I wouldn't have made the offer. Besides, you need to stay strong and able to do this work because you're not getting paid until you're finished." She adjusted the laundry basket and nodded him on. "Go ahead. I'll be out in a jiffy."

Bridger opened the lock on the shed and stepped inside. In the light of day, layers of dust made the shop look like one of those newfangled photographs he'd seen during the war—everything still and frozen in some shade of rust. The morning light allowed him to see more than the lantern had shown. A box of rags under the workbench would get him started.

By the time Lola knocked at the doorjamb, Bridger had cleaned the worktable and settled into the corner on a high stool to inspect and wipe down tools. He slipped off to take the tray from her, noting with a little disappointment it contained lunch for one.

He smiled his thanks, feeling his scar pull tight.

Lola glanced around. "It seems you've made a good start here," she said, her voice choked and tight. "I haven't touched the place since…"

"That's understandable." He set the tray on a cleared space. "Did your father keep the finished coffins somewhere else?"

She drew slender arms around herself, glancing around. "No, no, they were stored here. I always asked Ike to send someone to move one inside as I needed it. I can't believe we've used so many since Papa died."

Bridger frowned. "That so?"

Lola nodded. "Lots of new faces passing through, and not all of them interested in following the law. Why, we had a gunfight right in the middle of town a few months ago. Quiver Creek is growing faster than we're able to handle. Pete tried to convince the town council to hire on a couple of deputies, full time."

"That doesn't sound like a bad idea. What happened?"

"The council said they couldn't afford it right now and praised the fine work he was doing on his own. Pete couldn't even stir up interest with the local business owners to hire more help. They said it was Pete's job and he should focus on doing it."

Bridger leaned against the bench and crossed his arms. He'd been through plenty of these towns to know local lawmen often had enough power to break the laws they were sworn to uphold. "Did he?"

Fire sparked in Lola's gaze. A nervous lump lodged in his throat, as if he were a man facing a minister from a jail cell.

She stared him down, her expression like ice. "No man could have done it better. Pete McKenna was a strong, wise and Godly man, and we were fortunate to have him watching over this town."

He held up a hand in surrender, wishing he'd thought how the question might sound before he'd spit it out. "No offense, ma'am. I haven't always had such experience with the law out here. No doubt they have a tough job, but sometimes they take liberties that don't measure up to what a lawman should be."

She didn't retreat, and her voice grew low. "Pardon me if your vast experience with lawmen gives me concern!"

Bridger stood upright. "It's not like that, Lola. I'm just saying—"

"I'm saying *not Pete*." Her green eyes grew wider and

glassy with tears. "I'm sorry. I have no right to judge you. But you're wrong. Between the rowdies passing through, the town growing so fast and the accidents we've had around here, no one man could handle it all. It was bound to catch up to him, and it did, and we as a community allowed it by ignoring him."

Bridger stepped closer but refrained from reaching out. Instead, he dipped his head to catch her gaze. "I meant no offense, Lola. I can see you put great stock in him. I didn't mean to insinuate anything about his character. I didn't even know him, so I had no business suggesting he was anything less than honorable, as you say."

She brushed a tear from her cheek. "I'm sorry, too. I wasn't fair to accuse you so quickly, either. We've had more than our share of grief and sadness in Quiver Creek these past few months. I'm praying for a better season ahead."

Bridger nodded. "I hope for your sake that's the case." He turned to the tray, his appetite dulled. "I'm especially sorry to upset you after you went to the trouble of this fine lunch."

Lola managed a shaky smile. "I'm sorry I allowed my lack of sleep and temper to get the best of me so that you're forced to eat it cooled."

"Let's say we're sort of even, then, and start where we were a half hour ago," he said.

"Who's to say I trusted you half an hour ago?" Her eyes lit with humor, but he recognized the truth in her jest.

His breathing eased as he focused on her guarded expression. "You offered me lunch and gave me the key to your father's woodshop. At least I'm on the right track."

Lola clipped along the rough boards on her way to Anthony's General Store. The sun's long rays soaked into her soul.

But thoughts of Bridger cast a cool shadow. He seemed determined to tear her down the middle. How dare he cast doubt on Pete's character! The nerve he had, being able and willing to help when she wanted nothing to do with him! And then offering a sincere apology when he ruffled her, only to make her hearken to the window every time a wagon rumbled, hoping to talk with him again. Even his church attendance brought a sense of irritation. Her mind had never been so divided.

She drew a breath, sifting through the mingled scents of melted snows, mountain breezes and early growth. She determined to put the handsome carpenter from her mind.

Her heart lightened with thanks for the early spring. Papa would have been itching to turn ground for their small garden, though it remained too early for that yet. She looked at the rugged peaks and forced a smile. Papa wouldn't want her to be gloomy or vexed, especially on a day as lovely as this. She swung an empty basket on her arm and opened the door. A soft jingle announced her arrival.

"Miss Lola!" Mr. Anthony greeted her. "How-a you doing this fine day?"

"Very well, thank you, Mr. Anthony. It is a beautiful morning out there."

"You come to order your seeds?"

Lola laughed. "I was just thinking about that. Maybe next week. Today I'm only here for some staples."

"Ah, and perhaps to take a look through the new spring catalog? Just arrived last-a week…." Mr. Anthony drew his words out in a cajoling tone. "Latest ladies' fashions for any stylish young girl." A young woman of twenty-three could hardly be considered a girl by anyone in Quiver Creek other than Mr. Anthony, who had been an old man as long as Lola had known him.

She leaned over the counter and patted his meaty fist. "No wonder you've managed to stay in business so long, sir. You certainly know how to charm your customers into purchasing more than they intended. You know all too well I'll have to take the time to look through that catalog today, don't you?"

"I only know you always look-a so stylish, and that warm spring days make the ladies itch for a fresh touch to their wardrobe. My dear Maria, God rest her soul, she say to me every year about this time, 'Cecil, when you going to get those new bonnets for the window?' Then, soon as they come, she make the display in the window, and one of those-a bonnets come home with her and never make it to the window." He smiled fondly, rubbing strong hands along the counter and giving it a gentle thump. "My Maria, she always such a beautiful woman."

Lola squeezed his hand. She never knew the late Mrs. Anthony, save through the love this man still held for her. "Then you must have made quite the handsome couple."

"Beh!" Mr. Anthony waved a gentle hand at her. "You charm an old man. Anything else I can do for you?"

Lola stepped among the tables and shelves, picking up the toiletries she needed. "Not today. I only need a few things, but I will take a look at that catalog."

Mr. Anthony bent to pull the thick volume to the end of the counter. Often the latest trends weren't practical for any woman of Quiver Creek, let alone a woman of her profession, but she still enjoyed looking to see if there were any she could accommodate for her own wardrobe. She thought of women like Mattie, her flamboyant style, compared with her own plain shirtwaists and skirts. No wonder men like Bridger Jamison took more notice of Mattie than her.

Lola stopped short, glancing at Mr. Anthony as if he read her thoughts...or noticed the blush crawling across her face. Instead, she found his back to her as he dusted cans stacked on high shelves behind the counter. The twinge in her chest caught her off guard. Why should she be jealous of Mattie? Or of anyone, for that matter, who could catch the eye of Bridger Jamison and rowdies like him who wandered through town?

But it did remind her, he had skills she needed. And Mr. Anthony had the supplies. "Has a Mr. Jamison been in to order pine boards? I told him they could go on my account. I'm anxious to have him start his work for me."

Mr. Anthony's head snapped around. "The order should be in by early next week." He adjusted his spectacles over his firm gaze. "This man, he is doing a good job for you?"

"He needs the supplies before I can check his skill, but he appears to be a hardworking sort. He's been in the shop for several days, cleaning and organizing the tools to his own liking. I know Ike keeps him busy with the hotel construction, too."

Mr. Anthony landed his fist on the counter with a thud. "Oh, yes, Mr. Tyler keeps him very busy these days. Is he bothering you?"

Lola shook her head. She felt his care wrap around her like a grandfather's sweater. "He only stops in to get the key and return it most days. He's there for an hour or so, early in the mornings before he starts work for Ike. Longer on Mondays."

"You a big girl, Miss Lola, a smart girl. But you watch yourself with this Mr. Jamison. He hides something, and he works for Mr. Tyler, and that's two-a strikes against him already!"

Lola bit back a smile. Mr. Anthony didn't approve of Ike Tyler any more than her father had. Ike had proved himself a philandering cad, and to have discovered it before a walk down the aisle with him flooded her with gratitude.

But men could change. Ike had been nothing but helpful and supportive of her decision to continue her father's business after his death. Sometimes she wondered if he was giving her time to mourn before suggesting they take up where they'd left off. While she could not entirely forget the heartbreak he'd caused, nor excuse his choice of business, she couldn't deny he had done more than a mere friend would have in the months since Papa died.

"Miss Lola, you hear me? You watch yourself, and you don't trust Mr. Tyler nor any of his men any further than you can-a throw them."

"You know I'll be careful. Ike has looked out for me, just as you have, Mr. Anthony, but we're only friends." Lola smiled and moved her basket to the counter. "I appreciate your concern, though."

"They cause you problems, they have-a problems with me, you hear? I refuse their business!" Mr. Anthony's tone grew louder and more adamant.

"Please, don't do that! It would mean your retirement, and I'd hate to see it."

"Ah, Miss Lola," he said, placing warm hands over hers. "There are too many others who need me here to retire now. God has-a given me strength and health well into my years. I may not be able to do what truly needs done in this town, but I still am spry enough to make things not-a so easy until that man comes along."

Lola laughed. "I'm sure that's so, sir." She watched as he tallied her order. After paying the bill, she settled on the high stool at the end of the counter. She smiled, thankful for Mr. Anthony and other townsfolk the Lord had surrounded her with. "Now, let's see what the fine ladies back East are calling fashion these days."

Spring styles might be frivolous enough to tear her thoughts away from Mr. Jamison for a while. His lean image and dark eyes formed in her mind's eye. She shook her head. Because something certainly needed to.

Chapter Nine

Bridger rested against the headboard on his bed, the box and sheaf of papers from Lola's place beside him. He turned the lantern up as the skies became dark and the town grew quiet outside the window. Soon the rumble of Quiver Creek would be confined to the space next door. But with late nights and early mornings this past week, he doubted it would keep him from sleep.

Frank worked in his sketchbook at the desk. Sighs of frustration and tones of glee mixed with the sound of pencil scratching across the heavy paper. Bridger took advantage of Frank's preoccupation to take a closer look at Mr. Martin's information. He had wanted to get a feel for the work space first. Now that he'd organized the shop, he needed specifics to do the job right.

Not sure what he'd find, Bridger delved first into the box. The patina of the wood aged it more than the barely yellowed papers. It wasn't large, but even dovetails and sanded edges marked a quality of workmanship that matched the care of the woodshop in which he'd found it.

He sifted through several letters inside the box, among the cedar lining, which appeared to be from Mrs. Martin to her husband or perhaps her beau at the time, given the dog-eared corners. He flipped through the stack, amazed a man would hang on to such a memento.

"Pa never held on to anything so worthless. And anything valuable, he sold to buy more whiskey," Bridger said aloud.

Frank started, pencil held tightly above the picture of a flower he'd been focused on. "You ought not speak of him that way, Bridge."

His jaw clenched. He never knew if Frank sometimes forgot what Pa had done or if his forgiveness honestly extended that far. But it only upset him for anything bad to be mentioned about Pa, and living every day knowing Frank had been the one to suffer most at their father's hand in the end, he kept his thoughts to himself. Bridger set the letters aside.

"What are you working on?" he asked, hoping to distract his brother back to his drawings.

"Pictures." Frank moved his pencil gracefully over the paper, sometimes pushing hard and other times with a light hand that belied his size.

"Do you still have room in that book?"

"Lots of room."

They fell into silence again, and Bridger returned his attention to the box. He couldn't say he expected to find much in the way of instructions. Most carpenters worked in the same line as great cooks—without a recipe. But Lola seemed to think her father had plans written down somewhere.

Flipping through the pages of a worn copybook, he found neat capital letters written purposefully on the pages. Certain pages folded into the binding to mark different sections. Bridger noted titles such as *Basics of Human Anatomy, Burial Preparation* and *Business Accounting Practices* written along the creases—Mr.

Martin's school notes. Bridger scratched his head. "I hadn't really thought about a man needing schooling for undertaking."

"You need school for all kinds of important jobs, Bridge." Frank never glanced up from his artwork.

Bridger continued reading the headings, reluctant to search too far for fear he'd learn more than he cared to about preparing a body to be buried. Had Lola gone to a school like this? He shook his head. It seemed unlikely for a woman to be permitted into such a school, if they did exist.

The final section was labeled simply *Coffins*. The narrow section contained few words but several sketches with numbers for measurement.

He sat up in surprise. "Here it is, Frank. Doesn't look like Mr. Martin used it much after he took his course, but it gives me some idea of how to get started. Who'd have thought?"

"I knew," Frank said. He slashed the pencil lightly back and forth over the center of the page.

Bridger smiled. "You knew how to build a coffin and didn't tell me?"

"Nope, Bridge. But I knew you'd find how to do it, 'cause I prayed Jesus would help you find out how to do it."

He slid from the bed to peer over Frank's shoulder. The detail in the spray of flowers caught him by surprise. "That's good, Frank. Even better than your horses." He sniffed the air. "I believe I can just about smell them, they look so real."

"Except they aren't colors. I saw a bunch down by the creek today when I was going for a walk—I didn't bother no one, either," he defended.

"I didn't say you did," Bridger said.

"You would have, though. I know."

Bridger thought back over the number of times he'd reminded his brother not to be in anybody's way or to attract attention in the weeks since they'd settled into Quiver Creek. Too many to count. Maybe he should back off a mite. Between the mess in the last town that could have landed Frank in jail and his own repeated warnings, maybe the message had finally gotten through.

"I guess I have been telling you that a lot, and I'm sorry it's got to be this way for a while yet. But we barely escaped big trouble last time. I have to keep you safe."

Frank turned back to his work. "I know, Bridge. We're a scary-looking pair, and I'll do what you say. But I still have an idea that Miss Lola would like a pretty bunch of flowers like that. Except she'd want colors."

Bridger punched Frank lightly on the shoulder and slouched on the end of the bed. "We can't really be thinking of giving flowers to Miss Lola or any other lady around here. But I might be able to do something about finding some colored pencils."

Frank's face lit up like candles on a Christmas tree. "Honest?"

Bridger nodded. "Anthony's General Store has a lot of different things, and if he doesn't carry them, I'm sure he could order them for you. I'll see if I can place the order when I stop in Monday to check on the wood I ordered."

Frank looked doubtful. "But they cost lots of money, right? And we can't eat them or wear them, even."

Bridger felt his insides twist. Apparently Frank remembered more about Pa's teaching than he figured. Their father had often pointed out that if a purchase wasn't something to be eaten, or worn, it was a waste of money. Except, of course, the alcohol that Pa claimed kept him warm enough to save the price of a coat and filled his gut better than flour and steak. Only it hadn't done much for the rest of the family.

"I have money for it, Frank. I told you, this is a good job. Mr. Tyler pays better than anyone I've ever worked for, and with what I'll make once I get started on those coffins for Lola…why, we'll be out of here with our own little spread in no time." Though maybe not too far away.

The time he spent with her, helping her, had become the best part of his days. Even after leaving his job with Ike, wouldn't Lola still need his skills? Would she want him to stay?

He shifted on the saggy mattress, feeling the thrum of new opportunity for the first time in a long while. "But I know it isn't easy for you staying hid around here. If some colored pencils for your drawings make it easier, well, I think we can spare a few bits to get them, all right?"

A broad smile bloomed on Frank's face. "Thanks, Bridge! You're the best!"

"Well, it may be a while before we can get them, so don't go puffing me up just yet."

Frank stood and threw beefy arms around Bridger's shoulders, almost knocking him back to the mattress in his excitement. "That don't matter. You're the best for even thinking of it. I wouldn't trade you for the handsomest brother out there!"

Bridger laughed as Frank settled down at the desk again and turned to a fresh page. He made a mental note to add a new sketchbook to the list but didn't mention it. He wasn't sure he'd survive another dose of Frank's gratitude.

Bridger copied information he needed from Mr. Martin's notes onto a separate sheet. Then he unclasped the sheaf of loose papers. It only made sense to look through everything, in case Mr. Martin had made changes or noted what to do for various sizes that might be needed. He shuddered. Hopefully Lola would never have need for any tiny ones a young child might require. Too sad to think on, let alone build.

The pages contained the same precise writing, but now they were numbered to maintain their order. Here he found information he could use on figuring amounts and prices of supplies to buy ahead, should he need them. He'd keep them to study further.

Continuing to flip through, he found copies of business statements for families Lola's father had helped over the years. Mr. Martin ran a modest business—several slips marked *paid* before the balance read zero. Toward the bottom of the stack, Bridger found a thick set of papers in a separate, smaller folder marked *Sheriff McKenna*.

He fiddled with the clasp for only a moment before curiosity got the better of him. Inside he found loose ledger sheets of some sort. The top of each paper had *Q.C. Business Association* written. The dates ran from about a year before to about six months ago—right around the time Lola said her father had been killed.

He ran his finger down the smooth pages, noting the amounts deposited at monthly intervals. Next to most payments, a name listed someone from Tyler's outfit. Who would trust Ike to handle finances for such an organization?

About halfway through, he noted other names occasionally written in all capital letters. Some were scratched out with a steady black line ending in *moved out*. Names like Mr. Anthony's he recognized as other business owners in town.

He flipped to the front of the folder again. He'd be the

first to admit he knew little about ledger sheets and less about business associations, but a group that ran with a bottom line of zero classified as unusual, and seeing the file labeled for local law enforcement seemed downright strange. Did Lola know anything about this? Whatever this was?

She seemed adamantly sure about the sheriff's respectability. Then again, he doubted she knew about this file, either. Why would her father keep it hidden in his workshop, mixed in with everything else?

"What's wrong, Bridge?" Frank's look told him he'd been frozen for a moment.

"I found some papers that look funny."

"Like a joke?" Frank asked, reaching for the papers with thick fingers.

Bridger waved him off. "No, no, not laugh-at-it-funny, just strange-funny, the way this arithmetic looks."

"Funny numbers?" Frank asked, his brow wrinkled in confusion.

"Maybe." Bridger checked the clock. He stashed the papers, placing the separate sheaf on top. "I have to get over to the hotel site for guard duty. Listen, you watch yourself walking out there this evening. The sun's sticking around a little later every day, makes you easier to spot, you know? Just don't—"

"Bother nobody. I know." Frank pulled his cap low over his eyes. "I never do."

Bridger tied his holster securely to his leg and covered it with his long coat. "Sorry. I guess I can't help worrying enough for the both of us. Just…be safe, all right?" He blew out the lantern, leaving them in almost complete darkness.

"All right." Frank nodded solemnly.

Bridger checked for a clear hall, but rarely saw the

other men, to the point he wondered if most didn't take rooms elsewhere. "Remember, I'll be late, but I'll try not to wake you. You try to do the same until the sun's up, at least."

Frank's grin shone from under his cap brim. "In time for church, though, right?"

Bridger thought about a comfortable pillow and what it must be like to sleep until a body had its fill.

"Yes, in time for church," he said. If it kept Frank content for a few weeks longer, he could sacrifice a little shut-eye. But the cost of Frank's safety grew by the day.

Lola fastened the last of the bedclothes on the line with a wooden peg as it caught the breeze and billowed. The snap of the wet corners blended with the rhythm of pounding inside the woodshop.

Bridger had worked like a desperate man from the day the supplies arrived, starting early in the morning and working through lunch before heading over to work on the hotel, which had made excellent progress over the past few weeks. Lola had not been in favor of the plan for such a large, ornate building. But a fine hotel likely attracted a more respectable crowd than the seedy rooms of the boardinghouse. And didn't it prove Ike's interest in moving toward a more respectable business?

She swiped loose hair from her forehead where it clung from the steam of hot, soapy wash water. She checked the time on her brooch. Early for lunch, but some cold lemonade would taste good.

Bridger's soft whistle carried through the air. Perhaps he'd enjoy a break, as well.

Inside, she squeezed the tart fruit, arrived fresh from California, and stirred in sugar. She remembered the molasses cookies she'd made the day before and placed some of those on a tray, too.

Sharing a lunch or at least some midmorning refreshment with Bridger had grown into a daily routine. Lola took a deep breath as she carried the tray out the door. A brief flutter of sanity cautioned her every day. She held more questions than answers about this man and prayed every evening for Marshal Anderson's quick return—surely his investigation would settle her anxious thoughts.

On the other hand, Bridger worked diligently, and his soft-spoken conversations—though mainly filled with appreciation for her father's work and questions about the town—gave her a sense of companionship she'd lost after Papa died. Walking the balance of caution and neighborliness wore on her nerves.

Setting the tray on a stool just off the porch, she heard a bark of pain echo inside the shop. She paused, but only muffled sounds of rattling tools followed as she stepped closer.

She waited only a moment after her sharp rap at the shop door before creaking it open. In the light filtering through the windows, Bridger's lean frame curled around his hand. One end of a white rag hung from his teeth as he tried to tie a knot, but blood quickly spotted it.

"What happened?" she asked, turning him with a shove to get a better look.

"Just a scratch. I got it."

"Let me see," she said, pulling the loose bandage away. A deep gouge cut across his middle finger, from the joint to the fingernail, almost clean through. Blood streamed across his hands and spattered on the workbench. "A scratch?"

"I got it." His tone called her attention to his face, pale and determined.

"Sure you do." She shook out the rag he used and folded the loose scrap of skin into its place before wrapping it tightly. Then she squeezed—hard. Bridger's cheeks grew paler, accentuating the jagged scar.

"Come on!" She dragged him outside and pushed him to a stool. Grabbing his rough right hand, she placed it over the rag and squeezed it hard with both of hers. "Hold that tight, you hear me?" He nodded, still looking dazed and a little woozy. "I'll be right back."

She raced into the mortuary and selected materials she needed from the cabinet, tossing them into a pan as she moved through the door. Outside, she watched Bridger's jaw clench and his eyes blink furiously, head tipped back.

She grabbed his hand as she fell to her knees and pulled him upright. "Not that way. Are you light-headed? Going to pass out?" she said, removing his fingers pressed to the wound. She slowly unraveled the cloth.

He nodded. "Don't much like the sight of blood, ma'am."

"Tip your head low, like this." She tugged his head down below his shoulders. The soft hair at his nape tingled warm against her cool fingers.

She laid a fresh rag across his hand and replaced his other hand on top for pressure. Dumping the supplies from the pan, she ran to pump cool water into it.

"Here," she said, returning to his side. "Put your hand in this. It's cold, but that'll help slow the bleeding and clean it out."

He did as she bade, his normal dusky tone returning. "Sorry about this, Lola. I didn't mean to cause a fuss."

She added carbolic to the water and rubbed more over her hands. The flow of blood slowed before she pulled his hand from the pan and covered it with another dry cloth. She rinsed the bowl and returned with fresh water, added more carbolic and placed needles and scissors in to disinfect.

"You're looking better," she said, blotting his hand dry with the cloth that covered it.

His smile returned, growing with the flush along his jaw.

Dousing her hands with carbolic one last time, she threaded the needle with catgut and stabilized his arm between her elbow and ribs in a firm hold. She wedged her left hand around his fist, raising and separating the torn finger to work on.

Blowing loose hair from her eyes, she pursed her lips and pulled the needle through his skin, gently tugging the loose edges together. Another stitch. "You still with me?" she asked, glad to avoid his view, but concerned with his silence.

"I'll be fine," he said. A chuff of laughter blew warm against her neck. "Although, some doctor you are. No whiskey to dull the pain of the needle."

She smiled, though she knew he couldn't see it. "I figure the pain of whatever sliced this finger had to be worse than this little needle. What happened?"

"Let's just say your father's chisels are plenty sharp."

She nodded but still couldn't picture exactly how he'd done it. She kept adding stitches, forming a perfect hook along the edge and across his finger.

His solid chest warmed her shoulder as he peered over it, watching her work.

"You're pretty good at this. You ever think of being a doctor instead of the undertaker?" he asked.

"To be honest, I have," she said, even more grateful to not have to look him in the eye. Not even her father had known. "But there's a lot more to it than a few little stitches in a clumsy carpenter's finger."

She made her final stitch and tied off the end before moving to her feet and facing him. "There you go. Try to move it—gently. Make sure there isn't more damage."

He drew his fingers into a claw a few times, but his brown eyes focused on her face. "Why didn't you ever try to go to school to be a doctor, Lola? Any woman as smart as you, doing what you do, why, you'd be a fine one."

She broke his gaze with a laugh. "Nice as it might be to try and keep folks away from the job I do now, it's not that simple. Colleges that allow women are rare as it is, let alone medical school. And even if one could be found, they are plenty expensive to attend."

"So how'd you get into this?" His square chin pointed to her home, her business, his voice still steady and serious.

"Papa taught me. His uncle was an undertaker back in Boston, and he learned by helping out as a boy, I suppose. But there wasn't as much to it then, from all Papa said."

"You do more than most," Bridger said. "How'd he learn all that?"

"Papa tried a lot of things, but folks always called on him when someone passed on, even before Mama died. When the War Between the States broke out, Papa felt called to help, though he was old for the fight. Uncle Joseph and Aunt Betty came and lived with me here, and Papa went to war."

Bridger shifted on the stool. "A lot of young men didn't come marching home again."

"You?"

"I fought," he said.

When he offered nothing further, she continued. "They put Papa to work with the doctors as a medic, due to his age and background. If a soldier died in camp or not so far from home, sometimes they or the family would try to get him home for burial. After the war, Papa heard of a school opening up to teach the science behind it, all they'd learned over the course of the war. The teachers traveled around the country, I guess, offering classes. Not everyone goes about it that way, of course. Most towns, I suppose, just wake and bury the dead right quick."

Bridger nodded. "That's been my experience."

"Anyway, with more people heading West but having family back East, greater need for Papa's services came. Without Mama around, he needed my help, and so I learned."

"You do a fine job, too." Bridger held up his fist and examined her work. "You'd make a pretty fair seamstress, as well." His lopsided smile teased her and his conversation brought familiar warmth.

She grabbed his wrist and cradled his hand, scrunching her face, feigning close inspection. But she couldn't hold it when he roared with laughter.

"I must apologize for interrupting this cozy scene—"

Lola jumped to her feet as Ike sauntered around the corner of the house. "Ike, you startled me!" She dropped Bridger's hand, and heat blazed her cheeks.

Bridger also stood, though not so fast. "I cut my hand up pretty good, Mr. Tyler. Miss Lola stitched me back together, you see."

Ike smirked, that all-knowing expression she recognized from their days of courtship. It still set her teeth on edge. "I saw enough to assure me you'll be in fine shape for longer hours on my projects," he said.

"He'll need to keep an eye on that hand, make sure it doesn't get infected," she said. She crossed her arms in front of her. "Was there something particular you needed, Ike?"

He brushed his mustache with a finger and stepped closer. He looked down at her, eyes sparkling and lips quirked at the corner in that way she'd found so appealing years ago. "I always need to make sure you're well and have all the assistance you require. After all we've been through together, and for friendship's sake, you know I'm only teasing, right?"

His sincere, kind tone always brought that queasy flutter to her chest. He teased as a brother might, but really, wasn't his concern from the heart?

"I know, Ike." She gave him a warm smile that faded as Bridger's gaze drew blank. "I also know you have the propriety to come to my front door if you're looking to speak with me."

He tipped his hat and laughed. "I'm caught! I heard Mr. Jamison's voice as I walked up, so I hope you'll pardon me this once."

"Oh, I see," Lola said. "You gentlemen go ahead and discuss what you need to. I'll pick up my things and get out of your way."

"Here, I'll get it," Bridger insisted, stooping to gather the bloody rags at his feet.

She bent to pick up the materials she'd been using. Her hands brushed his as they grabbed for the pan together, and Lola found herself staring into his eyes, no longer dull and closed, but deep brown with golden flecks lit by the sun. Her breath caught.

"There," Ike said, tossing the remaining ball of catgut into the pan. He glanced between them. "Send me the bill for your service to his hand. After all, he is my employee. Besides, you'll both be busy for a while. Bridger, I have another delivery for you. And, Lola," he said, looking her square in the eye, "you have a body to care for. We found Cecil Anthony dead this morning."

Chapter Ten

Bridger steadied a nail with his bandaged finger and pounded it into the boards. Standing on top of the second-floor roof gave him a good view of the town, and he imagined what it would look like from the third and final story. Tall building for this town, but given the number of folks moving in and about Quiver Creek, it wouldn't be the last.

He wiped his sleeve across his forehead, peering across to Lola's place. Her tears at Ike's callous announcement had proved his undoing. Guilt and gratitude had swelled together when Ike had ordered his escape and sent him to help Toby retrieve the body and deliver the old man to Lola's place.

By the time they'd returned, she'd donned a fresh apron and enough determination to cover her grief and do her job. She'd pulled the white sheet down to reveal purple bruises covering the storekeeper's face, and her fingers had traced the edge of his head with loving care.

Given the fierce protectiveness the man had shown for Lola, their relationship had been a close one. How could Lola bear to do her job, when it came to preparing loved ones for burial?

"How long you think one nail will hold that beam, Jamison?" Toby called from the ground.

Bridger refocused and reached for another nail. Ike had sent the other men on extra patrols around town, leaving him to deal with Toby's grumpy disposition alone. "We'd finish twice as fast if you'd come on up and pound a few yourself."

"I got things to attend to on the ground," Toby said. He'd never set foot on the second floor until they completed the walls, and his tone confirmed Bridger's suspicion: the man feared heights.

Ike sauntered along the street, clearing the bend from the mortuary. Frustration spiked in Bridger's chest. He pounded another nail in two heavy swipes and moved for another board.

"You're making good progress," Ike said from the street, hand shielding his eyes as he tilted his head. "Good to see your injuries aren't holding you back from the work you're being paid to do."

"How's Lola?"

"I just left her, poor thing. That old man meant something to her, I suppose."

Bridger glanced down before setting another nail. "He watched out for her, that's for sure. Between her father, the sheriff and now Mr. Anthony, she's had a lot of tough work lately."

Toby grunted. "Woman like that best get used to it."

Bridger dropped the board he held and hunkered down to get as close as he could at this height to Toby's swarthy face. "What's that supposed to mean?"

"I don't reckon she has any business taking on a man's work like she done. She gets a mite more personal with her 'guests,' like she calls them, than Mattie does with ours. She ought to find a man and get married like any respectable woman—"

The hammer flew from Bridger's hand, narrowly missing Toby's head. "You lousy, judgmental—"

"Whoa, now!" Ike raised hands toward him, stepping closer to Toby and picking up the tool. "Back off, Jamison. A man has a right to his opinion, and it's not like half the town doesn't agree with him."

"You're supposed to be helping her!"

"I do. Lola and I go way back. At one point, we were betrothed, and if I have my way, we will be again. That would be the greatest help she could get. She just isn't of a mind to see it yet. But she will. Soon."

Bridger's finger throbbed with every heave of his chest. His jaw clenched until he almost choked with the desire to rage on. He stood and stepped away from the edge, never tearing his gaze from Ike's. His memory burned with the knowledge of his father's temper. "Miss Lola seems to be a woman of her own mind, if you ask me," he said, taming his furious tongue.

"She's in mourning now—her mind's not thinking clearly. She'll come around," Ike said. He tossed the hammer high and it landed with a skid across the floorboards. "The point is, it certainly isn't any of your concern either way. You're hired—by me—to help her out. So don't go thinking you're anything more than the handyman, you got that?"

Ike's fire lay low, but steady, like it had the night he'd been hired. Bridger recognized it and the warning it delivered. He couldn't imagine the hows or whys of a woman with the class and beauty of Lola Martin even considering marriage to a snake like Ike Tyler. But Ike was right. He needed this job and the pay if he were ever going to provide something better for Frank than a stuffy room next to the noisy saloon of a growing town. He had no claim on Lola and no right to do any more than he'd been hired for.

He swallowed hard and nodded. Picking up the hammer, he turned for another board and some extra nails to tuck under the edge of his lip. "I got that—boss," he mumbled around a mouthful of nails and began pounding. He'd be no better than Frank, getting involved where he wasn't wanted. On the other hand, maybe Lola ought to be the one to say so. She certainly hadn't given the impression she found his presence difficult to tolerate this past week or so.

"I'm glad you understand your position, Jamison," Ike said. His smile shone below his oiled mustache, that instant calm as infuriating as his possessiveness. "It never pays not to follow my orders, though you'll have to take my word on that. There's no one still around that's had the audacity to try."

Lola returned her teacup to the saucer with a delicate clink. As much as she hated to burden Grace with more thoughts of death, the comfortable spot at her friend's table soothed her sadness. "I'll miss Mr. Anthony so much. I can't imagine what happened," she said.

Grace's hand fluttered over her growing belly. "Where did they find him?"

Lola bit her tongue, thinking how weak her loss must seem compared to her friend. "The bottom of his stairs, Toby said. Like he'd fallen on his way down. But Mr. Anthony wasn't a tottering old man, Grace. He wouldn't just—"

"Accidents happen, Lola. You know that better than most, I'd say. Besides, our time is appointed by God, and when He calls, we go. We can take comfort in the fact that Cecil knew the Lord and was ready for Heaven."

She couldn't stop a small smile that grew with the thought of Mr. Anthony seeing his dear wife again, but glanced away to the window, the notion too heavy to share with her friend.

"I'm sorry to burden you with this all. It's just been so…difficult these past few months, harder than I'd have thought. I know we had plans for later this week, but I needed to get away from my house for a while. Does that make any sense?"

Grace stretched a hand to pat her arm. "You were right to come here. I would have wanted to know, and sharing a sorrow lightens the heart."

"But maybe not so much for you," Lola said.

Grace shook her head, swirling her tea in the cup. "Losing Pete hurts so bad, nothing can make it worse."

Lola squeezed her hands together as tears filled her vision and threatened to fall. "I'm sorry for being so selfish. We must discuss brighter things. How has it been, having your parents here?"

Grace sniffed and dabbed her eyes with a lace-edged handkerchief. "They're a godsend. Pa's management skills have transferred to the ranch as well as they worked in his store back home. I believe he's gotten younger since they arrived, out surveying the herd and such, getting things ready to brand calves and move them to summer grazing."

"How is your mother adjusting?"

Grace smiled. "Better than I expected. She's never lived outside of town, but there's something about the air and the mountains, she says, that gives her new vitality. I think she's falling in love with Wyoming the same way I did. It's been good to hear word from home, family and friends, too. She's stepped in to care for me like I'm a little girl again, and maybe it's wrong, but it's been a great help."

"I'm glad."

"Me, too," Grace said. "At first, I wasn't so sure. But it's given me time to grieve Pete without being overwhelmed by everything else."

Lola nodded. She'd been more alone than ever after Papa died, and taking time to plan what she should do had proved impossible. She'd had to step into Papa's shoes from the start, with he and the man responsible both to bury right after it happened.

She fingered the delicate crochet of the tablecloth. "That's good news after this hard spring we've had in Quiver Creek. So much bad news…too much."

Grace's eyes widened and she slipped around the table to edge the curtain back from the window. "Speaking of—here comes that marshal!" She brushed her skirt and moved toward the door at a speed surprising for a woman with her baby girth.

Lola followed behind as her friend opened the door. Jake Anderson reined to a stop and dismounted, greeting them with a doff of his hat.

"I heard I might catch you here, Miss Martin, and was happy to take the advantage away from any prying eyes in town, if that's all right. I won't take long—I just wanted to let you know I'm back in town."

"I'm glad to see that," Lola said, squeezing past Grace to stand on the bottom step. "There's been another death in town, and we wondered when you'd be able to return."

Jake removed his notepad from an inside pocket. "I heard the local mercantile owner was found this morning. He was elderly, though, correct?"

Lola crossed her arms before her. "He had more years

on him than most around here, but 'elderly' hardly suited him, either." She thought of the round bruises across Mr. Anthony's dusky skin. "It doesn't seem right he should be taken that way."

Jake gave a wry grin, rubbing his hand along his wide jaw. "All in the Lord's timing?"

Lola sensed his question, thinking again on the pattern of black-and-blue splotches. "To be honest, I'm not entirely convinced, Marshal." She glanced up at Grace, thin wisps of blond hair blowing across her hollow cheeks. Images of death slowly molded together in her mind. "What are the chances a young sheriff would die in the mountains the same way an old man died in his store?"

Chapter Eleven

Bridger shifted in the back pew as Pastor Evans delivered the eulogy for Cecil Anthony. While he barely knew the man and had not earned a fair impression from him, he attended the service to pay his respects. He hoped to have the same kind of fire in his belly at Mr. Anthony's age.

Ike told all his men to be at the service, and they obeyed, standing in a gang at the back of the sanctuary, looking as comfortable as a cat in a pond. Bridger focused on the minister, glad he'd arrived on his own.

Mr. Anthony's daughter, a petite middle-aged woman, had traveled with her son for the service. He heard she planned to take the body back East for burial next to her mother.

Bridger never considered anything further than being buried where he fell. Fighting in the war, men were fortunate to get a marker for their graves. Home had been the dust under his feet for so long he doubted a soul would remember him back in Indiana. But as he offered condolences to Cecil's family, he considered the peaceful rest upon the businessman's face. The coffin he'd fashioned, his first attempt, had turned out well. Lola did important work, and it gave him a good feeling to be part of it.

He caught Lola's profile as she sat in the front pew, focused on the minister. The black velvet hat and cape she wore could not outshine her hair, the length of it curled and twisted in a rich mass at the base of her neck. Her dark lashes and wide eyes were noticeable even at this distance, and her pale skin spoke of the sadness she felt as well as her beauty. Who would look out for her now, with Mr. Anthony gone?

"Saying goodbye is not easy. We don't like to do it even when we have reasonable expectation and intention of seeing our loved ones again within a few days," Pastor Evans said.

Bridger clasped the top of his hat in his hand and nodded in agreement. Ike had put him in charge of seeing Mr. Anthony and his family to the rail depot with another supply order to pick up for the return trip. Frank wouldn't like it, and Bridger knew he'd taken the coward's way by waiting to tell him just before he left. But the money had been too good to pass up.

He thought of the savings that grew in the little pouch stashed in his saddlebags. Before long, he'd need to consider a bank at this rate. If he held on to this job for several more months, he might have the funds to get his own place and set up shop. A year or two, he'd afford that little ranch Frank dreamed about.

If only Frank would listen to reason and stay put. Bridger didn't like the idea of leaving him for what might be the better part of a week, holed up in that room. But it had to be…for a while longer.

"But the Lord does not leave us comfortless. He sends His spirit in special ways at these hardest times. He will not leave our minds weary and our fragile hearts without protection," the pastor continued.

Lola bowed her head into her gloved hands, but the sound of her muffled sobs traveled to where he sat. Ike swept a handkerchief from his suit coat with grand flair and tapped it against her shoulder.

Bridger's scar pulled taut as his jaw clenched. He shifted forward in the pew, irritated with Ike's hovering. Irritated, too, with the way Lola allowed it.

He stiffened in the seat. Ike said he'd once had a claim on her heart and planned to again. He couldn't picture a fine, Godly woman like Lola with a barkeep, though. People and circumstances changed, and he grudgingly admitted Ike possessed qualities a lady might mistake for charm. Except something more rang false when it came to Ike. Bridger couldn't nail down anything for certain, but it didn't dovetail.

Pastor Evans drew his attention again with his gentle smile and direct way of saying things. "Cecil lived a good life, he'd be the first to tell you, and a Godly one witnessed by we who knew him. Our town will miss him, but he isn't lost forever. To those who love and serve Jesus Christ as he did, Cecil has only moved into the storehouse of God, and we'll see him again someday."

Bridger tapped his hat brim with his bandaged finger. Could that have been what riled Mr. Anthony about him? He'd believed in Jesus, the Son of God, from the time he'd been a little feller at his grandmother's knee. But that foundation seemed to lack a first story, let alone whatever built up beyond that. Did the old man sense the lack in him?

He stood with the rest of the town for the minister's final prayer. Trusting Jesus was real didn't seem nearly so hard as believing that mattered in his daily life. In the same way, Frank knowing their need for money came easier than understanding why he'd be gone for a week. Bridger squared his shoulders at the thought of the coming fight.

Lola opened the door for Bridger and Ike's men to carry Mr. Anthony in for one final night as her guest. "Place the casket on the table." She unpinned her hat and set it on the stand in the corner.

Toby and Jasper Ferris dropped their end with a careless thump. "Be careful!" she said. "Mr. Anthony deserves more care and respect!"

Bridger and the other men lowered the foot of the coffin with a gentle slide against the leather-covered table. She took a deep breath and held the door open, her nerves working overtime. "Thank you, gentlemen," she said, fighting tears from her throat.

Her head bowed, she blinked tears away as they filed out without comment. One pair of boots stopped in her vision. Bridger.

"That was a real nice service, Lola. You do a good thing here."

She smiled, pleased he'd made a point to tell her so. "You did, too. Most men would not take as much care with something so...practical."

His grin came gentle, lifting the edge of the scar. "Every piece of wood deserves my best work, the way I see it. Maybe even more so for such...practical things. Besides, your pa left clear instructions. I can tell he took pride in his work, too."

"Thank you." She'd missed Bridger over the past few days, busy with arrangements for the Anthony family and meeting with Marshal Anderson. "It was good of you to come, being new to town and all. I'd be happy for you to continue your work for me, if you're still of a mind."

"That's what I wanted to tell—"

A sharp knock drew her attention to the door, still open in her hand.

A broad figure filled the entry. "Lola, I wonder if I might speak with you a moment?" He glanced at Bridger. "Is this a good time?"

"Of course…Jake. Uh, come inside." She motioned him in, closing the door partway. Bridger stood frozen, a blank, uncertain look on his face. She sensed tension building from his squared shoulders to his rough hands, resting where his gun belt would be.

"Jake, this is Bridger Jamison. He's the gentleman I spoke of before. Bridger, this is Mar—Mr. Jake Anderson, from up Montana way. He's come to Quiver Creek on business."

"What kind of business might that be, sir?" Bridger asked. His tone drew out soft and low, belying his stance.

Jake waved his hand in a friendly gesture. "Any business that proves exciting. A little bit of everything to get what I need."

"Sounds interesting." Bridger's tone fell flat and his eyes glazed. He appeared…suspicious.

"I'll be in town for a while now, Mr. Jamison, and I'd enjoy learning more about your work."

"That so?" He shot a hard glance at Lola and she flinched. "Miss Martin must've had plenty to say about me. You have need of a carpenter?"

"I may. One never can tell which acquaintances might be most helpful," Jake said, his tone cool.

"Bridger has shown himself to be a fine craftsman." She closed the door to a finger-width to prevent their voices from carrying to any passersby. "In fact, in working with him over the past week or so, I feel confident that you might share with him the nature of your occupation. We could use Bridger's help."

Bridger's gaze threw daggers her way. What was he thinking?

His jaw quaked. "Is that right? Sounds rather cozy, now, doesn't it?"

Did he think…? Was Bridger jealous?

Jake looked between them, and she bit her lip. The marshal had wanted to introduce himself in his own way and time, but he'd have to question Bridger at some point. The sooner he sorted out Bridger's story, the sooner he could focus on his other matters, right?

Bridger drew a deep breath and squared his shoulders. "You don't need to tell me anything, Lola. You're a grown woman running a business of your own, and I'm the hired hand. I'm smart enough to figure this without any explanation. You don't have to worry about me flapping my gums about it, either. The company you keep is up to you." He stormed to her side, hand on the door latch.

"No, Bridger, listen!"

"Hold up," Jake said. He stretched his long arm out to the door and pushed it completely closed, Lola's fingers slipping out of danger at the last instant. "Let me introduce myself properly, Mr. Jamison. I'm Jake Anderson, U.S. marshal. And I'd be mighty interested in hearing just how you wound up with the body of a dead sheriff for delivery."

Bridger stepped away, glancing between Lola and Jake in the darkening morgue. Muscles relaxed and calm wariness overtook frustration, as he offered to shake the lawman's hand. "I'm glad to meet you, Marshal. I started to give up on you."

"That so?" the man said, his deep tone laced with doubt.

"You don't know how anxious I am to clear this matter." Not to mention the strange relief he felt knowing the man's true interest in Lola.

She looked flustered, eyes darting about the room. "Would you like to move this conversation into my parlor, gentlemen?"

The marshal waved her off, facing Bridger. "This is fine. So, Mr. Jamison, tell me your story." He pulled a tablet from inside his coat pocket.

Bridger removed his hat and ran fingers over his hair, drawing them down along the scar. "There's not much to the story. I came through the pass on my way into Quiver Creek and stopped for the night to set up camp. When I went to get firewood, I found the body a few feet off the trail. Loaded him onto my horse and brought him to town, here to the undertaker."

Lola gave a tentative grin as she lit a lantern. The warmth of the flame reflected off the cedar shelf, adding a rosy glow to her cheeks.

Anderson wrote a few things, then flipped back a couple pages and read something written there. His boots shifted, the pencil scratched, every sound magnified by the solemn bareness of the room. Then the marshal looked up and tried to stare the truth from him.

Bridger held the man's gaze, steady and hard. He had nothing to hide on that account. It made little difference that Frank had discovered the body first.

"You think you could show me the place?"

"Yes, sir. I'm heading out of town tomorrow early,

be back by week's end. I could ride up there with you Saturday."

The marshal's stare went from cool to frozen. "What's calling you out of town?"

"I'm to deliver Mr. Anthony's body to the train depot in Ralston and run a few errands on the way back."

"Did the Anthony family secure your services?" He kept writing, fingers moving nearly as fast as the questions, not bothering to look up.

"No, my boss is helping them. He's sending me."

Anderson flipped to the back of his notepad, scanning through with his pencil. "I understand you work for Ike Tyler. He's accommodating the family, you say?"

Bridger glanced at Lola again, her slim brow quirked as she focused on the marshal. "As a favor to Miss Lola," he said.

The warmth of her hand on his wrist surprised him. "Let me say something here." Her voice rose, firm and light. "Mr. Jamison arrived at my door late in the evening as a stranger. Then he brought in the body of not only our town sheriff, but a dear friend. Having conversations with him over the past few weeks, and seeing his work and concern for others, I no longer doubt his story is true."

"You're vouching for his character?" the marshal asked, his gaze just as firm and direct with her.

Eyes wide, Bridger watched her vision waver from his too-long hair to his worn collar. She shivered when her gaze followed the trail of his scar, and he looked away.

"Yes, I suppose I am," she said. But the tremor in her voice couldn't be missed.

Marshal Anderson made a few notes and then closed his tablet with a cool smile. "Mr. Tyler helps you a lot, doesn't he, Lola?"

She nodded, her cheeks painted a faint blush. The coolness of the room brushed Bridger's arm as she removed her gloved hand. "We're friends from way back," she said, but her tone held defense.

"So I understand," Jake said. "In fact, word through town is, you were engaged at one time, isn't that right?"

Color blossomed across her face. "Years ago."

Bridger planted his boots into the floorboards, fighting his desire to protect her. But the lawman's eyes turned kindly, and he patted Lola's crossed arms. "I don't mean to throw past choices into the present, Lola. But I'm here to ask the questions and discover if any crime has been committed."

She returned a tremulous smile. "I understand."

Bridger understood, too, with sharp, sudden clarity. A woman who had feelings for a man wasn't always the best judge of character, he knew from experience. No matter how many folks tried to step in and help, hadn't Mother denied them all to stay with their father? Despite the alcohol, the fighting?

He looked at Lola. Knowing so much but still trusting. Maybe too much so. Enough that, in spite of whatever caused their wedding to be called off, she still didn't fully see the kind of man Ike was.

And if her judgment had proved wrong once, how much merit did her confidence in *his* story hold? Her forgiving nature, Ike's renewed attentiveness and Lola's vulnerability caused her suspicions to wane, it seemed— while the marshal's questions focused his own. Ike eagerly helped anyone who could profit him in some way, he noticed. Lola's beauty and community ties would advance Ike's standing, just as Toby's construction knowledge established a fine hotel and Mattie's vivacious personality drew business. Ike paid well, for certain—

and held it out like a carrot on a stick to make a mule move. Which begged the question—how was Ike using *him?*

Figuring it out mattered more than ever. Because Jake Anderson wasn't here only to ask questions about the sheriff's death—he intended to investigate Ike Tyler, too.

Chapter Twelve

Lola drew her shawl. Burdens of the day weighed heavy, and she longed to slip into cool blankets and sleep until the sun blinked in her eyes.

A soft knock at the door provided welcome distraction from her cares. At least this call came to her home, not the business. Maybe Bridger needed something before he left in the morning, or perhaps Jake had more questions. She didn't know what else she could tell him. Her thoughts were foggy and jumbled from their discussion earlier in the day. What was happening in this town?

She peeked out the window. Ike waited at the front step, his tall frame rocking from heel to toe. At least he didn't bring business. She hoped. She opened the door to the cool night air.

"Good evening, Lola!" He leaned toward her with his hand against the doorframe above her head. "I'm sorry to disturb you. I know you haven't had an easy day. I wanted to see how you're holding up. I hope I didn't startle you."

A sigh escaped as weariness flared. "No, though I am surprised to see you running patrols."

His eyes glowed in the faint moonlight, shadows casting an unpleasant ring around them. "Mattie can handle the saloon for a while, with my men to back her up. Besides, this is a patrol of a more personal nature." He grinned, a hint of the boy she once knew. "I wanted to remind you that my care for you far outreaches my concern for this town."

She rested against the opposite side of the jamb, warmed by his thoughtfulness. "It hurts to say goodbye to good people—so many dear friends—but I'll be all right. It's what I do."

It eased her heart to talk, but considering the impression Mr. Anthony had held of Ike, it felt wrong to share too much. "I appreciate you stopping by, Ike. But it has been a long day, and it's about time for me to turn in. Everything here is closed up tight."

"That's good, good," he whispered. He shifted closer, his gaze searching her face. "I wanted to tell you again how sorry I am about Cecil. He and I didn't always see eye to eye, but I know you had a soft spot for him."

The knot in her chest slipped loose and tears washed her eyes. "He was the grandfather I never knew. I'll miss him terribly."

Ike's cold fingers grasped her elbow within her thick cape. A shiver quaked through her, and she drew the cover close about her neck.

Ike smoothed his mustache. "I'm sure he felt the same about you. He made it his mission to keep any would-be suitors away, that's for sure," he said. "I propose to do the same, Lola."

"I appreciate the thought, but you have a whole town to watch after, until a new sheriff can be chosen. I'm sure you'll be glad to have that position filled so you can focus on your own business."

"We want to be sure we have the right man for the job, so there's no hurry to find a replacement. Besides, my men and I have done fairly well, wouldn't you agree?" He slid his arm to her shoulder. "I'm tempted to apply for the position myself. 'Sheriff' is a more acceptable title than 'saloonkeeper,' is it not?"

Papa certainly might have found it so. "I'm in no position to judge you, Ike. There are those in this town who would say it's not honorable for a woman to do the job I'm doing. What matters is that your intentions bring honor to God."

Ike smiled, but it didn't carry to his eyes. "I do hope, my dear, that you'll consider me on the path to reformation. We are friends, aren't we?" He tipped her face toward his with a thumb against her chin. "I don't know if there is anyone else with whom to speak regarding you, but isn't it possible we might return to where we were? I'm making changes, Lola. Trust me, I'm doing all I can to return myself to your favor, to prepare a life for you, for us together."

Lola backed away, but the joy they'd felt together overwhelmed her tired mind, pushed the empty ache of loss and loneliness to the darkest corners. "I'm still in mourning, Ike, please…" She drew a deep breath, feeling his fingers caress her cheek. "I still need time."

He drew so close the shadows hid his features, only the warmth of his breath filling her senses. "If it means I still have a chance, darling, time is something I can afford to give."

She closed her eyes, exhaustion bearing down. She thought of her papa, Mr. Anthony, Pete and all she had lost. Loneliness stabbed her heart, and wrong as it was, she knew if he tried to kiss her now, she'd have no energy to stop him.

A clatter at her back door jolted her eyes open, and she breathed hard with surprise. "What—?"

Ike drew away, a flare of irritation bordering on anger striking his face. He raced around the side of her home. "Who's there?"

He disappeared from sight, only to return a moment later, his usual grace lost. "I saw no one, Lola. Perhaps a cat."

She shivered in the breeze, thankful for the interruption. No temptation beyond what she could bear, she recalled. "It's all right, then. It's all right."

Ike stopped, poised as if to return to his previous stance. But she shook her head. "You have a town to protect, Mr. Tyler." She drew her arms around her waist. "It's best you be off."

"I won't apologize for what I was about to do, Lola."

"I wouldn't expect you to." She grinned in spite of herself. "But it is well that the cat came along when it did."

Ike backed away to his horse and then stared at her a moment, hand on the pommel. "I'll consider that a sign of hope for my future, then, ma'am. Good night, and rest easy."

She watched him ride off and slipped into the warmth of her dark house. Her tired limbs ached, but at odds with her heart and mind. Easy rest would be an unlikely blessing tonight.

Bridger peered at the dented clock for the hundredth time since settling into his bedroll at the foot of Frank's bed. He needed sleep for an early start.

Frank's heavy tread finally echoed up the stairs. Bridger sat, hoping his brother remained unseen. He hadn't noticed how loud Frank's boots could be.

As Frank stepped through the door, breath ragged, Bridger turned the lantern wick higher. His brother flinched to find him waiting. "Where have you been?"

The door closed with a soft snick, and Bridger sensed Frank's purposeful slowness. "Just walking, Bridge."

"Just walking where, Frank? You're usually in by now." He hated his accusing tone.

Frank set his hat on the desk and moved to the bed, which groaned under his broad build. "Around town. I didn't talk to nobody, either. I even ran—"

Bridger shot to his feet, gripping the foot of the bed frame in each hand. "Why did you need to run? What happened?"

Frank smacked his hand on the flat pillow and drew it across his midsection. "He didn't even see me, Bridge. I'm fast. So don't growl at me!"

Bridger gentled his tone against the frustration in his chest. "Who didn't see you?"

"Mr. Tyler."

Bridger rubbed a knuckle across his lips, holding back angry words that threatened to bolt. They would get him nowhere with his brother. "Where *didn't* he see you?"

Frank stared at the door as if judging his chance of success for escape. "At Miss Lola's," he said, voice a bare whisper.

"I told you to stay away from there! What do I have to do, Frank, chain you inside this room all day?"

His brother flinched again and rubbed his head. The exact spot where Pa had knocked him with the skillet, all those years ago, still gave him fits at times. Memories flashed through his mind—the pinch of Pa's tight grip around his arm, shaking so hard Bridger thought it would rip right out of the socket, while blood ran down his face from the cut of the broken bottle… Frank stepping in and breaking the hold, sending him into a sprawl against the rough wall…

"I said I won't do it again, all right? Don't be mad,

Bridge. And don't lock me in—please. I ain't no dog." Frank knelt in front of him, rocking the bed in his desperation.

Bridger stepped back. "I wouldn't, Frank. I didn't mean it—honest, I didn't. You have every right to walk around here free as any other man. But you have to blend in awhile longer, you see? And snooping about the homes of beautiful ladies isn't what men do if they're lying low!"

Frank slumped, his chin bobbing in agreement. "See, I knew you thought she's pretty, too!"

Bridger squeezed his temples between his thumbs. "But you don't see me sneaking around trying to catch sight of her!"

"You sound like those men in the last town, like I have bad ideas about her," Frank accused. "I never would hurt her, not any woman. I know what the Bible says about treating women right, and I remember what Grandpa taught, same as you. We got to protect 'em, right?"

Bridger's ire cooled as he acknowledged, with shame, that his brother's insight held more truth than he wanted to admit. "I'm sorry, Frank. I didn't mean to make you feel that way." He knew better than any other soul on earth the lengths Frank Jamison stretched to offer protection for any living creature in need. His every breath served as proof.

"Besides," Frank continued, "I was not either peeking at her. It was spying, like making sure she was okay."

Bridger pulled the chair from the desk and sat, watching Frank unlace his boots and toe them off. "What makes you think she needs you to 'spy,' then?"

"She had sad eyes."

"Well, she is sad. Her friend died, which is something else I have to tell—"

"That's not the only thing."

Bridger rubbed his neck. Of course it wasn't the only thing. But he felt certain Lola hadn't realized her former fiancé was under investigation by the federal marshal.

"What else?" Bridger asked.

"Mr. Tyler saw her."

"You mean he was visiting her?"

"Talking to her. Out on her front step."

"They're friends. He probably checked on her," Bridger said. He stood and moved to the window, as irritated at himself as toward Lola. Since when did her evening conversations make any difference to him?

"He looked real friendly, though. Like some of those men back home looked at Ma after Pa died, her being so pretty. He got to standing too close, so I—"

Bridger grabbed his brother's shoulder and tried to look him in the eye, but Frank gazed at his stockinged feet. Worry flared. "What exactly did you do?"

"Nothin'!" Frank twisted his shoulder from Bridger's grasp. "Well, nothin' bad. I kicked the porch to make a noise."

"Then what happened?" Alarm pounded in Bridger's chest.

"Mr. Tyler came and checked, but I was out of sight, Bridge. Honest. He told Miss Lola it was a cat."

Bridger released his breath in a tight whoosh. Now to hope Ike believed that, too. "All right, Frank. I'm glad you told me. I can't smooth things over if I don't know what you've done, so you need to tell me."

Frank looked dejected, and Bridger's conscience pricked him. His brother had to understand, somehow, how difficult this was, and how much more so it could get. Especially when he'd be gone for a few days.

"Listen, Frank. You have to be careful, and it scares

me to think you could get into more trouble. I mean, there were those who wanted to hang you in that last town."

"I know!" Frank said. His face puckered, tired and petulant.

"Then you have to do what I say and stay away from Miss Lola." Bridger broke his brother's focus. "'Cause I'm leaving town for a few days on a job for Mr. Tyler, and I won't be around to keep you out of trouble."

"Why are you going this time?"

"I'm to deliver Mr. Anthony's body for the train back East. I head out early in the morning."

"How long?" Frank's resigned tone spoke more of irritation than acceptance.

"I should be back Friday afternoon if nothing goes wrong. Until then, I need you to stay put. No snooping around in town. Promise you'll stay off the streets while I'm gone."

Frank slipped off his shirt and stretched out on the bed in his undershirt and denim pants. "I won't cause no trouble, Bridge, I promise. I know I'm a scary-looking fellow."

His dejected tone curdled in Bridger's chest. He patted Frank's leg. "I know you won't, brother. The problem is, you never do."

Chapter Thirteen

Bridger slipped from the room while skies remained misty gray and Frank still snored.

He hadn't bothered to light the lamp, afraid to disturb his brother's hard-won respite. It served as a reminder that Frank's hours in the room would be largely spent in the dark, fear of fire keeping him from lighting the lantern. And his meals would be reduced to trail rations—some jerky, crackers and a wedge of cheese, with water from a canteen filled daily in the creek. Frank wouldn't starve, but he'd likely be a few pounds leaner by the time Bridger returned.

Bridger balanced his saddlebag across a shoulder and slipped into the saloon through the back door for some last-minute supplies. The long bar gleamed in the reflection of the mirror behind it, clean and at rest with the tables and chairs after another lively night.

The door of Ike's suite creaked open. Mattie tiptoed through, hair disheveled and wrapped from neck to toes in a thin robe that in some strange way left less to the imagination than her usual costume. Bridger stood frozen, as heat blazed across his chest. He'd never considered himself a man to be swayed by a girl like Mattie, but she did hold her own charms. He cleared his throat so as not to startle her.

"Good morning, Bridger." Mattie's greeting came at a whisper, sultry and rough from smoke that filled this room each evening. She subdued a hank of curls behind one ear with a silky caress and smiled, her dimple flirtatious beneath sleepy eyes. "You're up and at 'em early this morning, sugar," she said, smoothing her robe over her hips. "Jasper leaves coffee for me, if you want some. It's stale from last night, but plenty hot, and strong enough to stand a spoon."

She wound past him, pulling the faded blue cloth tighter around her narrow waist, and moved toward the kitchen. Glad for dimness that he hoped hid his blush better than it hid her sway, he started to refuse. But she paused at the door to face him, her features bare and sweet, looking younger than he'd have thought her to be. "Please? It'd be nice to have a talk with you."

Bridger nodded agreement and she flounced to the stove, her smile bright. He found it harder to stand his ground with this innocent version of Mattie than her usual flamboyant self. Sunshine struggled its way through the gray sky outside the swinging doors, likely a forecast of the rain he'd suffer through on the drive today. A few minutes to warm his gizzard shouldn't cause much delay. His boots echoed across the floor.

Mattie returned with two chipped mugs, steam rising from the top of each one. Setting his coffee on the bar, she propped herself on a corner stool and patted another.

Bridger passed up the seat to lean against the bar. Mattie pulled a bottle of whiskey, doused her cup with a shot and raised her brow in question.

"No, thanks," he said. "Kind of early, don't you think?"

"Ah, but this is late night for me, sugar." She replaced

the cap and sipped from her mug, eyes closed as her smile melted into pleasure. "Besides, this is a habit from my grampa Finnegan."

Bridger took a swallow, which burned a trail of fire down his throat. "Funny, I've been thinking of my grandfather a lot lately, too." He coughed. "He tried to teach me to be a man. My father did all he could to undo it." Bridger barked out a laugh.

Mattie squeezed his arm, her touch warm. "Your grampa must've done the better job, then, because you are one of the few gentlemen I've met in this town." She slid her fingers away and wrapped them around the mug. "I know I've tried harder and been rewarded less with you than any other man."

Her slim brows rose, and her alluring glance held hope.

"I got more problems than you need, Mattie," he said. "Besides, Mr. Tyler might not take it too kindly."

She waved her hand. "He doesn't own me like he thinks he does, like he does half this town, anyway."

"He does seem primed to gain a lot of money, the way this town is growing," Bridger agreed. Maybe wealthy enough to fool a strong, beautiful businesswoman into believing he'd changed? The coffee churned in his gut at the notion.

"Ike does have a knack at pulling providence and timing together. Smart enough to play on the folks he needs to help him, too."

Bridger looked across the room to Ike's door, closed and silent. "You don't sound too fond of him for someone who…"

She set down her cup and pulled her robe closer to her slender neck. "I work for Ike, but not like most folks think. This town doesn't know it, but I run this place. Ike owns the saloon, but I'm the one to make sure it turns a profit." She leaned toward him, her voice low and confidential. "It wouldn't suit Ike for everyone to know, mind you. But it's the truth. Anything else between us is, well, so we aren't stuck being alone, I guess."

"I suppose the Quiver Creek Business Association wouldn't be so interested in having women on the board, is that it? Even if you could teach them a thing or two?"

Mattie blinked, drawing up on the stool as if she'd been struck. "I didn't think Ike planned to tell you. He seemed to think it would be easier if you weren't familiar with that part of his business."

Her disappointed tone confused him. "He didn't really tell me. I figured it out when I saw some records. I'm not as dumb as I look, you know."

"I never took you for dumb, sugar, but I may change my mind if you tell Ike you know." She raked long fingers through her silky curls.

"I don't see the harm in me knowing." Bridger tamped down his rising excitement. Something about the business association wasn't on the up-and-up, and Ike Tyler's hands were mired in it up to his elbows, at least.

"No," she said, but the curl in her lip said otherwise. "I thought I judged a man's character a little sharper than that, and I didn't figure you for… Well, that's neither here nor there. It's not like I have any room to talk."

Bridger scratched his chin. "Maybe you should talk more about what's important, let the fellows who come in here know how smart you really are. You could do better than Ike, Mattie," he said, keeping his voice low. The call of a magpie wafted through the air.

"Sugar," she said with a laugh, "I can't wait around forever for another cowboy like you to come through Quiver Creek. Besides, once he convinces that lady undertaker he's good enough for her, well, I don't suppose Ike will be interested in anything but business after that."

Bridger buried his face in his mug, gulping the last of the bitter drink. Had Frank really interrupted something between Lola and Ike? Could Lola's father have been part of Ike's scheme? Somehow he couldn't line up the daughter Mr. Martin raised with his growing certainty of Ike's involvement in illegal gain. The marshal's interest, Ike's bottomless finances that failed to match a saloon's profit and now Mattie's comments only added to his nagging suspicions of the man. But he needed more. Marshal Anderson may have questions about Ike, but wasn't it suspicion about himself that had actually brought the man to town? And what did it all mean for Lola? Bridger shifted his saddlebag again, avoiding Mattie's gaze.

"Oh, no, sugar, not you, too."

"What?"

"I'm not some blithering fool, honey, and I ain't blind. You're falling for her, too, aren't you?"

Bridger pushed upright from the bar. "I don't know what you're talking about. Besides, Mr. Tyler has his own ideas about her. I'm only helping her the way he asked," Bridger said. "He also wants me to run some deliveries, so I'd best be on my way."

Mattie slipped off the stool and stood between him and the doorway. "Don't rush off. I don't blame you, you know. She's a beautiful woman—smart, classy…respectable, you know? She'd be a heap further ahead with you than with Ike, that's for sure."

"I'm not sure she believes that."

"She will," Mattie said. She stood on tiptoe in her flat slippers and pressed her warm, soft lips against his jaw. "I can't help it, Bridger Jamison. I still see you as one of the good guys."

"Thanks, Mattie. Any man with eyes ought to see what a lady you are. A smart one, to boot!"

Mattie flushed. "It's nice to know there are men out there who care to find out."

He glanced at the angle of the sun starting to peek through the windows. "You'd best get to sleep, and I'd best get my delivery under way. I don't want Mr. Anthony to miss his last train ride."

More important, the sooner he left, the faster he could return. The press to get back already weighed heavier on him than it had a few moments ago. Until he figured out what was happening in this town, the closer he stuck to Lola, the better.

Lola dumped a mass of dried flowers behind the wood-shed and pumped water for a fresh bouquet. This morning silvery lupine waited at her back door, still damp with spring dew.

Secret flowers didn't seem Ike's style. His grand conspicuous nature had once held her attention, like the striking flash of a long blade, until she found herself on its cutting edge.

Her first thought had been of Bridger. His rough exterior hid tenderness, but she witnessed it in so many little ways—the care he took with the tools, his soft knock at her door each time he came for the key, his adamant concern for maintaining a gentlemanly distance as he worked. How could she have dealt with Mr. Anthony's death without his help? His comforting presence?

Heat flooded her face without another soul around. She had no business thinking of Bridger as any more than an associate.

She remembered his golden-brown gaze locked on her face and a tingle warmed its way up her spine. She shook her head. No business at all. But schooling her thoughts grew more difficult as the days passed.

The slender wand of purplish-blue blossoms waved and bounced as she clipped the bottom stems and slid them into her mother's vase. Their delicate scent wafted on a breeze as she carried them into the kitchen. She set them on the counter and stepped back to admire them. Just lovely.

Maybe Ike deserved reconsideration. Was he really trying to change? He'd been nothing but solicitous since Papa died. Without his help where would she be? A flush tingled up her neck and across her face. Had he truly intended to kiss her the other night? Would she honestly have allowed him?

She gathered a dustrag to clean the house. But action didn't prove strong enough to call her thoughts away. No, she wouldn't be so foolish as to take up with Ike again. Papa had never fully approved of him, and fortunately she saw his reasons firsthand before she said, "I do."

It had been the emotions of the day and Ike's surprise visit that caught her off balance. Pastor Evans had preached last Sunday about temptation being stronger when one became too hungry, angry, lonely or tired. She thanked God for the timely reminder.

But if she had led Ike to believe his chances for reconciliation had improved that night, she needed to quell the thought.

She shook out the crocheted antimacassar from the chair and settled it in place. Soon as she finished, she'd try to find Ike and ask if the flowers came from him, at least. She also needed to pick up a few supplies from Mr. Anthony's store. It wouldn't be the same with Ike's men running the counter. But until affairs were settled, they had taken over the business.

It certainly provided Ike a tighter bottom line in getting supplies for hotel construction. For the saloon, too, for that matter. She adjusted the new bonnet from her last visit over coiled hair and picked up her reticule. It was a wonder Ike hadn't thought to open his own store long before this. No one could accuse him of a lack of enterprise.

Lola removed the shawl she had grabbed as she stepped out the door when she cleared the bend into the town's main thoroughfare. Sunshine warmed the cool breeze blowing down the rocky peaks enough to make it comfortable without a cloak.

Neighbors waved in greeting, but more new faces appeared daily. Population would demand a dedicated rail spur in no time at this rate, and Ike would be poised to reap a killing on pocketbooks as the only true hotel owner in town.

Hammers pounded even now, echoing between buildings, and the progress amazed her. Ike stood outside, head tilted toward the imposing height, proud smile on his face.

"Good morning, Ike."

He angled his grin her way, eyes alight. "Good morning to you, Lola. What brings you this way?"

She was relieved to see none of his men lurked about. "I need to pick up a few things at Mr. Anthony's store. But I'm glad I ran into you. I wanted to thank you for checking on me the other night, but—"

"I know I said I wouldn't apologize, Lola, but I will. A gentleman should never press his advantage with a lady." He slid closer, hand grasping her elbow in careful fashion. His voice lowered to a whisper. "But I wanted to press it, very much. I hope you'll forgive me. I lost myself for a moment in your eyes and the moonlight, but I promise you, it will not happen again. Not without your permission, that is."

Lola breathed deep, glancing around as people passed them, most with knowing smiles. "While I appreciate the flattery, Ike, and I accept your apology, you have to know—"

"Shh!" he said, placing a finger gently to her lips. "Don't say anything more, Lola, please. I know the wrong I've done to you in the past can't be undone, and I grieve what I lost. I'm not asking you to take me back. But please, say you'll consider me going forward. Give me a chance to show you the new man I've become." He slid his finger away.

"We will always be friends…schoolmates…neighbors… but I can't allow anything more to come between us—"

"Yet. But I pray I can change your outlook. For the sake of friendship, you can give me that chance, can't you?"

She focused on her hands, as if they held the answer. Could she? The Lord God could change men—she believed that. Didn't Ike deserve the opportunity to prove it? She wavered, arguing with her own thoughts and faithlessness.

Ike leaned into her line of sight, drawing her chin up. "You won't be sorry this time, Lola. You'll never know how I've been working to earn your attentions again. I've been doing all I can to show you we're meant to be, and I'm closing the saloon as soon as the hotel is finished."

Shock froze her a moment. "But, Ike, I—"

"I am poised to make my mark on this town. With you beside me, well…" His voice trailed off as his eyes searched her face. "I won't push you. I know you've been dealt a lot these past few months, but you'll see that all things work out for the best in the end."

Lola smiled at his earnest expression. "You're still an old charmer, Ike Tyler."

He stepped away, a broad smile peeking below his thin mustache. "Not charming—sincere. I'll prove that to you. All on your time. I assure you, I can be patient... for a while, at least. But say the word, my dear, and I will shower you with flowers, candy, all your heart desires and more."

Lola raised a skeptical brow. "But not before?"

Ike held his hand over his heart, bowing slightly. "I promise."

She considered his words, his expression. She believed him, probably more than was wise at the moment. But he hadn't been the one to leave the flowers at her door, either. Somehow that thought didn't comfort her as much as she thought it would.

"If you've changed, really changed," she said, "I'll be glad to see it. You deserve as much opportunity for redemption as any man. As for the other..." She searched the streets, wishing a clear sign would swoop down and tap her on the shoulder. "We'll have to take that as it comes. But I appreciate your promise to not push the issue and allow me to discover the truth about you in my own time."

His hands covered hers, and his face brightened. "That's all I ask, Lola." He dropped his hands as if suddenly aware he'd breached his intentions. His coy smile broadened. "Just a chance."

Lola nodded, resigned in his exuberance. "Every man deserves that, Ike." She smiled.

His gaze lingered a moment, then he spun on his heel and swept his arm toward the hotel with a grand bow. "What do you think? Will this gain the attention of visitors to our fair town?"

"I don't see how they could miss it. It certainly looks impressive. When do you expect to have it finished?" she asked, catching on to his excitement.

"Another month or more, I'm afraid. Hopefully we'll convince the railroad to bring a line this way. It would increase profits for ranches to the north, too."

"Not to mention your own?" she said, peering under the porch roof from the steps.

"I am a businessman, after all," Ike defended. "I'm waiting for shipments of some fine appointments to go in the rooms. Tasteful, distinguished—"

"Is Bridger to bring them?" She missed him not being in the woodshop each morning to work.

"If they've arrived in Ralston, yes. Why?"

Lola drew her arms around herself, holding the shawl close. "I wondered when you expected him."

"By week's end, another day or so at most. How's he coming with your projects?" Ike's tone held more nonchalance than his features.

"He only finished the one casket, and I needed it for Mr. Anthony. I hope he can finish more before I get any more guests." They had been used too quickly of late.

"How long do you plan to continue this…your…the business?" Ike asked.

Lola whirled, the momentum of her bustle forcing her down a step. She tapped a finger against her chest. "My *business* has been better than I'd prefer these past months, Ike. Instead of thinking what else I should do, the Lord has shown me how valuable the service I provide is to this town. I expect to continue it until He shows me otherwise."

Ike held both hands up. "No reason to turn on me, Lola. I'm not arguing your decision, only asking." He leaned against the stair rail. "Besides, it's a fair question. I may be the first to bring it to you, but I'm not the first to have asked it."

Lola gave a polite nod to a group of women passing on the sidewalk, her lips drawn tight. "I know what they think." She slumped, descending the rest of the steps. "To be honest, I wouldn't be able to continue without all the help you and your men have given me. If you hadn't sent Bridger my way, Pete might have been my last guest."

"You're one of the few homegrown gals still around, and people are concerned about you. Don't blame them for that." Ike twirled his mustache, pulling the end into a fine point. "After all, you can hardly call what you do 'conventional.'"

"Not conventional because of what I do, or not conventional because I'm a woman doing it?" She demanded an answer, her hand sliding to her hip in a most unladylike stance.

"I'm not trying to argue with you, Lola. I'm asking you to consider appearances."

"Are you saying you won't help me anymore?" Her heart pounded. What would she do if he didn't?

Ike swooped close, his voice firm but quiet. He glanced at the bustling shoppers moving around them. "No, I'm not saying that, not at all. But I care for you, and it hurts me to hear what people say."

"I don't need you to speak for me." Her tone rasped, weak and unsure even to her own ears.

"I won't presume to. Not yet, anyway. I only meant to see if you were aware." He breathed deep and released it with a huff. "And possibly to find out for myself."

"I'm not some half-brained ninny, Ike. I know what some folks think about this job. I grew up with it for most of my life. I know it's not common, what I do, and less so for a woman. But the business has to continue. I have nothing else to——"

"Yet. I'm hoping to change that, too." He smiled. "Don't be cross with me, Lola. Not when we've decided you ought to give me another chance. But don't be surprised to find me at your door more often. I want to watch over you. After all, you're not only a dear…friend." He grasped her wrist and drew her close, the pressure firm. "Your business deserves my protection as much as any other in this town. I intend to keep my eye on you…whether you appreciate it or not."

Chapter Fourteen

Bridger stood ramrod-stiff, afraid of bumping shelves of glasswork in the sweltering room. He'd found Axlebee's Glassworks a few streets off the main road, and while the sun barely topped the trees, he determined it would be his last stop.

Heat from the glass furnace blasted through to the front room, adding to his weariness. Traveling with a full wagon and an order of glass windows didn't ease his restlessness, either.

He couldn't get to Quiver Creek fast enough. Time had dragged like an ant pulling a moose this past week, and even busy days of loading supplies and rumbling through towns to find what Ike needed didn't help.

A short, round woman poked her head through a side door and bustled toward him. "I'm sorry to keep you waiting, sir. How may I help you today?"

"I'm here to pick up the order for Ike Tyler, over in Quiver Creek. Is it ready, ma'am?"

The woman blanched as she tied an apron around her ample girth, then blazed a glance his way. "You're a new one, laddie. A far sight more handsome than any of the others I've had the misfortune to meet, but 'tis no matter if you're working for the likes o' that one."

A back door slammed. "Woman, you'll hold your tongue!"

The smithy limped his way around shelves of glass with careful tread. The older man stooped, thin spine bent from years of work.

Bridger shifted his boots, trying to find a stance that didn't make him feel like the devil himself under their stares. It seemed Mr. Anthony wasn't alone in his low opinion of Ike Tyler—or anyone who worked for him. And between the greetings he'd garnered and the realization that the marshal had questions about his boss, Bridger suspected folks had more reason than Ike's too-slick, off-balance personality to hold a thinly veiled wariness against him.

He needed to get back and talk to that federal marshal… and check on Lola.

"Mr. Tyler sent me for his windows. Are they ready?" Bridger handed the order slip to the woman.

She ripped it from his grasp, never breaking her fiery gaze. Her lips clamped tight and Bridger braced for another blast.

Mr. Axlebee stepped forward and pulled the paper from his wife's grasp, handing it back to Bridger. "I'm afraid the order isn't ready," he said. "Train was delayed last week with a spring flood, and I didn't get the materials I needed to finish on time."

Bridger removed his hat and raked a hand through his hair. That would mean another trip, not to mention the delay in setting the windows in the hotel. "When can I tell my boss to expect them, then? They were to be ready for this week."

The man glanced at his wife before answering. "We need two more weeks to get it all."

"Isn't there part of the order I could take today?"

The man nodded toward his wife, who carefully withdrew a metal box from behind the shelf and opened it with a rusty key. She fumbled inside a moment before pulling out a wad of bills. Her icy stare drilled through Bridger. She licked her thumb and thrust each one to the counter, like a punch to his face.

"Here!" She settled the bills together and tucked them into an envelope before shoving it under his nose. "It's all we can pay for now."

Pay? He picked a vase off a shelf, admiring the fine quality. He wasn't sure what they owed Ike, but he hated to leave them penniless.

"Please, sir," the old man rasped, "don't break it. We'll make up the difference in two weeks, when you come back for the windows."

Bridger settled his hat back on his head. Lola might like the vase. He'd been thinking of her a lot this week, wishing he worked in her woodshed instead of doing Ike's errands. The delicate strength in the design of the glass reminded him of her. "I'm not sure what interest—"

"We'll pay the interest, too," the man assured him.

His pulse jumped. Ike's true nature of business grew crystal clear.

He set the decorative vase on the counter and took a deep breath. He couldn't tip his hand. "If you have something you need delivered to him, I'm happy to oblige. But I'm not about to take your last penny, and I'd like to buy this vase for a friend of mine, if that's all right." His voice bounced against the glass items, making his words louder than intended. Or maybe frustration caused it.

The woman glanced at her husband, then turned her

skeptical eye toward him, eyebrow curled in disbelief. "Now you listen, sonny. You want that vase, it's five dollars. You can add it to this envelope and take it with you, because the sooner we square up with your Mr. Tyler, the sooner we don't have to look at ye."

"It's good to see you, Grace!" Lola greeted her friend as she stepped out of the general store. "I didn't know you were coming into town today."

"Father sent me for some special liniment for his horse. Can I give you a ride home?"

Lola swung her parcel into the wagon and scrambled over the wheel. Ike's man Toby stood on the walkway, arms crossed, a scowl etched across his face.

Grace chirped to the team and moved into the flow of wagons rumbling through town. "Not the same cheery little store, is it?"

Lola glanced back. "Toby is none too happy about minding the customers and doesn't care who knows it. As if going in there without Mr. Anthony wasn't hard enough." She swallowed around the lump in her throat.

Grace clenched the reins as they passed the hotel. "Everything in this town is hard anymore." She shook her head. "I'm sorry. I shouldn't have said that. Mr. Anthony's service was real nice, but it opened the memory of Pete's funeral like a fresh wound."

Lola wrapped an arm around her friend's shoulders. "I know," she said. What else could she say? Quiver Creek had suffered a miserable year, and it didn't seem the Lord had finished whatever lesson these trials were supposed to teach.

Doc Kendall waved as he crossed the street in front of them. "Good morning, ladies. How are you feeling, Mrs. McKenna?"

Lola leaned forward as the wagon slowed.

"Much better than a few weeks ago, Doctor," Grace said.

"Glad to hear that. I plan to be in town for the next few weeks, so stop into my office sometime. I like to keep an eye on my future patients," he said.

Lola smiled. "I'm glad you'll be home for a while."

"As am I, Miss Lola. I'm sorry to hear about Cecil. I know how special you were to him." He pulled out his pocket watch. "I apologize, ladies, but I'm on my way to Mrs. Adamson's place. She was feeling poorly last time I came through, and I want to see how she's progressing."

"You're a busy man," Lola said.

"As are you, my dear. I hope to talk more with you soon!" He bowed and tipped his bowler, then hurried off at a fast clip across the road to his horse.

"That man spreads himself thinner than a coin on a railroad track," Grace said.

"We're blessed to have him. But a town this size, what we really need is a full-time doctor," Lola said, watching the man trot down the street. "He can't be but a few years older than we are, but he'll work himself to an early grave."

Grace's soft gasp drew her attention. "I remember saying the same thing to Pete," she whispered.

Lola closed her eyes. Why did she forever say the wrong thing? "I'm so sorry. I didn't mean—"

"I know. But I did. I was angry when he left, gone looking for some big cat when he should've been home mending fences, checking the stock, finishing that cradle..." Grace's voice grew softer. "Being with me."

Lola hugged her friend. Hadn't she thought the same about Bridger? She needed him to finish work for her, but she had to admit, she missed his company more.

Grace shuddered as they rounded the corner. The lines of wagons thinned as her home came into view. "The funny thing is," Grace said, the edges of her lips tilting in a sad smile, "I loved that about him. Pete was forever helping other people, and that's part of what made me love him so much."

The team slowed to a stop in front of Lola's door before Grace faced her, unshed tears threatening to spill. They only added brightness to the desperation in her eyes. "I don't understand why God had to take him, Lola. I don't. I've talked with Pastor Evans, with Mother and Father, with God Himself, and it makes no sense, not now."

Lola's heart gripped with the strength of a grieving widow's handclasp. What comfort could she offer her friend, when she didn't have any answers?

"When? When would it have been a good time, Grace? Five years from now, when your baby is old enough to know his father is gone? Five years ago, when you were courting? Or fifty years from now, leaving you alone after he'd grown fifty years more dear to you?"

Grace blanched white as if she'd been slapped, but Lola pushed on. She coughed, throat tight with tears. "There's never a good time to die. I've learned that. Not for those of us left behind. But think of Pete, Grace. He's enjoying all the glories of Heaven right now. Would you want to call him back from that?"

Grace bowed her head, and Lola thought she'd have curled into a ball if the roundness of her belly hadn't prevented it. Lola rubbed a hand over her shoulders, soothing the muffled cries that escaped.

Lola rested her head on Grace's shoulder, shedding a few tears of her own. She battled through the same questions with no answers. But she had experienced the

Lord with her through the sorrow. She'd also come to realize the depth of her selfishness, because her first response to the question had been an adamant yes. She still hadn't reached the point where she saw any goodness in her father's death, but her faith and trust in the Lord had grown.

Moments passed before Grace shuddered in her arms and sat against the wagon seat. "I just miss him so. I'm sorry."

Lola patted her shoulder and handed Grace a handkerchief. "I know, and that won't change. But with the Lord's help, you can accept it and grow through the pain. That I can promise you."

Grace's mouth wobbled, as if she intended to smile but her lips refused. "Your father once told me the comfort you provided families couldn't be taught. He was right."

Warmth filled Lola at the gift of her father's praise through Grace. "Do you have to hurry home? I could make some lunch."

Grace looked at the sky, judging the time. "No, I really ought to get home. Mother's feeling a little under the weather and I don't want to be away too long."

"Nothing serious, I hope? Maybe Dr. Kendall should check on her."

"No, no, nothing like that. Just the spring sniffles, I'm certain. I'm sorry I've taken our entire visit. How have things been with you?" Grace grasped her wrist as Lola stood to leave the wagon.

Lola examined the trees standing like sentries on distant ridges, knowing Bridger rode among them. She sighed. "It's been a quiet few days."

"No more strange noises?" Grace's eyes squinted with concern.

Lola's gaze snapped to her house, the woodshop door barely visible from this angle. "Not exactly."

Grace tugged her to the wagon seat. "What's that supposed to mean?"

Lola looked down rather than face her friend's alarm. "Well, I haven't heard anything, but I've had a fresh bouquet of wildflowers at my back doorstep every morning this week."

"Bridger's still out of town?" Grace asked.

Lola's gaze flicked toward her friend. "He's to meet with Jake Anderson on Saturday, so he'll return by then." Or hopefully sooner. "Why?"

Grace smiled, showing a row of perfect white teeth. "My heart has eased about him, you know. I'm glad he's around to keep an eye on you. I guess I hoped he brought the flowers."

Warmth toasted Lola's face despite the brisk air. "Why should he? I'm his boss, after all. It wouldn't be proper."

Grace bit her lip. "I can't help it if I'm a hopeless romantic."

"We hardly know him! He's under investigation by a federal marshal!"

"Yes, because you alerted the authorities. At the time, I thought it wise, and I guess I still do. But I've seen him in church, around town, and I'm telling you, Lola, he has a good soul. Don't get me wrong, there's dangerousness about him, but the kind that makes you think he'll stop at nothing to see that right is done."

Lola stared at Grace, wishing a stiff breeze could blow the heat from her cheeks. "You've hardly spoken a dozen words to the man and you know that about him?"

Grace nodded, the wisdom of experience shining in her blue eyes. "I saw it in Pete enough to recognize it."

"Ike's been keeping an eye on my place, too," Lola admitted.

Grace's lips drew a firm line. "But the flowers aren't from him."

"No," she said. "I discovered it in a roundabout way, but no, they're not from him."

Grace huffed. "Not his style to give a woman something nice without gaining credit for it."

Lola thought of their conversation earlier that morning. "He's trying to change, Grace. If the Lord won't remember his sins against him, how can I?"

"Because God gave you memory for a reason," Grace said. "Ike had no right, what he did to you. It's irksome to see him prospering, I'll tell you that."

Loyalty and shame swirled in her chest so that Lola lacked the muster to provide a convincing defense. "He doesn't expect me to forget that, only to give him a chance moving forward," she said.

"Then you be sure you use your God-given memory to stay wary. I don't trust him."

Lola rubbed a hand over her wrinkled brow. "You're telling me you feel better about a virtual stranger hanging around my place than you do Ike, whom we've known for years?"

"Yes," Grace said, her voice a harsh whisper. "Just as you have learned about care and compassion from watching your father in his line of work, Lola, I've learned from watching Pete. Sharing his experience and the Lord's discernment have made me a good judge of character. Bridger may be facing some rough circumstances, but there's something solid at the core of him."

"But not Ike?" Lola asked.

Grace shook her head with vehemence. "The only thing solid about Ike is his bank account," she said. "And that only adds to my reasons for not trusting him."

Chapter Fifteen

Bridger jarred from a doze as the wagon bounced over a deep rut. He rubbed his jaw, feeling stubble that only added to his rough appearance. The lack of sleep didn't help, either. He'd been a fool seven ways from Sunday, to have gone so long without figuring Ike's scheme. How could he allow the lure of money to blind him?

Still, more questions plagued him. The Axlebees had fallen on rough times with the mister laid up from a bad fall, when Ike swooped in to offer the loan they needed to tide them over. But it came at high interest and no room for delayed payment. How many others had fallen for similar deals? Or did Ike operate on a case-by-case basis, using whatever means necessary to gain control? How many people were being hustled? And did Ike have any partners?

Bridger carried more questions than answers, but Ike's bankroll blinded him no longer.

He rolled into town in a dust cloud, all sluggishness drained from him in his frustration.

He dropped the materials at the hotel site and stormed toward the boardinghouse. He froze at the top step. Ike waited at his door, and Bridger sent a silent prayer that

Frank had slipped out or managed to remain silent until he left.

"How'd the trip go, Jamison?" Ike asked, cigar swinging from his fingers.

"You know that better than I would," he said, not bothering to hide his irritation.

Ike drew to full height with a cultivated sense of calm, adding to Bridger's fury. "What's all this? I understand none of the men like being away from the comforts of home, such as they are," Ike said, waving the cigar toward his door. "But it's my business transactions you were conducting, and—"

Bridger stepped forward, hating that he had to tilt his head to look the man in the eye. "Let's just say I learned a lot on this trip, Ike. More than I care to know."

Ike slumped against the doorjamb, twirling his cigar between his fingers. "It seems to me you didn't learn as much as you forgot, if you think I'll tolerate that tone from you or any of my men."

Bridger formed fists in either hand, muscles tense and ready to pounce. "I'll grant you, I'm not the sharpest chisel in the toolbox, but you're not as smart as you'd like to think, either."

Ike's hand rested at his shoulder, cigar at Bridger's ear as he drew closer.

A solid punch across his chin a second later sent Bridger into the opposite wall, his advantage lost in fatigue, Ike's greater height and the factor of surprise. He kept his footing and lunged, only to be shoved back.

"Hold on, now," Ike said, holding his hand up, palm toward him. His frustrating, controlled smile returned. "Before you go getting all riled, let me tell you why I'm here."

Bridger followed Ike's gaze to the door of his room,

and cold dread sank in his chest. "Go ahead. What are you doing here?"

Ike took a slow puff, blowing a smoke ring toward the low ceiling. "It's no concern of mine who a man keeps in his room, you understand…"

Bluff! "I agree, but what's that to do with me?" Bridger fought the urge to glance at the door, his heart beating hard, high in his dry throat.

"Let me prove to you how smart I am. I don't involve myself in the private lives of my men. I don't expect them to involve themselves in mine, and it works out best all the way around."

If Ike detected the twitch of his fists, he chose to ignore it. "When a man works so hard to keep something… or someone…a secret, tucked and hidden away like a gold piece, well… A man doesn't do that kind of thing without reason. That makes the secret a powerful one, and gives me a valuable commodity. Do you understand me now, Mr. Jamison?"

Bridger squared his shoulders and widened his stance. Silence reigned behind the door, but he didn't dare challenge Ike's assumption by opening it. "I suppose I might," he said, crossing his arms. "If what you're saying is true. As for what I'm saying, a man can die for what he doesn't know around here."

Ike smoothed his mustache over his growing smile. His laugh rumbled down the otherwise silent hallway. "I reckon you're right, Bridger."

His shoulder shook at Ike's slap, but he held his ground. Thoughts shaved off in all directions through his mind, but the solid core remained focused on protecting Frank… and Lola. Best to stay on as one of Ike's men, for now. "I'm glad you understand my position. So tell me. What exactly have you hired me for? Stop keeping me in the dark."

Ike wavered upright from his over-calm lean against the doorjamb. He flicked the butt of his cigar and turned toward the stairway with a heavy hand at Bridger's shoulder. "No rush, Mr. Jamison. Now that we understand each other, we have plenty of time to discuss the fine details."

Ike sauntered down the narrow stairway and around the corner before Bridger opened his boarding-room door. The room remained dim in early afternoon, but Frank sat at the desk, solely focused on the paper and colored sticks in his hand. Bridger tossed his saddlebag onto the bed and moved to wash the top layer of grime off his arms at the dry sink.

"Bridger! You're back!" With a wide smile lighting his face, Frank looked like a child who'd found a lost puppy.

Bridger dipped his hands in the lukewarm water and reached for the soap, fighting the fury in his chest with slow, deliberate movements. The heat it radiated could melt a candle. "Not a moment too soon, either. What have you been up to while I was gone, Frank?"

His brother showed enough wisdom to avoid his direct glare, at least. "I walked away from town so's no one would try to talk to me, and I drew lots of pictures. And I didn't talk to one person the whole time."

Bridger winced. Being trapped in the room for long periods of time over the past weeks had been hard for a fellow who liked to talk as much as his brother. No other soul to run his mouth off to must have been nigh onto torture. Bridger scrubbed his face, groaning his frustration into the washcloth. Its mustiness drowned the soapy scent.

Frank stood at his side in an instant. "You hurt, Bridge?"

He stared a long moment at his brother's pale, blank eyes, full of concern. Frank had no part in the problem he'd created. "Not like you think, no. But I'm in a big mess here, Frank. Bigger than the last one."

Frank's gaze traced over his face before his big frame crashed to the bed with a bounce. His broad shoulders slumped and his whole being sagged. "You mean we got to leave here?"

Bridger scooped water in his hands and raked it over his dusty hair, the ends dripping down his collar. "That's part of the problem, you see. We can't leave this time. Not yet, anyhow. But it's not going to be easy to stay, either."

Frank's face took on a slack expression that foretold a rare moment of clarity. "Are you worried about me?"

Bridger nodded. He choked at the utter dejection on his brother's face, forcing his thoughts over the grit in his throat. "I always worry about you. But even more with this."

"We ought to pray, Bridge. Ma would tell us to pray for what to do." Frank's firm declaration came on a husky whisper. "We ought to go to church, too. People could help us."

Frustration forced Bridger to the opposite wall. He groaned and rubbed rough fingers over his eyes. He swiveled to face his brother. "Did Ma's praying ever save me from one of Pa's whippings? Did her prayers keep Pa from drinking every spare cent we had?" Anger welled from his gut. His words burst louder, colder, more hateful than he'd ever allowed. "Where were those fine church people when I showed up at Sunday school with a black eye? Do you have any idea how many times I prayed to God that Pa wouldn't find me for another beating?"

He strode across the room, bending low into his

brother's face, grasping a meaty shoulder in either hand. "Where was God the night Pa sliced my face?" Words spat out like firecrackers in the flames, and his grip tightened. He leaned closer, his nose a breath away from Frank's. "The night Pa turned on you?"

Frank blinked, drawing back only a fraction before Bridger released his grip. "He was in me that night, Bridge. That was the night Pa might've killed you, and that was the night God gave me the strength to step in and call Pa out."

Bridger shook his head. "What are you saying?"

"I don't remember much about…before. But I remember some about that night. I know he hit you. Don't know why he never took to me that way, 'cept I was bigger." Frank drew a deep breath, his eyes lost in the long-ago nightmare. "I remember he beat you something fierce. Especially that night. I knew I couldn't watch that no more—so I stepped in."

Frank blinked and shuddered. "I wish he hadn't messed your face, Bridge. But I grabbed him right after he cut you with that bottle. Then I don't remember much after, except waking up and seeing your face all bandaged, and Ma telling me Pa was gone for good."

"They found him drowned in the creek after that night," Bridger whispered. "I was too little to remember much, but it was a long while before you woke up." His chest constricted as he stared at Frank, thinking of all he had cost his brother. "God has a strange way of answering prayers."

"Lots seems strange to us, but He did answer," Frank said.

Bridger looked out the window, unable to face his brother's faith any more easily than his flat gaze. "But look what it cost you!" he whispered into the glass.

"I'd do it again, Bridge. I'd do it again. I just wish I had done it sooner." Frank stood. "But you got no call to blame God, nor those people at the church."

"How can you not?" Bridger asked. Pleaded.

"'Cause that hate makes me just like Pa was," Frank said. "And I don't want to be nothing like him."

Bridger leaned his pounding head against his arm at the window. Hadn't he spent all his life trying to be anything except what Pa had been? He huffed a deep breath, feeling wearier than when he'd first ridden into town. "None of this changes the problem we have now. And church can't fix this. I can't take you, Frank. I'm sorry, but it's how it has to be. Especially now."

"Why? We've been here a long while, Bridge. You have a good job and all, right? Can't you tell folks about me even yet?" Frank's tone came as close to whining as he'd heard.

"No! That's part of the big mess we're in! Ike, my boss—he knows you're in here." He paced the narrow gap at the end of the bed.

Frank's brows curled. "How could he know?"

"I don't know!" Bridger moved to the only chair in the room and dropped, rubbing his eyes with his hands. "I mean, he's not exactly sure, I don't think, but he knows there's someone here. You haven't been snooping around Miss Lola's again, have you?"

A slightly sick expression crossed Frank's face, and he flinched at the accusation. "He didn't see me!"

Bridger read the truth. "Maybe he did, or maybe someone else did. The point is, I told you to stay away from her, but you had to do things your way." He bit his tongue before he said more, feeling the anger press harder against his ribs. "You were careless, Frank, and now we're in a bad spot."

Frank sat still for a long moment, and Bridger could fairly see the wheels of understanding start to crank, his wide eyes darting back and forth. "That's not enough to put us in a bad spot, no worse than before, at least."

Bridger groaned, heat burning up his neck in what he couldn't label as anger or shame for a certainty. Because even in his dimness, Frank hit this nail on the head. His brother's infraction paled in comparison to the trouble he'd pounded them into.

"Our only way out of this trouble is to—"

A knock at the door interrupted what might well have been the dumbest, most unfair comment he'd ever make about his brother. But the sharpness of it jolted them both to high alert.

Lola could hear muffled odd scrapes and rattles through Bridger's room door as she waited. She glanced along the dim hallway in both directions and shifted her feet. The stuffy air pressed against her, heavy with the smells of musty curtains, old cigars and cheap liquor. Hopefully no one would be about this time of day. She knew by the heat her face must be pinker than a wild rose.

What had given her such a notion, to come to Bridger's room? She'd been raking the flower bed for spring planting when she saw his wagon rumble by, loaded to the gills. He hadn't acknowledged her wave, which sniped at her heart with sharp disappointment.

But this was a business matter, she reminded herself. He'd been gone almost a week and she had not one spare casket. Didn't she have the right to know when he planned to return to her job?

A cough and rumble came through the door. "Just a minute," Bridger said, his voice thick with exhaustion.

Suppose she'd caught him preparing to…wash off the

trail dust? Embarrassment formed a heavy knot in her throat and the heat on her face grew to a full-fledged blaze.

The door swung open and she gulped. Her tongue froze stiff and she stammered. "Ah, I apologize for… for interrupting. You see, I—that is, I only wondered… Well, I can talk with you another time. I didn't mean—"

His brown hair swept boyishly across his forehead, damp and uncombed. Droplets clung at his high cheekbones and left faint trails into the stubble on his chin and along his jaw. The top button on his shirt was the only one undone, yet the overall appearance brought a hitch to her breath.

Surprise gleamed from his brown eyes and he searched around her, never budging from his stance at the narrowly opened door. "What's wrong, Lola? Is there something you need?"

Of course he would assume something was amiss, her standing at his door like…like some witless female. "No! I mean, I saw your wagon rolling into town and wondered how your trip—when you might be able to return…" A voice floated from downstairs, and she glanced around the hall again. She felt like those spring bonnets on display in the window of Mr. Anthony's store. She squeezed her hands together and stepped close, lowering her voice. "Could I come in and speak with you?"

His eyes grew wide. His gaze darted around before spearing her. His throat bobbed as he drew a deep breath. Then a grin tipped his lips just enough to tug at his scar. "No dead bodies here, Miss Lola," he said.

She stepped away, slipping in a tangle of boots, and certain the skin on her face blistered at this point. "Oh! Of course not! I'm so sorry. I—"

An odd groan rumbled from his lean chest and he

wobbled as though he'd been kicked in the shin by a mule. "No need for apology. It's you who's owed one." He coughed, gripping the door with thick, tan fingers. "I should've stopped on my way into town, let you know I don't plan to get back to the woodshop until Monday."

Her heart thumped once and then returned to a sluggish rhythm of disappointment. "I wondered—"

Another groan came from Bridger, this time followed by a wince as he quirked to the side.

"Are you all right? You weren't injured in your travels, I hope?" she asked.

"Nothing like that," he choked out, as if the breath had been poked from his lungs. "This isn't the best place to talk, though. No sense in giving folks reason to question your propriety over me, not like this."

"I understand." She backed away, hands fluttering for a place to go that didn't add to her awkwardness. "I'll see you Monday, then—"

"Wait!" Bridger slipped one shoulder through the door, arm stretched toward her. "Maybe we could talk over supper?"

Her bustle bumped into the opposite wall of the narrow hall, halting her flight and stopping her short. "Supper?"

"Next door. I know it's the saloon, but Mattie's the best cook in town, so…?"

Mattie's a fair cook compared to me. She argued in her mind, but it didn't prevent the delight that helped cool her face. "I'll meet you outside. Say five o'clock?"

A wide smile of even teeth seemed to relax his whole stance. "Let's make it six," he said. "I will need to clean up first if you're going to sit at a table next to the likes of me."

* * *

Bridger tucked the string tie into his pants pocket. He and Frank had debated for half an hour whether the situation called for him to wear one, and he'd left the room in agreement with Frank. But by the time he'd reached the bottom of the stairs, he'd realized it went too far. The necessary bath made him feel at least worthy of her company again. But he didn't want Lola thinking he believed this to be anything more than business, a chance to hammer out a better arrangement regarding his absence.

Finding her on the other side of his door had blown sense away like sawdust in the wind. Frank's nudges hadn't helped. But she'd seemed too focused to notice. He hoped.

She had to wonder how he expected to manage both jobs when he'd left her high and dry for almost a week. She had the right. Thankfully, she hadn't needed another casket in the meanwhile. Once he managed to work ahead and complete a stock, he knew he could handle it. He had to convince Lola to give him the chance. Not only to maintain the appearance that nothing had changed for him with Ike, but to keep an eye on her.

Toby met him before he rounded the corner into the main area of the saloon. "Just the fellow I come to look for," he said, a sneer on his swarthy face. "Ike wants to see you."

Bridger huffed. Lola would likely be waiting for him as it stood. But he couldn't ignore Ike. He had to play along. "What's he want?"

Toby laughed and pounded him on the back. "Well, well, looks like the blinders are off, huh? No more 'yes, sir, Mr. Tyler, sir' from you."

Bridger threw Toby's sweaty arm off his clean shirt.

"I had the right to know from the start. But I'm still here, aren't I?"

"Of course you are," Toby said, stepping close enough to choke him with his foul breath. "I reckon Ike thinks you're more useful now. He told me he has big plans for you, boy."

"I'm no one's 'boy,' but I do want in," he lied, meeting Toby's leveled gaze.

"Then you'll hightail yourself into Ike's office before you meet that pretty little undertaker's daughter." Toby stepped back, sweeping his arm toward the door in a grand gesture. "You keep your mind on what Ike tells you. Otherwise I'll be babysitting you the rest of your born days."

Bridger headed straight for Ike's office. He didn't bother looking to see if Lola waited. His mess with Ike took priority. He stepped in without a knock.

Ike's head snapped from the papers he studied when Bridger creaked the door open, but he showed no other signs of surprise. "Have a seat," he said, directing Bridger to the chair opposite his wide desk.

He sat, and Ike did the same, leaning back in his leather chair and steepling his fingers. "I've given your position a lot of consideration lately, Bridger. I debated how to pull you into my organization on a more permanent basis and decided this little trip made the perfect initiation. So tell me, how did you figure it out?"

Bridger rubbed the polished wood trim of the cushioned seat. The fear in Mr. and Mrs. Axlebee sprang to mind. With them as a scapegoat, who knew what added pressure they might face? "I'm not an idiot."

Ike stroked his mustache, not bothering to hide a smirk. "Come, now, don't be cross. Someone had to tip their hand."

Bridger leaned forward. "Fine. I figured it out from Mr. Anthony, weeks ago."

Ike's smile dropped off his face and he lurched forward, shifting the papers into a single pile. "That old man never knew when to call it quits."

Bridger filed Ike's reaction away. "I assume you wanted to talk about something more than how long I've known about you."

Ike paused, lost in thought. Then he shook himself to attention. "Certainly, but it is worth consideration. I wanted to tell you about your new opportunity working for my outfit. I think you're ready for a regular route. You hit these businesses once a month." Bridger took the paper Ike passed his way. "That whole 'just doing my job' act may work for you a good long while."

Bridger studied the list. The Axlebees were on it, along with others he'd visited on this journey, plus several more. "This will have me gone a full week every month. Why so far?"

"You're the new man. In time, you work your way closer. Besides, you won't always have supplies to haul, so you'll be faster on horseback," Ike said.

Bridger folded the paper twice to fit it into his pocket along with the tie. "What's in it for me?"

Ike tilted his head back with a hearty, high-pitched laugh. "I liked your style right from the start. I'll take guts over brains any day, and if you're telling the truth, I can assume you might have some of both."

"So, what makes this better than what I've been doing?"

"Better pay, mainly. What would you say to ten percent of what you deliver, on top of your regular pay? That will increase by one percent a year for five years, plus additional routes."

Bridger skimmed dirt off the sole of his boot and lowered his gaze to hide surprise as he calculated the total in his mind.

Ike smirked. "I told you I take care of my men."

Bridger fought to school his features. "What if I want out?"

"Do you?"

Bridger shifted to narrow the gap between them and faced his boss. "Not now, but I might not take to it. I haven't been tied down in a long while."

"When you leave my employ will be contingent on when I'm inclined to relieve you of your duties," Ike said.

"Aren't you worried about the authorities?"

Ike laughed. "In case you haven't noticed, my good man, there aren't any 'authorities' around here."

Bridger knew that had been part of Ike's plan. "That federal marshal is to come around, right? What of him?"

"Federal marshals aren't all that interested in the little happenings of these territory towns. Even if one bothers to venture our way, he won't give more than a cursory investigation and be on his way back to civilization. So you needn't fear for your stellar reputation. Besides, most of these folks owe me for legitimate loans." Ike's feet clapped on the gritty floor. "But I have a feeling you aren't in any hurry to leave my employ."

Bridger stood but didn't dare tip his hand by mentioning the high interest rate Ike charged, impossible for most businessmen to pay. "Not for that kind of money, I'm not."

Ike shook his hand and pulled a cigar from his pocket. "See? Smart. And I like that. Now, you go on out there and find what Lola needs you to do. I appreciate you keeping an eye on her. I really do." His handshake tightened to a crushing grip. "But make sure that's all you keep on her, you understand? Or all your newfound wealth will be used to pay the balance on your funeral."

"I don't move in on another man's girl," Bridger said. Revulsion for Ike's oily personality curdled his stomach. *But a lady has a right to choose for herself....*

"Glad we reached an agreement. We'll talk more soon," Ike said, following him to the door.

Bridger stepped out, scanning the growing crowd. He spotted Lola waiting at a nearby table. Her glossy hair streamed down her back, glorious in its thickness, with small twists framing her face as she turned to send him a small wave. A deep green dress matched her eyes, and she smiled with a rosy blush against her cheeks.

Bridger choked, his next breath forgotten.

He should've listened to Frank.

Chapter Sixteen

Lola's breath flew like a dry winter wind at the sight of Bridger Jamison. His brown hair gleamed in the lantern light, wonderfully straight and still damp, but combed with a careful part to the side. His skin had darkened over the days he'd been gone, his eyes bright in their brown depths. A stiff white shirt accented his coloring and rangy frame.

He skirted the crowded tables of the saloon with ease, lips quirked as he drew close. After a slight bow he sat in the chair across from her. The scent of wood and soap and fresh air still clung to him. "You look lovely this evening, Lola, if it's all right for me to say so," he said. His smile widened to show even rows of white teeth.

She took a sip of cool water from the heavy tumbler. "Thank you. I hope it's not too overdone. Ike's saloon doesn't require fuss, but I don't often have reason to dine out."

Mattie slipped behind Bridger with pencil and paper to take their order, trailing long fingers across his shoulders before standing between them. Her fitted shirtwaist, little more than a corset with sleeves, accentuated her womanly figure. The satin skirt sported a small bustle but ended just below her knees, exposing slender legs. "Well, now, sugar, what can I get for you and the lovely miss?" she said, a broad smile on her painted lips.

Bridger's glance held a scant moment before his attention returned to Lola. She knew it had to be a struggle. Mattie's beauty caught the eye of most men in town, without her even trying. Did Mattie deem Bridger worth a little effort?

"We should be early enough to have our pick of the menu," he said. "I'll take the thickest, juiciest steak you can fire up, with the largest baked potato you can dig and a big scoop of buttered carrots on the side. And a cup of coffee as strong and dark as you can make it." His eyes danced and Lola's breath caught when he leaned toward her with a charming, crooked grin. "What about you, Lola?"

She glanced around the crowded room, thankful she'd chosen a table near the wall, where dim lighting better hid her blush. The new green dress she'd pulled out for the evening sagged matronly compared with Mattie's flounce. Served her vanity right, she supposed. "Roast chicken and vegetables, please."

"Sure thing, sweetie." Mattie's tone matched one she might use with a very young girl, instead of a community businesswoman. "You want this on your tab, Bridger?"

"Yes, thank—"

"No! I'll take the bill." She was the employer, after all.

Bridger and Mattie turned stares at her as if she'd sprouted wings. "Mr. Jamison and I have business to discuss," she explained.

"We can talk about my work as you like, Miss Martin. But our meals will be added to my account. I'm celebrating." Bridger's gentle gaze never left her face.

"Sure thing, sweetheart," Mattie said, tucking her pencil into the belt wrapped at her narrow waist. She patted Lola's shoulder. "You do look lovely tonight, sweetie. That green really brings out the fire in your eyes." She left with a swish, sashaying off to the next table.

"You don't have to do this," Lola said, picking at her napkin. She wasn't sure which irritated more—the fact she couldn't compete with Mattie, or the fact she wanted to.

Bridger made a show of placing a napkin on his lap, a teasing gleam in his eye. "Do what? Eat? I'll have you know I spent four long days dreaming of this steak, and boss or no, I aim to have it."

"You know what I mean. I am responsible for your business expenses, and—"

"I don't want this to be just a business expense, if you don't mind. It's not often an old tumbleweed like me has the opportunity to share a meal with a beautiful lady." He leaned forward with a conspiratorial whisper. "You wouldn't steal my rare opportunity to pretend I am a gentleman, would you?"

His finger tapping on her hand shot warmth along her arm and across her shoulders. She lost her resolve in his shy grin.

She nodded. "I don't suppose I could."

He glanced around, profile strong in the warm lantern glow of the room, then drew his elbow to the table to lean closer. "Besides, I need to convince you not to fire me. I apologize for leaving before I had a stock of…work… completed, but it shouldn't happen again. If you'll give me a chance, I can—"

"Hard to say 'casket' isn't it?" she asked.

He flushed, sitting upright. "I don't suppose your job is easy for anybody to accept or understand. I didn't mean to offend you."

Lola dismissed him with a wave. "I'm the one who is sorry. I didn't mean to snap." Sometimes the loneliness of her profession and the reasons for it were so clear, they pricked her like a needle. The worst of it was, she understood. Who would want to court a mortician?

"I admire what you do, honestly. My squeamishness is my own shame." He leaned back, nodding thanks to the girl who brought his steaming mug of coffee and a fresh cup of water for her. "But seeing what you do and how it brings comfort to people… Why, it's a testament to the person you are, Lola."

Warmth filled her from golden sparks in his eyes. "The kind of person I am is one embarrassed by her curtness. You are very kind, and no one has any business judging you as anything more than a fine gentleman. Now, shall we start again? Tell me, what are you celebrating?"

He paused for a large swallow of coffee. He savored it on his tongue and closed his eyes. "A return to town, keeping my job—I hope." He paused long enough to show an impudent grin. "Enjoying a meal with a fine woman…"

She laughed, lacing her fingers together at her waist. "Enough flattery, sir. You may keep your job, provided you can start first thing Monday morning and complete three coffins before your other job calls you away from Quiver Creek again."

"Consider it done," he promised. "I meet Jake Anderson tomorrow morning, then I should be in town until the first part of next month, at least. I'll see you don't run out of caskets while I'm gone by that time." Pride in his word choice tinged his voice.

"Very well." Looking at him now, eyes alight and shirt crisp, she wondered how she'd ever been so mistaken about him. Even his raw scar took a softened look in the muted lighting around them. "I wish I hadn't jumped to conclusions about you. I'm sorry to have brought you extra trouble."

"No offense taken," he said. His voice grew distant. "I'm a scary-looking character, especially given the circumstances of that night. You were wise to contact the federal marshal's office. In fact, I'm grateful you did."

Somehow she sensed he no longer spoke with idle flattery. "You'd think in my line of work, I'd be beyond the effect of 'scary-looking characters.'"

"I'd like to hear more about your business."

Lola rimmed the edge of her glass with her fingertip. "You know what I do. The science would bore you, I'm certain."

"But there are a lot of different angles to your job— the science, the caring for families, the accounting and business end of running a mortuary."

She shrugged, unsure where his questions were leading. How much could he care to know? "I've done so much of it with Papa for so long, I don't think on it in that sense."

"Are there any, I don't know—guilds, organizations— for your profession?" he asked.

Her heart skipped, sensing more to his questions than idle curiosity. Her profession was hardly proper dinner conversation, but the drone of the busy crowd made the quiet corner where they sat feel cozy, far removed from the other patrons. "Possibly back East. Nothing like that here. Even if there were, a woman among the ranks would not be a welcome addition." Ike sidled by with an interested stare. "I've only been able to operate here because people knew my father and need my services.

Even with that, I know Ike's had to run interference at several turns." Gall burned bitter to admit it.

"What about general business associations? Would they invite you into one for Quiver Creek if it existed?" An insistent press echoed in his tone. Why would he be so concerned?

"One time, I overheard Papa talking with Mr. Anthony about some such organization, but I guess nothing came of it. Ike would play a hand in it, and neither of them were too impressed with anything Ike did. After Papa died, I heard nothing more about it."

Mattie delivered steaming plates and set them on the table with a saucy wink. "You enjoy that, darling. And you needn't worry about who's to pick up the tab on this one. Mr. Tyler says your meal is on the house."

Lola met Ike's smiling face as he stood on the other side of the bar, pouring a drink. He raised it in toast to Bridger, who had swiveled to see him, too. She couldn't see Bridger's eyes, but his jaw worked into a stubborn set. Some unspoken message passed between the men as Ike crossed to his private door.

She gave a nod of thanks as Ike disappeared into his office. Bridger faced her again. "Suppose Ike had gone ahead and started an association? Would he include your father?"

She picked up her knife and fork to begin her meal but felt her wrist clamped in Bridger's tight grasp. Her pulse jumped. "He'd probably try. But Papa relied more on what a body did than on what a body had to say, and it would take more than an invitation from Ike to convince him."

Bridger released her and slumped back, his voice soft and muted as if he'd forgotten their meal or her company. "So he wasn't involved."

She backtracked the conversation in her mind, trying to find where she'd lost the path. "Involved in what?"

Bridger leaned close, his voice still low, his focus intent on her face. If she didn't know better, she'd say the outcome of the world hung on her next words. "Did your father owe Ike or his men any money?"

"What are you talking about? Papa didn't need a loan. If he had, he'd have borrowed from the bank, never from Ike." Was he trying to accuse Papa of something? Protective anger left a bitter taste in her mouth. How dare he suggest—?

His hand shot forward, covering hers with a touch that held coolness and warmth at the same time, soothing. "Then why in the world did he make weekly payments to Ike's men for the Quiver Creek Business Association?"

Bridger tilted in the saddle as his mount climbed the steep trail into the mountains, Jake Anderson close behind. The air cooled. A drizzle of rain slicked his skin, raising gooseflesh within his damp sleeves.

Riding around a sharp bend, Bridger searched the mountainside for the lightning-struck tree that marked his and Frank's campsite that night.

He trotted a few feet ahead to the dip in the trail where they had found the sheriff's body sprawled. "Here," he said, jaw clenched. Moving stiff and solemn, he dismounted.

Marshal Anderson slid to his feet and joined him, staring at the dusty earth. "You're sure?"

Bridger studied the trail, the trees, the rugged land. "Not exactly something you forget too easy, the spot where you find a dead body."

The marshal nodded and pulled his notebook from his coat pocket, gaze intent on the ground. Trees overhead blocked most of the light, but Anderson held the paper close to his face and reviewed what he'd written before he surveyed the scene further. "That rock, it was there when you found Sheriff McKenna?" He pointed toward a heavy stone.

Bridger toed it with his boot. "Yes, it seems to run underground enough to anchor it."

Marshal Anderson glanced from his writing. "A month past makes a cold trail, Mr. Jamison. What else looks to be disturbed?"

Bridger studied the area. He closed his eyes to recall the exact scene from that night. Lola no longer held suspicion against him, but did his mind hold any small detail to bring justice for the sheriff's death?

"We picked this spot because there weren't any signs of animals, but almost anything might've changed."

"Who's 'we'?"

Bridger stepped away and shoved his hands into his pockets to hide their shake. He glued his focus to the spot where the sheriff had lain. "My horse and I."

A low chuckle rumbled in the man's chest. "You're in the habit of consulting your mount on such matters?"

Bridger shrugged, hoping to loosen the rigid muscles across his shoulders and appear relaxed. "You know how it is, Marshal. A man wanders these mountains, it gets terrible lonesome sometimes. You saying you ain't never found yourself in a conversation with that gelding you ride?"

The man conceded the point with a smile, but his eyes gave nothing away. "Call me Jake, Bridger. If you're going to point out a man's foolishness, you might as well do it on a first-name basis."

Bridger rubbed a hand along his scar and released a

tight breath. He'd have Frank in jail alongside him if he weren't more careful.

"I need you to show me how you found Sheriff Mc-Kenna," Jake said, tucking his notebook away and falling to his knees by the rock. "Exactly how did he lie?"

The marshal leaned his shoulder into the damp ground, head against the guilty rock like a pillow, with his face toward the dirt trail. "Like this?"

"No, more on his back." Bridger directed him with a twist of the hand. "That rock was more to the side of his neck."

Jake jerked his broad shoulders around and dug into the spot where the earth came up around the boulder. Then he laid his head down and sprawled toward the upward side of the mountain, boots pointed toward its peak. "More like this?"

"Better. His head crooked to the side, made me realize his neck was likely broken." He directed Jake's head with a nudge from the toe of his boot.

"What about his arms and legs?" Jake lifted the limbs in question.

Bridger chewed his lip. He'd paid less attention to that once he knew the man was dead. What did it matter now? "He kind of lay toward his right shoulder, with his left arm more to the side. His legs pointed down the trail, the right bent a bit under the left."

Jake moved into position. "Like this?" he asked, taking off his hat.

Bridger glanced over the scene. The marshal was a fair sight longer than the sheriff, but… "I believe so."

Jake froze in place, his eyes closed and breath held. He looked dead himself. Then his eyes snapped open, facing up the mountain. Not one muscle moved out of place. A moment later he asked, "Any marks on him?"

"Cuts and bruises."

"Bruises? Do you remember where, exactly?" Jake's lips moved, but otherwise he remained still.

"He had a good-sized mark on his left cheek, near the eye, and another on the opposite side of his jaw. Otherwise, some scratches." Bridger wondered why the marshal hadn't talked with Lola. Surely she would have more information than he knew.

Jake rolled to his knees, scrabbling up the hill a ways before gaining his feet. "What about his hands?"

"What about them?"

Jake continued upward, only his outline visible in the diluted light from the drizzly sky above. "No marks on them, bruises?"

Bridger looked back at the spot where he'd found the sheriff, trying to see the details again in his mind. "I can't rightly say that I noticed, I'm afraid."

Jake nodded from his stance about twenty yards away. "You and your horse ever decide to cut through this way?"

"The trail winds around a far piece above where you're standing, and it's steeper than the section you just climbed. Do you think he fell up there and rolled down?" It didn't seem likely, but then, he hadn't ever considered a man's death much before.

Jake skidded toward him with long, awkward strides, trying to keep his footing. "What do you think?"

"I think if he had, he'd have run into some trees long before here." Bridger adjusted his hat for a clear view of the marshal's expression.

Jake met him on the trail but continued to scan his steps. "Where'd you find his horse?"

Realization dawned, but it didn't brighten his chances. A cold lump thudded in his chest. He coughed. "I didn't."

"You suggested a horse threw him but didn't see a horse?" Jake challenged.

His mind reeled. "I assumed his horse spooked, bucked the man off and headed for home. You haven't found it?"

Jake's eyes narrowed and Bridger felt his chances for help from this man crush under the scrutiny. "I did. The livery owner found it outside his stable, looking clean and cared for, two days after you brought Pete McKenna into town."

Bridger drew to full height and squared his shoulders. "I don't know anything about that."

Jake brushed his hat before replacing it on his head. "I thought Ike Tyler's men knew most everything going on in Quiver Creek."

Fire blazed in his gut. "I'm not one of Ike's men."

"Is that right?"

Bridger bit the inside of his cheek and flexed his fingers, considering his next words. "Yes. I needed a job, and Tyler offered one. That's all. But what he's doing is part of the reason I was so anxious to talk with you alone."

Water collected in drops over Jake's badge, giving it a gleam in spite of the frail sunlight. "What do you know about Tyler?"

"Plenty." He winced at the heat in his tone. "Enough, anyway. And I'm willing to learn more if it will stop him. But I need your help."

Jake stepped closer, a curious gleam in his eyes. "What are you thinking?"

Bridger drew a step closer, too. "I'm more interested in your opinion, Marshal."

Jake leaned to the side, a slow smile pulling his mouth with it. "I didn't think you had any hand in the sheriff's death when I asked you here, if that's what you want to know."

Relief filled him, like the first draft of fresh air after a blizzard. It hadn't been the intended question, but he appreciated the answer. "So then why did you want me to come?"

"The more I know, the better," Jake said. "Seeing the place of the crime, even a month later, often tells me information I'd not have found otherwise."

"You don't believe it was an accident."

Jake ignored his statement. "But I will say your offer to help with my main investigation is surprising. What exactly do you know about Tyler's operation?"

"I know he cheats people, and he preys on folks in several little towns around here. He controls several businesses and collects money from many of them." The dam of anger he held toward Ike started to crack. His breath heaved. "I know he's hurting people and needs to be stopped before things get any worse."

"Do you have proof?" Jake asked, his tone tinged with excitement.

Bridger shook his head. "Maybe. I found a ledger Lola's father kept of transactions he made with the Quiver Creek Business Association—which doesn't legitimately exist, far as I can tell. I think Mr. Martin was gathering proof against Ike. But there's more." He rubbed his face, strain from his time on the trail catching him in a sudden flood. "He's given me a promotion of sorts."

"Bringing you up the ranks?" Jake asked.

As hard as it is to admit... "Yes."

Jake's arms darted out, pounding his shoulders with a crushing shake. "This is the break this case has been looking for!" A broad grin split across the man's face. "You're already on the inside. Right now we have some complaints, but any time we go to investigate, folks decide not to talk."

"They're afraid. You can't blame them," Bridger insisted.

Jake smacked him on the back. "But you're not?"

"Only a fool wouldn't be," Bridger admitted. "But once he's out of business, we'll all rest easier. I want to help."

Jake sobered as he started a restless pace. "Before you agree to that, you need to know we think Tyler's behind several deaths in Quiver Creek already—including the sheriff's."

"So you don't believe it's an accident?" he asked again.

Jake ticked off the reasons on his fingers. "No sign of a tumble as far as I could see. The body wasn't found until many hours after death, even though this is a relatively well-used trail."

Bridger's mind pulsed. "So there are too many things out of place."

"And similar accidents happen to some of the folks filing complaints against Ike Tyler. I'd send the whole citizenry of Wyoming Territory against the man that says Tyler isn't connected to Pete McKenna's death."

Bridger released a breath into the moist air, long and low. He fought notions of Frank's—and Lola's—threatened safety from his mind. "Tell me what to do."

Chapter Seventeen

Lola shook the blanket from the line and folded its worn softness. "He wants to clear his name."

Grace stopped short, pulling the basket away. "Hasn't he done that already?"

Lola focused on a precise fold in the tablecloth she held. "Of course he has. I'm certain even Jake has no reason to suspect him by now. Bridger went this morning to show him…" She let her voice trail off. "To help him finish his official report on Pete's death."

But Grace smiled with satisfaction, lips smug and eyes gleaming. She raised the container for the next pins to drop. "I knew from the start."

"Knew what?"

Lola jostled from Grace's playful push. "I knew he was a good man."

Lola focused on removing the next linen from the line, thankful the full sheet hid her face a few moments. "I concede your point. Bridger Jamison is a fine and upstanding man. But what does it matter to me?"

Grace tugged on the sheet. Lola grasped the corner before it fell to the dust, but it no longer shielded her from Grace's too-knowing gaze. "Because I see the way you look at one another, and it does my heart good to see my best friend falling in love."

"Love?" Lola grasped the sheet in a twisted roll, wishing she could wipe the heat from her cheeks. She fumbled with the cloth and her words. "He's been very helpful, and I appreciate that, nothing more."

"You had supper with him last night." Grace gave a knowing smile.

"That was business!" Lola plunked the last sheet into her laundry basket and strode toward the door.

Grace stopped her with two hands grasped against her shoulders, the bucket of clothespins bouncing against her arm. "You're not honestly going to stand there and tell me you aren't the least bit interested in him otherwise. We've been friends too long for that."

Lola twisted for the breeze to blow strands of loose hair from her face. She caught sight of the woodshop door before looking her friend in the hopeful eye. Was Bridger becoming more than she could admit, even to herself? The memory of his smile in the lantern light across the table last night filled her with warmth and spoke truth to her heart. "You're supposed to be too preoccupied to notice such things," she said, feeling flushed.

Grace sobered. Lola dropped her basket to the ground and wrapped her friend in her arms. "I'm sorry. I didn't mean—"

"I know, and it's all right. But just because I'm grieving doesn't mean I stop feeling joy in seeing other people drawn together." The hint of a smile pulled her pink lips. "Perhaps it makes me look for it all the more. I'm happy for you!"

Lola picked up the laundry again, glad to have it off the line before gray clouds over the mountains made good on their threat of rain in town. "I know so little about him. I'm not even sure where he stands with the Lord."

"There's time for that. You're not betrothed…yet," Grace said, following behind.

Lola winced at the reminder. Her record of court-ship carried tarnish already. "I'm not so sure I can trust myself again," she said, plunking to the step outside the back door.

Grace lowered to the space next to her, and Lola shifted over. "God allows us mistakes to increase our wisdom sometimes. It's not like when the two of you shared a tutor and Ike seemed like the only eligible man on earth."

She slid away so Grace could follow her inside. "You make it sound as if I were desperate."

"Maybe you were, then. But look at you now. A beau-tiful, kind, intelligent woman of business in a bustling territory town where women are gaining opportunities all the time. You've come into your own, Lola. Your papa would be so proud."

Lola glanced around the tidy kitchen. The sturdy cup-boards and smooth sideboard carried her father's keen workmanship and attention to detail. "You make it sound as if Papa's death improved me." Hurt lingered in her tone and grief ached in her chest.

"Oh, Lola," Grace said, drawing her as close as her expanding middle allowed. "Not that! Not at all! I'm saying there is no great loss without some small gain. God never takes something from us that He doesn't use to draw us closer, to mold us into the people He wants us to become."

Tears escaped from Lola's clenched eyelids as she held her friend close. She thought over the hurt, grief and loneliness of the months since Papa's death. Over the new sense of confidence and satisfaction in her work, her secret hopes and her plans to somehow find a way into medical school. Would she ever have had the gumption to send those applications to the Woman's Medical College of Pennsylvania if Papa were still here? Would she have had reason to meet Bridger Jamison?

Lola leaned back, wiping her tears. "Isn't it shameful to be…glad?"

"Oh, honey," Grace said, drawing a handkerchief across her own damp cheeks, "it's not that. I believe it's what they'd want for us, your papa, my Pete…. They loved us so much, they wouldn't want us to just go on living…but to go on living better."

A sudden knock at her front door drew their attention. Lola pulled away to answer it. Doc Kendall's eyebrows quirked at her appearance, and she forced a cheerful smile. "Hello, Doc. To what do I owe the pleasure?"

Silas doffed his hat with a hasty glance through the door to Grace before nodding a brief greeting. "I'm afraid it's business and not pleasure today, Miss Lola. I came from Myrtle Stiles's place. She'd been feeling poorly, and her ranch hand rode to fetch me. She passed away this morning. Weak heart. The problem is, I've been called to help Mrs. Garrett deliver her baby. She lost her first only a year ago. I have to get there right away. I know it's asking a lot, but can you manage to bring Myrtle into town?"

Myrtle Stiles was no small woman. She weighed nigh onto three hundred pounds and stood almost six feet tall. Lola glanced at Grace, knowing she could offer no help. "Will her ranch hands be there to assist?"

Silas shook his head. "I'm afraid not. I was hoping you could find someone in town."

Lola's mind sifted through the men she knew who could offer a hand, but somehow she felt less comfortable asking Ike than she had in the past. Still, she pushed the doctor on his way. "I'll find someone," she told him. "You go on and help Mrs. Garrett. I wish I could be there to assist."

"I know," the doctor said. "But duty calls us in different directions this time, I'm afraid. I thank you, Lola." He hustled off with a quick wave.

"Let us know how things go with the baby!" she called after him. He mounted his horse and tore off through town, black bag bouncing against his horse's flank.

Lola closed the door and turned to Grace. "I'm not sure who—"

"Get Bridger," Grace said. "He would be back by now, I would think, and he'd be glad to help you. I know it."

Lola grabbed her cape and satchel, pausing at the mortuary door to gather her things. "I can't! What if he takes my request as a sign of interest? I don't want to push things if it's not what the Lord wants for me."

Grace stepped toward her, squeezing from the side with one arm draped across her back. "I'm certain," she said, a smile and a gleam lighting her face. "After all, this is 'just business,' is it not?"

Lola slipped into the boardinghouse and listened as the door creaked closed before making her way to Bridger's room. Heavy tread echoed through the crack as she raised her hand to knock. She released her pent-up breath, a smile escaping with it.

They'd had supper together last night, so why such eagerness to see him so soon? Lola squared her shoulders. This was business. She rapped her knuckles against the coarse wood and waited.

Silence.

Lola leaned her ear toward the door. She'd been certain she heard him inside. She waited only a moment before she heard another shuffle. She knocked again. "Bridger? It's me. I'm sorry to bother you, but I need your help."

A sharp creak of mattress ties sounded muted through the wood, and she regretted bothering him. Dark lines of exhaustion had ringed his eyes last night. And something more—worry, tension…she wasn't sure which. "I'm sorry, Bridger. I know you need your rest, but I didn't know where else—"

The door swung open, filled with the frame of a man much taller and definitely broader than Bridger's lanky build. Her heart thudded once, hard against her ribs. She jerked. "Who are you? Where's Bridger?"

The large man shifted his feet, glancing into the room and over her shoulders with an anxious gleam in his blue eyes. "I'm not supposed to answer the door," he explained.

So why had he? She sized the stranger up, his strong back, wide shoulders—a large, strapping man who would be able to lift Myrtle Stiles single-handedly. "Who are you?" she asked again.

He bent low, almost as if she were a small child. "You're that pretty lady Bridger works for. I know you," he said, his voice soft.

"Where is Bridger?" she asked. "What have you done with him?"

"He went with that marshal fella up the trail to show him where we found that lawman." His stilted manner of speaking drew her curiosity.

Confusion swirled in her mind with her eagerness to complete the task at hand. What did this man know about Pete? Why would he be in Bridger's room? *Dear Jesus,* she breathed. *"Who are you?"*

"Shh…I'm Bridger's brother, ma'am," he whispered.

He closed the door so only the wedge of his wide face could be seen. "You shouldn't know, though. Bridge'll be mad."

She understood the feeling. Why hadn't he mentioned a brother? "Bridger keeps you trapped here, all by your lonesome?"

The man nodded. "Just for a while longer."

Something both simple and foggy in his tone tugged at her heart. Bridger must have his reasons for hiding his brother. Had this lumbering fellow killed Pete? Perhaps accidentally, forcing Bridger's plan for protection?

She stared into his blank eyes. Somehow she sensed this man was too guileless to lie. *Guide me, Lord,* she prayed.

"Did you hurt that sheriff, mister?" she asked.

He slid back and the door opened wider. "No, ma'am. I'd not hurt him anyhow. God says we have to love folks and treat them kind."

Lola felt her spirit ease and puffed out her held breath. "Then I need your kindness now. What's your name, sir?"

He laughed, shaking his ruddy head. "I ain't no 'sir.' My name's Frank—Frank Jamison."

"Well, Frank," she said, peace and necessity forging clarity to her mind, "I came to ask your brother, but you're a big, strapping fellow. Will you help me since Bridger's not here?"

His dull eyes widened, his gaze shifting. "He wouldn't like it, ma'am. See, we're a scary-looking pair, only I'm even scarier."

Seconds ticked away on the timepiece at her neck. His desire to help her and escape his prison fought against fear of his brother's reprisal on his open face. She sensed his innocence. Was she taking advantage of that?

Bridger certainly would not be happy, but what right did he have to treat his brother this way, even if it were to protect him? Besides, she needed help he'd be well able to give. "I promise to smooth things over with your brother. What do you say?"

Still he paused, weighing her offer against his brother's ire. Then a smile grew on his face, showing a fine set of white teeth so like his brother's. "If you explain it to him, he'll see I had to, ma'am. Pretty lady like you, he'll have to see I didn't have any other choice."

Bridger trudged the steps to his room. Days of travel, late nights and early mornings exacted a toll, but maybe now he could rest. Jake Anderson believed his story, and together they would bring Ike to trial. He had worried the marshal might not allow him to have a part in it, but once they'd developed a plan, Jake had agreed.

Bridger opened the door, the room already dim as the sun slipped down, and tossed his saddlebag on the bed. He had to clear his name. Not concerning the sheriff's death, but for all those people he demanded money and goods from in the course of doing Ike's dirty work. Not to mention he'd never be able to look a man in the eye again if he didn't have a hand in bringing his boss to justice. He'd never be able to face Lola.

Lola...and Frank, he pondered. He slumped to the bed, rubbing gritty hands over his stubbled face. They were the real snags in the plan. Ike already monitored his interaction with Lola. Would he hurt her if they grew too close? The thought brought him to his feet, restless. He poured tepid water into the bowl of the dry sink and rubbed lye soap into calloused hands. No, Ike seemed to care for Lola in his own twisted way. That should provide enough protection for her.

But what of Frank? Bridger shook water and grabbed a dingy towel, wiping dampness across his weary face. He blew a frustrated huff. Trouble just seemed to work its way through Frank first.

But not this time. He owed Frank a big apology. He didn't know how, but the damage Pa had caused his addled brain cleared Frank's manner of feeling for people in a way Bridger couldn't hope to match. If he'd had a stronger sense of people as Frank did, they might not be in this mess at all.

Bridger stared through the window across the rooftops of town, glazed by rays of evening sunlight. Where had his brother gone? He should be back anytime now. Darkness came around six o'clock.

Moments passed. His sole focus on Frank, Bridger paced until the walls crushed against him, oppressive in the darkness. Frank hadn't failed to miss the chime of their grandfather's pocket watch, he reminded himself. Frank would saunter through the door at any minute, and Bridger would be the grateful fool for his worry.

He hung his coat and hat and stretched out on the straw tick with weariness in his bones. "Lord Jesus, we're in a mess. Frank sets a lot of store in talking to You, so I'm trying the same. Keep my brother safe," he said. "And Lola, too. I'm not asking for myself, mind you. But I sure wouldn't mind the extra help watching over the two of them."

His muscles eased at the notion of having backup with the power Frank so fully believed in. Who knew? Maybe before this was all over, he'd believe a little more, too.

Bridger smiled and closed his eyes. Minutes passed as his limbs sank into the mattress beneath him. Frank might be forced to use the blanket on the floor tonight, because Bridger wasn't sure he could move.

The tiny clock on the wall chimed half past, rousing him from a light doze. Breath caught, ragged in his chest. Frank was late. And right now, Ike was the only cause he could think of for it.

Chapter Eighteen

"You were a great help to me today, Frank," Lola said. "I would never have been able to move the body without you."

His wide smile shone amid the reddish stubble on his chin. "I helped, huh?" he said, pride in his tone. "I wasn't scary-looking to you at all! I'm glad I opened that door, even if Bridge will be mad."

She bit her lip, suddenly unsure. Nothing to do for it now. She patted his thick arm as they rounded the final bend into town.

Lola pulled her wrap close as the sun dropped behind ragged peaks. Frank held the reins of her wagon loosely in his hands, and the horses seemed to float above calloused ruts in the road that might jar Myrtle's wrapped body on the wagon bed.

What would make Bridger want to hide Frank away? Such a large, rough-looking man to be so gentle. Sure, folks weren't always understanding of anyone…different. But wouldn't the people of Quiver Creek be willing to give him a chance?

Bridger raked his hair and replaced his hat with a frantic huff. Where could Frank have gone? He'd looked around every corner of the saloon, walked the length of town and searched through the empty and almost finished hotel. No sign. He'd visited the mercantile under Toby's curious glare then wandered to the creek's bank and followed it through a line of trees to the clearing near church.

Surely his brother wouldn't explore farther. The sun sank well below the mountains, leaving only a brilliant gleam of pink behind the peaks as twilight fell. Maybe Frank waited for him in the room, and his worry stood for naught.

Maybe he'd gone farther and been hurt—accidentally, or by someone who preyed on those of feeble mind. Bridger rubbed his tight chest. Maybe Ike had found him.

Bridger increased his stride to reach the church. It held his last hope.

He found the glow of a lamp coming from the rear. Surely Frank hadn't sneaked inside? Or perhaps the minister had seen him. He knocked softly at the back door.

Pastor Evans's eyes blinked in surprise above spectacles perched on his nose. "Yes?" he said. The same peaceful smile he wore every Sunday morning lined his face. "How can I help you, son?"

Bridger grabbed his hat and held it clenched in his fist. "Are you here alone, parson?"

The man's bushy eyebrows drew toward his eyes, which held a skeptical stare. But he opened the door wide and nodded him through. "That I am. Just the Lord and I chatting a bit this evening. I like to have this time to prepare for the morning message."

Bridger moved toward the warm lantern light of the simple room before realizing his intrusion. "I'm sorry to bother you, sir. I didn't mean to startle you, either. I'm looking for a…friend, and I wondered if you'd seen him."

Pastor Evans adjusted his glasses as he padded his way to a tiny desk and sat. "This is certainly the place for seekers to come, friend. Would you refresh my old mind as to your name? I recognize you from my congregation but can't say I've had the pleasure of a formal introduction."

"Bridger Jamison, sir." He glanced around, hoping Frank would appear in the midst of the tiny room.

Pastor Evans snapped his fingers. "That's right! You're the man Lola hired. She speaks highly of your work."

The mention of her name caught him off guard. "She's a fine lady, and I'm glad I can be of assistance to her."

Pastor Evans's gaze bored into him until Bridger figured the man had a sense of everything about him. From the way he lived to the way he took his coffee in the mornings. He shifted his feet and searched the room, noticing an open Bible on the man's desk and a hand-whittled cross on the wall behind. He should've kept looking outside.

"Your friend, he's the type that might be found at the house of God?" Pastor Evans asked.

Bridger shrugged. "I suppose not this time of night. I looked everywhere else, though, and hoped."

"Well, I haven't seen anyone since I came over around five o'clock, but it's plain to see how important it is that you find your friend. Nothing dire, I hope?" The minister rubbed his slender pale fingers together at the tips. "I'd be glad to pray with you, that you find this person."

Bridger scoffed before his brain kicked in to where he stood, and to whom he spoke. "I'm sorry. I am worried for my friend. I'd pledge to never miss a service again to know he's safe at this point."

Soft laughter rumbled from the little man. "So often we wish the Lord worked that way. I suppose because it would give us some measure of control over things, we think. Don't take this wrong, but you seem to me a man who's lived his life trying to control things. How's that worked out for you?"

He stared at his hat. He wasn't here to discuss himself, only to find his brother! But he had been the one to ask for help. "To be honest, it ain't working so well at the moment. But if you haven't seen my friend, I really need to be on my way, to keep looking."

Pastor Evans nodded, slipping his glasses farther up his nose. "I'm afraid I can't help you there, son. But how about a quick prayer that you'll find who you're looking for? Can't hurt, right?"

Desperation clawed in his chest as he noted the darkness pressing harder at the window. He worried the brim of his hat between his fingers. "I reckon not. What do I do?"

"Stand there and talk to God, son." The pastor bowed his head and started before Bridger could think to close his eyes. "Heavenly Father, I come and ask for help for my friend Bridger Jamison. He's feeling terrible worried for his friend and hopes to find him safe and sound, if that be Your will. We trust he's safe in Your care. While I know all is in Your timing, Lord Jesus, it would ease our hearts considerable-like if Bridger were to find him before it gets any darker. In Thy Holy Name we ask this, Amen."

Bridger stepped toward the preacher. "That's it?"

Pastor Evans smiled. "That and faith are all it takes. Though the Lord and I would both be glad to see you here every Sunday, regardless."

He swallowed hard, remembering his promise. But if he found Frank, that was all that mattered. He shifted his feet, boots scuffing against the plank floor and antsy to leave, but more at peace than when he'd arrived. "Thank you, then, parson. I'd best be on my way."

The minister closed the door behind him, warm light only a glimmer in the window again. Spring peepers along the creek announced the fullness of the season, but they only served as a reminder that the time grew late. Where else might he look for Frank?

Bridger rounded the church. He'd make one more loop through the boardinghouse and see if Frank had returned to their room, then get a horse and ride out. He didn't know what he'd do if anything happened to his brother.

"Bridger!"

Jake Anderson rode along the street, his eyes constantly searching. Bridger glanced around. It wouldn't do for Ike's men to catch him talking too friendly with anyone outside of Ike's posse. Even if Jake's true purpose wasn't suspect yet.

He lowered his voice. "Everything look all right tonight?"

Jake leaned over his saddle horn. "I make my own rounds before I turn in. Helps me think, and you've given me plenty to keep my mind occupied. What are you doing out this way?"

"Bridge!"

Frank's voice startled him, coming from the darkness of the road ahead. And nothing had such a welcome ring. He stepped away from the dirt path as Frank drove the wagon closer. Lola perched at his side and his relief became squashed with fear. What was Frank doing with her? How had Lola found him? Why were they sitting there together smiling when Frank should be in their room right now, staying out of sight?

He met the wagon in three strides. "What in the wide Mississippi are you doing out here?" His voice rose only steps away from a yell. "Do you have any idea how long I've been looking for you?"

Bridger waved his arms to the inky blackness above, then thrust a finger in his brother's face. "We had an agreement, Frank, and I trusted you to abide by it. Who knows what might have happened to you out there, gallivanting around this town like you're the founding father of Quiver Creek?" Stars burned in the sky above, matching the fire in his chest, and provided a canopy for the rage inside him. Frank's lips formed a stern line, but he didn't attempt to speak.

Bridger lowered his voice to a bare rumble. "I'll lock that door from the outside next time, Frank. You hear me? I can't believe you'd be stupid enough to—"

"He was helping me." Lola's voice carried firm and furious on the night wind. "I needed someone to help me move a body I couldn't have managed alone. I came for you, but you weren't there. Frank did a fine thing today."

"You had no right dragging him along, once you saw what he's like. If you have so little notion of what's going on in this town, you're a bigger fool than he is, and I'll thank you to keep him out of it." Couldn't she see the danger she put Frank in? And herself?

Ire coursed like hot flint into his stiff limbs. He faced Jake. "Marshal, I'd appreciate it if you'd help Miss Martin finish whatever job needs doing. I'm going to get my brother under wraps before she puts him in more danger than she already has." He whirled again toward his brother, grabbing the beefy arm still braced against the reins. "Come on, Frank. You mind me, now."

"No, Bridger!" Frank's voice echoed in its fullness. Leather creaked as his jacket strained against his barreled chest. "You shouldn't speak to Miss Lola that way, and I won't let you. I think you forgot how to treat a lady, and I'm gonna teach you. You mind me on that!"

Bridger stepped back, the force of Frank's words like a punch to the face. "Listen, Frank, I—"

"No, you listen, Bridger. Did you hear her?" he asked, his voice growing softer. "I *helped* today. I did something good for someone else and it felt *good.* And it didn't hurt nothin', either."

"But—"

"If you can't see that, you're no better than Pa!"

Bridger jolted, his gaze never dropping from Frank's proud, angry glare. He loved his brother and hated everything about his father's legacy of selfish fury. But hadn't Pa done the same to him? Kept him trapped in a prison of fear, secrets and doubt? Was that how Frank felt? He looked at his brother, who stood in the wagon, arms crossed at his middle to make his point. How could he have taken so much from him?

Shame the likes of which he'd never felt staggered him, but he forced a nod toward Jake, who had witnessed this family discussion. The marshal had the grace to nod back without comment.

Facing Lola proved more difficult. "Forgive me. I had no call to talk to you like that, and I'm sorry it took a public reprimand from my brother to recall my manners. I'm thankful he could be of service and grateful you both are safe and sound." He broke his gaze from her tear-rimmed eyes. "I let worry gnaw on my good sense."

Lola's chin rose, her full lips drawn in a tight line. But soft forgiveness glittered in her eyes, and a crease in her cheek flooded his heart with hope.

Frank dropped his arms and returned to his seat. "Miss Lola, if it's all right with you, and the lawman—" he nodded toward Jake "—I'll go on back with my brother. It's getting late and we put a scare on Bridge. But—" he paused with drama, that rare teasing light in his eyes twinkling with the stars overhead "—I expect we'll see you in church tomorrow morning. Both of us."

Lola ran ahead of the marshal to open the mortuary door and laid a fresh sheet on her examination table. She lit the lantern hanging overhead as Jake sidled through the door with his heavy burden, carrying Myrtle Stiles's body with tender care. Together they tugged the tightly wrapped cover loose, and Lola donned a fresh apron. She hoped Bridger's latest project would be large enough. Sorrow twisted in her chest at the thought of using the caskets as fast as he could build them.

The task at hand should have kept her mind focused. But Bridger's angry words echoed in her thoughts. How could he believe she'd intentionally do anything to hurt anyone? How dare he talk as if she were some mindless ninny!

Perhaps her request for Frank's help had been born of need, but not only hers. Frank wanted—needed—to be a contributing part of the community around him, and Bridger was wrong to deprive him of that for any reason.

Jake wiped his hands against each other and adjusted his collar. "You need to consider things from Bridger's point of view, Lola."

She laid cloths and sponges on the table, too upset to face him. "He kept his own brother locked up like a common criminal. It's pretty plain Frank Jamison hasn't an ounce of meanness in him, so why would he do such a thing? Too embarrassed that his brother isn't perfect, that's why. He ought to—"

"Calm down. Bridger had his reasons, I suppose. But

he's a good man, better than most, from what I've learned."
Jake hovered near the door, his hand on the knob.

Lola stomped across to the cupboard, pulling bottles of embalming fluid. She slammed the doors in irritation and ignored the rattling jars. "You heard the way he spoke to him!" *To me.*

Jake flopped his hat against dusty pants and moved into Lola's path so she had to look up. "Jamison's under a lot of pressure. He was right when he said you don't know everything going on in this town, and he's right to be concerned about his brother. Give the man slack, Lola, because he's worried about you, too."

She stepped back, arms clenched around her waist, and huffed loose hair from her eyes. "I agree. I've sensed his tension, too, and thought it perhaps his nature. But it's been worse the past few days. What's going on?"

Jake's face blanched and he made a hasty retreat for the door. "It's best you don't know until and unless it becomes absolutely necessary, Lola. The fewer folks who know, the safer you are and the easier I can investigate."

Why did men insist on making things more intriguing by saying less? "You can't tell me anything?"

Light flickered across his wide face and glowed along the wooden walls behind him. "Only to be cautious, same as I've been. But you have no reason to be leery of Bridger. Don't add to his concerns."

"Mr. Jamison needs to learn he doesn't own the market on problems, sir. You say he's under pressure? Well, he's not the only one!" She swept forward, almost pushing Jake out the door with the motion. "Now if you'll excuse me, I have a job to do."

Lola closed the Bible in her lap and leaned in the rocking chair, setting it to a gentle sway. The late hour required only one dim light in the great room, enough to read but not so much to destroy her sleepiness. Her confrontation with Bridger and laying Myrtle to rest had left her mind too full to head straight to bed, but her body yearned for sleep. If she didn't soon turn in, though, rising in time for tomorrow's—today's—services would be impossible.

A knock startled her from a light doze. Who would be calling at this time of night? She slipped to the window and peeked out. Ike?

"Is something wrong?" she asked, opening the door a narrow crack as she grasped her night-robe at the neck. "It's terrible late."

Ike flashed a grin, no trace of tiredness in his face. "That it is, and I apologize for disturbing you. I saw your light and wanted to make sure all is well."

She glanced at the soft glow cast by the lantern against the window. Still, any light at this hour was uncommon. "I'm fine, Ike. It was good of you to make certain."

His smile gave away his pleasure. "It's my job to assure your safety, Lola. I care about you. I heard about the widow Stiles. I'll be glad to help. She's a hefty job, I'd guess."

She was, but it was unkind of him to mention that so callously. Lola sighed. With her thoughts so wild and raw over the day's events, she needed sleep more than anything.

Ike clasped his cool gloved hand over hers at her neck. His touch startled any lethargy from her.

"Forgive me," he said. "I can see you're upset as it is. I'm sorry, but Toby said he overheard Jamison yelling at you over near the church this evening." He removed his hand to stall her protest. "He'd been on rounds and heard voices but left when he saw another gentleman there at your aid. Still, he described it as quite a scene. Are you all right?"

Consternation racked her chest. How dare Toby claim such a thing! Her hands fluttered in the night between them. "It was a misunderstanding, Ike. Your men would do well to focus on the safety of the town and stop spreading gossip. That's the only help I need."

His eyes gleamed, a burst of fire quickly swallowed but not prevented. "I won't apologize because I've learned one of my men treated you like the insensitive cad he is, Lola. The men I hire aren't noted for gentility and civility, but they're the best I've been able to find in this rough town." He smiled, raising his hand again to brush against the softness of her cheek. "Even those of us born to gentility can be improved by a woman's touch."

Defense of Bridger tightened her limbs, but she blushed in spite of herself. "Bridger Jamison is your best man, Ike. He's proven invaluable to this town and to me."

His voice grew quiet, gruff. "He's nothing but a lout, although given the general nature of the men we must employ in this town, I suppose he's worth his keep." Ike slid closer, smelling of whiskey and tobacco from the saloon. "I understand he has a brother he's been keeping locked away all this time. Lying by omission at the very least," he said with a tsk. "Makes me wonder what else he's lied about, what other crimes he's hidden."

Lola slipped away from the door, narrowing the gap. "He's entitled to keep his own counsel. It's his family, after all. I'm certain he had good reason." Hearing her own doubts repeated from Ike's slick tongue cleared her mind. At least Bridger's reasons had nothing to do with selfish whims and heedless treatment of others, as Ike's transgressions had been. "Neither of us is in a position to judge."

Ike straightened, smoothing his mustache. "You don't hide family that's harmless, Lola. That's all I'm saying."

"But sometimes you try to hide them from harm. Bridger had his reasons, and he's entitled to them." She couldn't stifle the yawn that overwhelmed her. She didn't try. The night air crept through her housecoat, bringing a shiver across her shoulders.

"I'll be on my way, Lola. I don't want to deter you from well-earned rest. It's only that I've seen the two of you together a great deal since he returned, and I'm worried about you. As a gentleman and as caretaker of this town, I feel it's my duty to protect you from his kind and their ruffian ways."

Ruffian ways? Bridger wore gentility like a pair of boots—worn and dusty from use, but as much a part of him as his teeth. The clock on the mantel gave a single soft stroke. "I must get to sleep, Ike. I'll see you in church tomorrow, and I'm sorry for being so cross. It's been a long day, but I do appreciate your concern and the things you've been doing to help the people of Quiver Creek."

Ike smiled and gave a gallant bow. "I appreciate the recognition, Lola," he said. "Good night."

She closed the door and fastened the latch and lock. Most homes didn't use them, but she'd had them installed after Papa died as a measure of security to her mind, if not in the physical sense. She'd been glad of it many times over.

But as she made her way up the stairs and slipped between cool blankets to finally rest her head, the nagging question lingered: Why was Ike so interested in Bridger at all?

Chapter Nineteen

Lola clipped up the steps behind the Jamison brothers as the church bell pealed across the narrow valley. "Good morning, gentlemen." She greeted them with a smile as she shook out her shawl. "It's wonderful to see you this fine morning."

Frank looked as fresh as a new penny, his copper hair tamed by water and parted with care. His bright expression drew her awake after a short, restless night. He clasped her hand, shaking it with a staccato beat in his eagerness. "Good morning, Miss Lola. I'm so happy Bridge brought me today."

She recalled the verse: *"I was glad when they said unto me, Let us go into the house of the Lord."* Behind his brother, Bridger stood worrying his hat brim, his bleary eyes proof he hadn't rested any more than she had. "I can see that. You must have slept well."

"I was almost too excited," Frank said, fussing with his string tie and brushing his worn wool suit jacket. "But Bridge said if I didn't shut up and go to sleep, he wouldn't bring me no matter what. You look awful pretty, Miss Lola."

She smiled at his flirtatious ways. "With these rings

under my eyes, you speak with more flattery than fact. But thank you, Frank. It makes a girl feel good to know her attempts to fix herself up aren't entirely in vain."

Frank's eyebrows dragged down, curling at the edges like a question mark.

Bridger nudged him from behind. "She means it was nice of you to say," he said. He peered at her over his brother's shoulder, the message in his brown eyes clear. "But don't push her kindness."

Frank glanced at his brother and then turned his subdued grin toward her. "I won't. You're welcome, Miss Lola." He leaned close, yet his conspiratorial whisper echoed in the tiny vestibule. "Thanks for what you did, asking me to help. I wanted to come since we got here, but after you needed me, he couldn't hardly say 'no' no more." He patted her forearm and stepped to the entry, waiting for Bridger.

Bridger drew closer. The caramel-colored shirt he wore under a tan vest lay crisp over his lanky frame, accentuating his dark skin and coffee-shaded eyes. Everything about him spoke of earth and strength and ruggedness, and he had no business appearing so handsome when she intended to keep her distance.

He leaned closer, his breath warm at her ear. "I owe you an apology," he whispered.

She refused to meet his gaze, focused instead on Pastor Evans as he made Frank's acquaintance. "You did, last night."

She risked a glance. He tipped his face away, his deep scar more pronounced with the angle, then swung back, frustration or embarrassment in his eyes. Maybe a bit of both. "But after having last night to ponder on it, I'd like to apologize properly."

His eyes glittered, and her breath caught in her throat.

A narrow grin tugged his lips. "Now that I mean it."

His smile, his scent, his nearness…they drew her senses awake better than the church bell. Heat crept along her neck and tingled in her chest. "It wasn't right of me, either, to drag Frank along. I don't understand why you wouldn't tell me—people—about him, but you're entitled to your reasons."

Bridger turned at her shoulder to keep Frank in his sights, which drew him closer to her side. "I can't tell you everything yet, but I hope you trust me enough to work it all out."

She nodded, not daring to look his way again. She kept her voice low as more members of the congregation filed around them. "In the meantime, I really could use Frank's help from time to time. Do you think he would like that?"

His shrug brushed against her shoulder. "I reckon he'd like anything that gets him out of the room more. But you don't have to, Lola. Frank, you see, he takes a lot of patience, and folks aren't always—"

"Folks aren't always right. Or kind, or fair. But give them a chance, Bridger. Give Frank a chance to prove himself to them."

His shoulders relaxed with a tight exhalation of air, and the warmth of his hand at her elbow ushered her through the church door. Frank jostled from boot to boot in his excitement, watching the minister take his place at the platform and waiting for his brother to choose a seat in the sanctuary.

Bridger's voice sounded faraway and thoughtful. "I guess that's all any man wants."

Bridger appreciated the quiet of Sunday afternoons as he wandered down the sidewalk. Frank rested in their room with a headache. Those weren't all that unusual for his brother over the years, and the excitement of being out and "in a real church" added to the cause.

He hated to admit it, but no longer having to hide Frank gave him a measure of relief. He worried about his brother's safety either way, but this removed one fear. And if Lola really could find use for Frank, it would keep him out of trouble and give some measure of protection while Bridger focused elsewhere. Maybe Pastor Evans's prayer had done more good than he'd intended.

Glass shattered as he passed the saloon's swinging doors. Toby's rumbling curses echoed from inside. Bridger poked his head into the main room where Toby worked setting up for the evening. "You be sure to put that broken glass on your tab."

A shard flew toward him but fell far short of its target. "Next time I'll shut your mouth permanently, boy." Toby stood from where he crouched over the mess. His glare could start a fire.

Bridger grabbed a broom from the corner. Too soon to antagonize Ike's most trusted hire. "I'll help. Smile at Mattie real nice, maybe you'll get away with your hide."

Toby wrenched the broom from his grasp. "I don't need your help—not with any of my business. So stay out of my way, you hear?"

"I guess it isn't up to you."

A flash of steel glimmered in Toby's hand. "I guess I can give you a match to that scar on your jaw if you get too mouthy with me. You have a long way to go before you don't have to take orders from me."

Bridger raised his hand but held ground. "There's plenty action here for each of us. No need to get all riled at me."

Toby drew closer, broad nose wrinkled. "I don't like

the smell of you, boy. Like expensive perfume on a painted dove—trying too hard to cover up something. Only worse, because I don't know which way the wind blows with you."

"What you see is what you get." Bridger's jaw ground tight.

"Right, and seeing is believing." Toby snapped his knife into its sheath. "Get along to that gal you're *working* for and your half-wit brother. And stay out of my way. Consider this your only warning."

Bridger clenched his fist. His arm ached with desire to smack Toby's superior attitude off his smug face. *Vengeance is mine,* he recalled. But providing the physical strength would be his pleasure when the time came.

He stepped through the door into bright sunshine. The air finally held warmth that spoke of spring's true arrival. He hated the thought of being tucked inside Lola's workshop this afternoon. Working on Sunday gave him an awkward feeling, but Lola needed another casket right away, and he owed her that.

Besides, wasn't this akin to pulling your donkey out of a ditch on the Sabbath? Pastor Evans had spoken in his message this morning about Jesus being condemned for the work He did, mainly because folks didn't really understand exactly what He was doing. Even Jesus hadn't been able to tell folks everything at the time, because they couldn't have handled it just then.

He hadn't thought much about Jesus and what He did during His time on earth in a long, long time. It surprised him to realize the Lord understood his place in the whole mess, at least so far as he stood in Lola's eyes.

Ike met him as he rounded the corner. "Bridger, just the man I hoped to see." His mustache twitched over a false smile. "Quite the surprise to see you bringing a stranger to church this morning. That's right Christian of you."

Bridger squared his shoulders. He forced his muscles to stay loose, fighting the tension Ike brought. "He's my brother, and he stays with me in the room. He wanted to go to church, and it was time."

Ike stretched his arm, pushing against a rough plank of the saloon wall and blocking the narrow path to the street. "Folks knowing your secret don't give your brother any protection if you cross me. You realize that, don't you?" His voice dropped low but held the same conversational tone.

Bridger ground his boot heel into the dust, gaze unflinching. "Why would I do that? I'm thinking you have a good system, sir," he managed to choke out. "I'm fortunate to be cut in on it. Why lose my shot at that kind of money?"

Ike's smile grew into a greedy laugh and he plunked his other hand on Bridger's shoulder. "I knew I had you pegged. I knew it."

Bridger wondered, but bit his tongue. "I've only been going for my brother's sake." At least, that had been the case up until a few weeks ago. "Besides, having one of your men attend services can only improve your image, right?"

Ike's teeth resembled fangs of a wolf as the notion grew to full thought in his head. "I suppose that's right. I like the way you think! But you make sure that Sunday stuff doesn't interfere with your job."

Bridger adjusted his hat to block the bright sun from his eyes. "You can be sure it won't, Mr. Tyler. I'm interested in moving up the ranks of your men."

Ike's eyes gleamed with the desperation Bridger threw into every word. "You're looking to oust Toby? Is that it?"

"I don't need to replace him," Bridger said. He didn't need Toby stirred against him any more than he already was. "But if you expand as the town grows, it might be more than one right-hand man can handle."

Ike fairly salivated with the praise, like a greedy dog with a large bone dreaming of his next meal. "I have been meaning to talk to you about another errand. If you think you're up to it."

Bridger allowed his own small smile, praying Ike couldn't detect his pounding heart. "I am. Trust me when I tell you, I know exactly what I want to do here, and there's no one who will turn me from it."

Chapter Twenty

Lola tested her hot tea with a sip. The earthy smell of sassafras filled Grace's cozy parlor with fresh sweetness. Visiting her dearest friend filled her heart with the same. She missed Pete's boisterous teasing, and more so Grace's wry grin of sufferance. Still, Grace's tranquil joy would not be denied.

"He was just so excited, having the chance to be in church. It was like watching a child at his first birthday party."

"Certainly makes you see things with new eyes, doesn't it?"

Grace looked down to secure her next stitch. "I think it's sweet the way Bridger watches over his brother."

"I agree." Lola bit her lip. Had she said that aloud?

"Well!" Grace dropped the baby sweater she knitted to her lap. "It gives me hope to hear you say so!"

She took another swallow of hot tea, using the gentle burn as an excuse not to answer right away. "Don't start," she warned, unable to prevent the smile growing across her face.

Grace rolled her eyes as if to say she hadn't the least notion of what that meant. "He's a good man, Lola. And gentlemanly and solicitous toward women and children, and those he cares for…"

"By keeping them locked away from the world for as long as he can." Lola set her plate on the table with a decided rattle.

"His heart is open toward God…."

Lola shook her head. "Frank pushed him into coming, from what I gather."

But Grace continued. "He's a good worker, holding two jobs to provide, and he's willing to take time to help others in need."

Lola shrugged. She had a point.

"And it certainly doesn't damage the eyes to look at him."

"Grace!" Lola spread her hands before her on the table. "You shouldn't notice such things!"

Her friend allowed one of those wide, teasing smiles that came less frequently these days. "But your reply tells me you haven't been prevented from noticing."

Heat engulfed her, tingling from the base of her neck until her ears singed. "No fair!" she said.

Soft giggles rolled from Grace until she held her rounded belly with a grimace. "Oh! The child steals my breath already."

"If you didn't tease, you wouldn't agitate him so." Lola stood, reaching toward her friend. "Are you all right?"

Grace waved her back. "I'm fine. He's growing and getting heavy, that's all. Makes it hard to breathe sometimes."

Lola settled into her chair. "I guess that's normal, then. You've been feeling all right otherwise? Did you see Doc Kendall?"

"Yes, of course. Everything's fine. Don't change the subject," Grace said.

"With all the new arrivals, there are several handsome men bound to be among them." Lola sipped her lukewarm tea over dry lips. She held her chin up with a regal tilt and fluttered her lashes, smiling. "Marshal Anderson is a fine-looking gentleman, as well, but perhaps it's not ladylike to say so."

Color rose in Grace's cheeks, making Lola wonder. "You have noticed," she said.

Grace shrugged, but her downcast eyes proved her forced nonchalance. "He stops by every few days to update me on Pete's case." Her voice grew soft. "There's nothing wrong with noticing. Besides, we were speaking of you."

Lola stared at her friend and stretched her hand to cover Grace's long fingers. "It only surprises me, so soon after Pete…"

Tears dripped from Grace's eyes and speckled her cheeks. "Out here, Lola, things are different. You know that. There's no timeline on love and loss."

Lola squeezed her hand and tilted her face into Grace's line of sight, rolling her eyes in a way that never failed to make her friend laugh. "So?"

"I'm not ready or in any way looking for romance, Lola. I get the idea Jake Anderson is a patient man, though. But that's neither here nor there at the moment. Now could be your time," she said.

Lola tapped her fingernails together, avoiding Grace's bright eyes. Then she rested her chin on curled fingers and slid a loose wisp of hair behind her ear. "I think…" She leaned forward, smile growing with her certainty. She faced her friend. "I think I'm hoping it is."

Bridger dismounted on the other side of a stand of trees outside of town. Quiver Creek wound its way through a nearby pass and farther down the mountain. Close enough to reach easily, but far enough from town to divert suspicion and avoid the eyes of Ike's henchmen.

The water gurgled and bounced over rocks and the sound of rapids ahead disguised any noise of the town left behind. The peaceful grove made a perfect spot to meet with Marshal Anderson but did nothing to ease the ache in his gut.

He drew into the shadows as a horse loped in his direction, until he saw the familiar bay. "Evening, Jake."

The marshal landed on his feet before his mount came to a full stop, glancing about the shadows with a casual gaze. "Good to see you. What do you have for me?"

Bridger tossed him a small bag that jingled as he caught it. "This is my share of the latest take Ike gave me from my weekend trip. I figure it's safest in your hands."

Jake rattled it before loosening the tie to peer inside. He let a low whistle fly. "You've been busy."

Bridger shoved his fingers deeper into his gloves. "Don't remind me. I haven't gotten this many black looks since I snuck a frog into Sunday school."

A gleam of a smile met him through the growing twilight. "You get used to it. I see them all the time."

Bridger huffed. "From criminals, maybe. But these are good, decent, working folks, and they see me robbing them of hard-won wages, nice as you please."

Jake stepped closer until his features became more distinct in the faint light of the quarter moon. "Only for a time, Jamison. We'll set the record straight, soon as we get all the information on Tyler and have everyone rounded up. Then we'll make it right."

Bridger jammed his hands into coat pockets and paced between two trees at the river's edge. "I haven't thought on my ma in years, but doing this…I wonder all the time what she'd think."

Jake stopped him short with a firm grasp to his shoulder. "She'd think of all the folks you're helping. You're not really doing this, you know."

"I know it," he ground out. "But these people don't." The marshal had no idea how he clenched his jaw to avoid a confession. He longed to explain his actions were only part of the plan to catch Ike. The need to tell Lola before she heard the wrong side of the story pressed against him. What if keeping his cover took more strength than he possessed?

"We can't risk Tyler catching wind of it, or else he could pull the whole operation and set up elsewhere. Then we'd need another year to put him out of business." Jake slid his hat back from his forehead and drew a deep breath. "If you jump the gun too soon, we lose him. Or worse, endanger them. You understand that, right?"

Anger flared in Bridger's chest. "I know my part." He stepped away, damp grass whispering against his boots.

Jake stood to full height, his hard expression showing how he generally dealt with that tone in others.

Bridger held up a hand. "I'm sorry. I have no call to blame you. I got myself into this mess." He rubbed his face. "I'm just happy you believed my story and were willing to help me."

Jake shifted the sack of money in his palm. "I promise you, Bridger, you're coming out a hero on this."

"I don't give a beaver stump about that so long as no one gets hurt," he said.

Jake's whisper carried on the evening breeze. "I know you're worried about your brother. We can move him out of town, somewhere no one needs to know."

Bridger shook his head. "That would be worse. Frank

and I haven't been separated since I walked home from the war and found Ma had died, left him on his own for the last year of the fighting. You should've seen him. I…" He drew a deep breath, thinking of conditions his brother had faced in the burned-out shell of their home. "He wouldn't do well, separated from me. He wouldn't stand for it."

"I could help you explain—"

"I can handle Frank. I considered all that before I ever talked with you. He would insist I helped you, anyway, if he knew." Bridger hunkered down, staring out along the rush of water heading far away from town, getting swallowed up into bigger and bigger streams and rivers until it mingled with the wide ocean. "I haven't told him anything because I figure the less he knows, the better off we all are." Lola's safety would be at risk, too. He wished he held enough faith in Ike's feelings toward her to believe she'd remain safe, but instincts told him otherwise. "Frank's not the only one who could be hurt by the time we're through."

"When do you head out again?" Jake asked.

Bridger paused before drawing his focus to the task at hand. "In a couple days. Ike wants me to take Jimmy's route this week, my own a couple weeks after that."

"Does he consider this a promotion?" Jake scribbled in his notes.

Bridger nodded. "Of sorts. Jimmy busted his foot when he dropped a bedpost while moving it to the top floor in the hotel. I figure Ike aims to punish him for his carelessness."

"This gets us a step closer. You'll get the information to me next week, then?" Jake moved to place the sack of money into his saddlebag.

"We can meet here when I get everything squared away with Ike."

Jake grabbed the pommel of his saddle but made no move to mount. "Take heart, man. We get closer to having all we need every time he sends you out."

Bridger agreed, but it didn't mean he could relax anytime soon. "I only hope it's not too late by that point."

Jake gazed toward the creek. "I wish I could tell you no one will be hurt and you'll be exonerated of everything in folks' opinions. I can't make their minds up on that, but I can promise they'll hear about the good you've done to restore true law and order in this town."

Bridger nodded. "I know I'll likely have to move on by the time we're done, and if it puts Ike out of business, it'll be well worth it. Besides," he said, climbing into his saddle, "I've been moving on my whole life."

Chapter Twenty-One

Lola smoothed gloves over her fingers as she trudged the steps to the Jamison brothers' room. The squeak and groan of a chair against the floorboards rattled through the thin door, and moments passed before Frank opened it.

"Good morning, Frank. It's Sunday and I've come to take you to church with me."

He rubbed his bleary eyes, glancing at the room behind him. A forlorn shadow crossed his face. "I don't reckon I ought to," he said.

"Whyever not? Aren't you feeling well?" She stretched the back of her hand against his cool cheek.

Frank stepped away and plunked down on the edge of the narrow bed, leaving the door open wide. "No, ma'am. I mean, yes, ma'am, I feel fine. But Bridge wouldn't like it."

Lola leaned her head against the doorjamb. He looked so pitiful, his disappointment keen. "He brought you himself last week. I'm sure he would want you to continue."

"But he's not here. He worries about me going without him." Frank bit his thumb. "He works too hard to worry so much."

Lola sighed. "I know."

Ike had kept him busier than ever this week and sent him away again. She didn't understand all of Ike's business dealings, of course, but he had taken a liking to Bridger. For some reason, though, Bridger didn't seem altogether thrilled with the prospect of becoming such a valued employee. Instead he'd grown more tense, more terse and less teasing.

But that shouldn't prevent Frank from taking advantage of his newfound freedom. "Church is exactly the place we should be, then, to pray for him and for strength to help him."

Frank's eyes clouded in deliberation. "I don't want to scare nobody if he's not around to fix it. That would make it worse."

"Well, you don't scare me, Frank Jamison. I'd be pleased to have such a fine-looking fellow escort me. Please say you'll come. We'll have a picnic with Grace after the service."

Frank rubbed his palms on his pants, then gazed at her, the smile he shared with his brother creasing his face. "You really think I'm handsome?"

She tapped her lips, giving him the critical eye. Frank's broad form and rusty waves would draw plenty of attention if not for the dullness behind his blue eyes. "I do. But more important, God doesn't look at that. He looks at your heart. And you, sir, have a good heart, focused on the Lord. So please come to church with me."

Frank jumped to his feet. "Thanks, Miss Lola! Thanks a bunch! Bridger won't be so worried if he knows you were with me."

She giggled at his enthusiasm. "Are you ready?"

He rubbed a hand over his smooth jaw. "I shaved and all, but let me slick my hair and get a tie and coat. I'll just be a minute, promise."

"There's plenty of time. I'll wait downstairs." She backed away and pulled the door shut.

"I'll be right down," he said, his voice rumbling through before it closed. "And I'm awful glad I picked you those flowers, even if Bridger didn't like it so much."

Lola halted, covering a snicker with her gloved hand. So Frank had been her mystery florist. She could imagine Bridger's reaction to that, but it eased her heart to know. Not only did Frank flatter her with his caring heart and charm, knowing who had left the flowers lessened the tension she worked so hard to deny.

She waited on the walkway out front. The saloon sat silent at this hour, more gray and unflattering than the lively music and pretentious lighting of the evening made it appear. She spotted the table where she and Bridger had met for supper and smiled. She hoped he rode with safety on the trail and returned soon. Drawing her arm around her waist, she held her Bible close. Frank wasn't the only one who missed him.

The creak of the saloon door drew her attention. Ike stepped through—tall, dashing, with his mustache precisely waxed. He carried a gallant quality that drew the eye. Such a shame it masked a cavalier and unfaithful heart.

Surprise dawned across his face. "Good morning, Lola! Is there something you need?" His gaze appeared hopeful, but for all the wrong reasons. How had she missed it before? Ike preyed on folks like the wolf in a fairy tale, pretending concern while using another's need for his own gain.

The thought rattled her, and his tilted head made her

realize she'd been caught staring. "I'm waiting for Mr. Jamison to escort me to church."

His smile broadened, his gaze deepened, and he stood by her side in two long paces. "Didn't Bridger tell you he'd be out of town?"

"I'm speaking of his brother, Frank," she said, keeping her tone cool. "Bridger mentioned you were sending him on business."

"I'm glad I caught you, then, my dear. A woman such as yourself ought not be found alone in the company of a man like Frank Jamison. I'll be glad to escort you both," he said. His hand rested at her wrist.

She shook free. "I have no fear for myself or my reputation in his company."

Fire sparked in Ike's eyes and he leaned close. "So I've noticed. Lately you have not shown yourself terribly discriminating as to the company you keep, Lola. My workmen, such as they are, aren't known as being pillars of society, and yet you're out dining with them."

Heat flared up her neck. "Mr. Jamison is hardly—"

"If you won't consider your personal reputation, at least think about your livelihood. I would hate to see your business affected by the town's opinion of Mr. Jamison." The smell of mustache wax and cologne assaulted her as he drew closer.

Disquiet fluttered in the pit of her stomach, like a moth caught in a cobweb. Ike's callous insinuation caused an unsettling mix of worry and aggravation. "My business is none of your concern, nor is my reputation."

He held his hand up. "But I'm afraid it is, darling," he said, his tone overly sweet. "Many folks thought something as unseemly as a woman undertaker should not be allowed to operate in Quiver Creek."

She'd suspected, but to hear the facts pricked her like

a needle. "People have need of my services here, and they see now it's good I kept Papa's business going." Her teeth ground at the thought of anything otherwise.

Ike waved both hands as though to calm her. "Forgive me for saying it that way. It's not my intention to quibble over your rights as a woman to do as you please. I'm trying to show you I've changed, Lola. I made an egregious mistake in allowing a trollop like Mattie to sway me from you. I've begged your forgiveness many times over."

Lola crossed her arms about her waist. "And you've been forgiven from the first." For months that truth rested solely on the Lord's command she do it. But now the sincerity with which she could say it made her realize, somewhere along the way, forgiveness she claimed had freed her to give it honestly. God's blessings in obedience never ceased to amaze.

"Because you're a good woman, Lola. But don't you see? I've changed. I'm a businessman worthy of you now. Together, we could own this town!" He slipped closer, drawing a smooth finger against her cheek. "I love you, Lola Martin. Won't you please take me back?"

Shock drew her gaze to his gleaming eyes. Hadn't she secretly dreamed of this moment? The one where Ike proclaimed his innate foolishness in having the affair, declared his undying love for her and begged her to come back?

At one time, perhaps. But not in a long while. She weighed him in the balance against the strength and goodness of her carpenter. Bridger had not done one self-serving thing in all the weeks she'd known him. What was more, where Ike stood hollow and empty at the core, something rich and strong and intimately attractive bore Bridger's life. He was a man who would never treat a woman—or anyone, for that matter—as cruelly as Ike had treated her. She'd been young and naive—and Ike preyed on it.

"I've learned a lot over the past year. You've taught me much." His feet slipped closer as she spoke, expectation ripe in his hazel eyes. "But first and foremost, I learned the Lord's plan is best for me, and He will stop at nothing to see me follow it. He was willing to see my heart broken, if it kept me away from you."

Ike sucked a breath and drew back as if she'd slapped him. "You can't think the Lord wouldn't want us together! Don't you see how perfect—?"

"No. God protected me from a wrong choice." She stepped away, taking a deeper breath than she'd felt in ages. "I'm sorry, Ike. I appreciate all you've done for me these past months. I truly do. And I hope and pray we can find a way to remain friends even now. But we will never be…what we once were. Do you understand?"

Ike slumped, stepping away with a dropped gaze. Moments passed before he squared his shoulders and faced her. "I don't blame you, Lola. I only hoped I could prove myself and build something new. But I waited too long." His lips pulled in a thin, grim line. "I won't bother you. Out of respect for the fine woman you are, I won't bring the matter up again."

"I appreciate that, Ike. I truly do." Her gaze lingered on his fine form once more, her heart pricked by the dashed hopes of what she thought he was, but stronger somehow for the pain.

"It won't prevent my hope you'll return of your own accord, mind you." His laugh came out shaky and strange. "You may find you have more need of me than you realize."

"We've known each other too long, Ike. I'll always need your friendship." He spoke of more, but that would be impossible. She saw it clearly now and prayed he would in time.

Lumbering tread caused the boardwalk to creak, drawing her attention. "We'll see you at church. All right?" She tilted her head, trying to throw his unfocused stare. "Are we all right?"

Ike smoothed his mustache and puffed his chest. "We will be, Lola. I promise you, we will be."

A thick steak, a thick bar of soap and a thick mattress sounded better than a banker's wages. Bridger shifted his saddlebag over his shoulder to balance the weight and promised himself all three—as soon as he met with Ike.

His boots echoed against floorboards in the empty saloon as he crossed to Ike's office. The scent of Mattie's cheap perfume and good cooking clung to the dusty air. Bridger rapped on the door and walked in. Ike sat at his desk between a pile of receipts and a ledger. Toby waited on a chair in the corner.

"Here's your take, Mr. Tyler." Bridger tossed a bag on top of the pile of papers. The heavy thud ended with a metallic jingle.

Ike's eyes surveyed him. "You made good time, but it shows in your face, boy. You're running yourself ragged." He grinned. "I like that."

Bridger smirked. "I get things done, sir." He didn't add growing concern for Frank drove him through the last sleepless night for home.

"Did you get it all?" Toby asked, loosening the straps to pull out the sack of coins and bills.

"Took a bit of convincing now and again," he said, feeling the bruise on his right cheek. "Some folks wanted to know why it wasn't Jimmy coming to collect. But after I explained, everyone paid in full for the month."

Well, most of them. He'd used part of his regular wages from Ike to make up the difference for some. One elderly widower and a man with four small children who had missed work to take care of his sick wife couldn't meet the demand. And Bridger refused any rougher tactics.

"You've done well," Ike said, leaning back in his seat and pulling a cigar from the humidor on his desk. "I might not have guessed you had it in you, Bridger. Looks like I'm a better judge of character than I thought." He handed another cigar to Toby.

Bridger shrugged, unwilling to pat Ike on the back any more than he did on his own. "You run a mighty attractive game," he said. *But not for much longer....*

"I'm glad you see it that way because I have a special client for you." Ike bit the end off his cigar and struck a match. Smoke puffed above his head like a sinister wreath.

Bridger's pulse jumped. Could this be the last stone to upset the whole cart? One last bit would give Jake everything he needed to close Ike's business and return Quiver Creek to a normal town. He fought the excitement from his voice. "Who is it?"

"Lola Martin."

His gut wrenched, his breath tight. "Lola? Why? I mean, I thought she and—"

"That's no longer the case. So there's no reason why she shouldn't have the same demands I make on any other business owner." Ike's lips tugged in a firm line.

His mind raced. "I thought you had some sort of hold on these other folks. Why are you so sure Lola won't contact the authorities?"

"I do have a claim against her. Who's been making sure she's safe out there on the end of town? Who's sure she has plenty of business coming her way?"

Toby barked a laugh. "She owes you, boss."

"Not only that." Ike rolled the cigar in his mouth. "Her father took a loan from me about a year ago, before his unfortunate demise. I haven't received payment in seven months. I'm due."

Even Toby took note, moving closer to the desk. "Why would he do that, boss?"

Ike waved the end of his cigar before flicking ashes into a tray. "He had some notion of sending Lola to medical school. He couldn't afford it, and no bank in the West would gamble on a lady doctor. He secured financing from me and sent some letters to see about her acceptance. The fool should have done more to convince her to marry me. I'd have seen her settled well before this."

The information staggered him. How would Lola bear the news? To realize her father's hope of helping her fulfill her dream would become her downfall? It explained all those payments marked in Mr. Martin's ledger.

Toby's slap on the knee drew his attention back to the room. "That's something, boss. Miss Lady Fancy-Britches will find out her old daddy wasn't so perfect after all, and if she'd taken you up on your proposal, she could've avoided the whole scandal."

Ike's slack expression startled him. "That's neither here nor there, now, is it, gentlemen? The fact is, I offer a service, and she had need of it. It's time to pay the piper."

Bridger braced his feet, hands balled into fists in anticipation of Toby's move. "I won't do it, Ike. Not...not a woman alone."

Tyler leaned all the way back, his chair clapping against the wall, and laughed long and low. "Did you hear that, Toby? The kid thinks he's in charge of picking his clients. Oh, you'll do it, Jamison."

"And what if I don't?"

Ike flew to his feet, gun drawn, chair wobbling in his sudden wake. "You owe me. You've been on my payroll a month now. Folks in these parts handed their hard-earned cash over to you, with your unforgettable face. If worse comes to worst, I'll take my lumps and drag you with me. I'll testify you took money on your own accord, after I decided to shut down the business."

Bridger clenched his jaw. "I'll take my chances."

Ike never blinked. "If it were only you, I'd believe that. But that brother of yours gives me an advantage, you see. He'd never get along without you, and he'd never survive in the asylum those folks up the trail fondly suggested to you before you hightailed it out of there."

"He didn't do anything," Bridger ground out.

Ike waved him off. "I don't recollect saying he had. Only that popular opinion didn't agree with you."

"Besides, he's family," Toby chimed in. "You'd hate to see anything happen to him."

"Or to Lola. If anyone hears so much as a whisper about your sudden attack of conscience, I may forget our prior relationship completely." Ike's eyes glittered with warning.

The muscles in his jaw twitched. Bridger weighed his options in the balance and forced a long, slow breath. His mind spun with responsibilities to Frank and Lola. His promises to Jake and Miss Grace to see justice and his determination to right all the wrong he'd caused pressed over him.

It also left him out of options.

Chapter Twenty-Two

Bridger's horse neighed and skittered, waiting in the stand of trees with about as much patience as he felt. Getting away from Ike and the others had proved more difficult than usual today. He couldn't be certain, but it likely wasn't by accident. How much did they suspect?

He hadn't slept, or eaten, or done much of anything except pace the floor and ride the perimeter of town trying to clear his mind and figure a way out of the mess. He hoped Jake could provide a different point of view because he'd wasted twenty-four hours with no ideas. Lola had to be on the books by Saturday.

A big horse trotted along the creek and Bridger slunk into the tree line until Jake came into view. "Bridger? You there?"

He stepped out of the scrub and threw the satchel in a direct hit to the marshal's chest. "I'm out."

Jake almost missed the catch in his surprise. "What do you mean? We're this close and you're bailing now? What happened?"

"He wants to hit Lola, start collecting from her."

Jake flung the satchel over his shoulder and rubbed his beefy hands together. Moonlight reflected from his triumphant grin, giving him the look of some ghoulish avenger. "That's perfect!"

"What are you talking about? I can't do that!"

"You're already collecting from other folks. And she could be the break we need," Jake insisted.

"She trusts me now, and if I do this—"

"We'll tell her, spell it all out." Jake pulled his notebook and jotted something down with the tiny pencil held in its loop. "From everything I've seen, Lola could be the perfect witness."

Bridger jammed fists into his coat pockets and paced. "What if he hurts her? I couldn't live with that."

Jake shook his head. "He's smitten with her. He won't do that."

Bridger halted and drove his finger into the lawman's chest, pressing the hard metal badge hidden beneath his coat. "You didn't see him. I don't know what changed things, but there wasn't one glimmer of feeling in his eyes when he told me to get her on the books. He said he'd hurt her if she ever found out it wasn't as much my idea as his."

Jake took a step back. "He threatened Frank, too, didn't he?"

Bridger nodded. "If it were only me, I'd find a way. You understand that, right? But Frank is all I have, and I need to get out now to protect him. Quiver Creek is on its own."

"I don't believe you have it in you to walk away," Jake said, his voice hard and tight.

Bridger rubbed a hand along his scar. Between little sleep and worry, his whole head throbbed. "I'm tired of hurting people, and I need out before Ike expects me to do more than intimidate and throw a few punches. I hoped to keep the problem from my doorstep, but now I'm thinking I need to find a new doorstep."

Jake bit his lip. "She'd at least have a measure of protection if it came from you. You leave, there's no telling which of his goons Ike will send to collect from her."

He pictured Toby's greasy smirk, and a bitter taste sickened him at the intimidation tactics he might choose to use against Lola. And Toby probably held more respect for women than all of the other men combined. How could he leave Lola to face them alone? He huffed. How could he endanger his own brother on her behalf?

"So we tell her and I take her and Frank away from here."

"Whoa, now!" Jake said. "That would tip our hand and we'd lose everything we gained in this investigation."

"So?"

Jake ran a hand over his face, the bristling of his stubble mingling with the rustling leaves. "He's not going to let her go that easily, Bridger. He'd likely come after the three of you, anyway, and you'd lose the protection of the town."

Bridger slumped. He'd exhausted his mind racing through all these scenarios already but had hoped…and prayed…that the marshal held the key to make them workable. If the Lord took any interest in the lives He'd given folks, it provided the only hope he could latch on to. "So what do we do?"

"We tell Lola. Quietly, mind you, and let her decide. I see her as the one person in Quiver Creek strong enough to stand against Ike Tyler."

Bridger pushed hair from his forehead and crushed the brim of his hat in the other hand. "But what if she's not?"

"Once other businessmen realize a woman is being

pressured, it might make them willing to come forward, band together," Jake suggested.

"Don't you think they could've done that already if they were willing?"

"Listen, Bridger. My chance to keep this quiet is about up. Tyler keeps close tabs on this town, and if he doesn't suspect me yet, he soon will."

Bridger replaced the hat on his head, rocking it back and forth to a proper tilt. "So let him. The town would at least be rid of him."

"What about people in those other towns?" Jake stepped closer, his voice low in the shadows. "What about seeing justice for all the people Ike Tyler has hurt and robbed in the name of gaining power and wealth? Good people who tried to get where we are in this case when Ike and his associates killed them? A friend of mine died here, pulling evidence. Mr. Martin was his contact person. I suspect Pete McKenna and Cecil Anthony got too close, as well."

Bridger groaned. The marshal didn't fight fair. As bad as he wanted to, he'd never be able to face himself in the mirror if he didn't do all he could to put Ike behind bars, where he belonged. And Marshal Anderson knew it.

Bridger conceded with a grim nod. "This plan of yours sounds like an awful lot of wishing and hoping to me, and not much else."

"That's where my faith comes into play." Jake had the audacity to smile with a look of victory. "The only way to win this battle is to fight on our knees."

Bridger slumped against a tree and rubbed his head in both hands. "I only have to convince her to give me the money? Do you have any idea what this will do to her, coming from me?" Not to mention what it would do to him delivering the terms of payment.

"I promise you, I'll be there within the hour to explain everything," Jake said. "But if we go in together, someone could see us. If I go first and she doesn't agree to help, you go back to Tyler empty-handed. It's got to be this way."

Bridger knew it made more sense than any other idea they'd kicked around. It didn't mean he had to like it.

Jake jotted some notes. "Be convincing, Bridger. I'll take Grace along and tell her and Lola both what's going on. If you and I can keep from crossing paths, Ike may not put it together right away, and that gives us a little time."

"Unless he already suspects you. Toby's barely lost sight of my backside since Ike told me to collect from Lola, Jake. I'm telling you, I don't like this."

Jake grinned, a little madness gleaming in his eyes. "All the more reason to conclude this case soonest."

Bridger nodded and rubbed his neck, muscles stiff as an oak board. "All right."

Jake climbed into the saddle, settling with a creak. "This isn't the end for you with Lola. She'll forgive you once she realizes why you're doing this."

"I hope so."

"Sounds like you could use some faith," Jake said. "You have until tomorrow to figure it out. I'll be at her place by eight o'clock. You be gone by seven."

Bridger threw a pebble into the dark ripples at the river's edge. "I know what needs done. I just want this whole mess behind me."

Jake trotted away from the stand of trees on his horse, leaving Bridger at the water's edge. Having a plan of action helped but gave him no certainty as to the outcome. The entire case could fall apart at his feet.

"Lord," he prayed, "it shames me to come to You now that I've made such a mess of things. Forgive me. I see where so much of this could've been prevented had I asked Your guidance from the start. But this is the tangle I'm in. I understand there are consequences for the way I've been living, turning my back on Your love and wisdom, and I'll accept whatever You, in Your mercy, send my way. But, Lord, let it fall on me. Don't punish Frank for my mistakes, and keep Lola safe. And please, Jesus, let this work."

He opened his eyes, the darkness of the day filling in every nook and cranny of the woods around him. The scent of grass and rush of water caught on the evening breeze. He'd never been good at those big, fancy prayers he'd heard growing up in church, and he'd been long out of practice before coming to Quiver Creek. But in spite of all that, his breath came easier and his shoulders felt lighter than they had in years.

He still wasn't sure how to accomplish what needed done, but his heart swelled with confidence the Lord would show him what to do and say when the moment arrived. It wasn't the instant response he might have preferred, but he accepted it.

He stood and brushed dew that dampened the ground by the river off his pants. Turning in early would give him the energy he needed to face tomorrow. Sleep wouldn't come easy, but after staying awake through last night, he didn't think worry would be enough to deter him from some rest.

Beefy hands grabbed his shoulders as he pushed a weary boot into the stirrup, dragging him to the dirt with a thud. The jolt knocked breath from him, and he struggled to his elbows. He kicked into the darkness, and he was rewarded with a curse and punished with a slug to the face. He fell, but brawny fists pulled him upright by the collar.

Bridger planted his feet and barreled forward. He landed a punch to the side of his attacker before strong arms hauled him back. His upper arms pinned, he kicked again with his feet, but the angle, exhaustion and surprise of the attack made him ineffective. A solid fist crashed against his ribs twice and slashed against his face. Hat long gone, the attacker twisted Bridger's hair at the crown and pulled, jerking his chin to face Toby's toothy grin.

"You fight pretty good for a scrawny runt, boy." A knife glittered in Toby's fist, edge tracing along the path of the scar Bridger had borne since boyhood. "But I've had enough fun for one evening."

Arms like logs squeezed his ribs and jostled him enough to crack his teeth. A raspy voice buzzed behind his head. "This is crazy, Toby. Either we need him or we don't, but—"

"This is what Ike ordered. We're all too deep not to stick with him at this point. Besides, we're not to kill him." Toby's eyes glittered. "This is just a friendly little reminder from the boss, Jamison. He thought you might need a bit more convincing before you went to visit Miss Fancy-Britches."

The cool blade rested against Bridger's chin and grazed his neck. He struggled to control his breath and firm his footing.

"I could extend this line for you. Slice you right down the middle. Or maybe Jim here could snap your neck, quick and easylike. More humane that way," Toby said.

"Like those others," Jim said.

"Shut up!" Toby moved the knife behind Bridger's ear, and his tight grasp slackened. "The boss managed to run the game this long. You want to cross him, you ain't the only man here can snap a neck. You got that, Jim?" The trees vibrated with Toby's roar.

The man behind him shifted. His hold against Bridger tightened as Toby focused him.

"You put that lady undertaker on notice and she pays up, you won't have to worry about anything else. If you don't—" Toby pushed the knife tip against Bridger's chest "—you'll never rest again, until it's permanent. Unless, of course, we take it out on that brother of yours."

Bridger struggled, his arm breaking free. He shoved Toby's wrist and knocked the knife but gained two clouts to his sore ribs and a fierce cuff to his head that dimmed his vision. "I said I'd do it, didn't I?"

Toby stepped back. He nodded and the men loosed him. "Then I suggest you practice your delivery. Because if you don't convince that woman a little better than you did the boss, we'll be back."

Bridger tried to draw a deep breath. Pain sliced across his ribs like a match on flint. But he stood straight, determined not to give Ike's men the satisfaction of grabbing his side. "I know my job."

Jim brought the knife to Toby, who held it up, then made a show of returning it to its sheath. "So long as you and the boss have an understanding you'll stick to," Toby said. He dipped his head, backing away as the others slipped out through the trees. With a cold, narrow smile, he joined them, escaping into the dark.

Bridger leaned over, hand pressed to his side. His breath crept painfully over damaged ribs. Nothing broken, only bruised.

One thought came as he fought his hazy vision and shuffled to his horse.

He hadn't expected an audible response to his prayer. Especially not one delivered by Toby.

Lola tucked stockinged feet beneath her on Mother's rocking chair and settled into the cushions with a favorite book. While the days had warmed considerably into May, evenings still made a fire necessary. She enjoyed the coziness of the house, quiet after a busy week.

A knock drew her from the story with a start. She waited, listening for another to tell her which door to answer. Ah! A visitor!

She scrambled to the door, wondering what might have Grace out so late. No one else from town came to mind, especially since she'd cleared the air with Ike.

She cracked the door open. Bridger paced on her porch in the shadows. It brought to memory the night they'd met, but now the thought brought a small smile. How wrong she'd been to judge him on appearance alone. "It's rather late to start working in the woodshop tonight, isn't it?" she teased.

His feet shifted and he glanced about. "I know it's not exactly proper, Lola, but can I come in?"

She blinked, her smile falling flat. His tone sounded strange, low and tight. The door wobbled from her grasp and opened wider. "All right. Sure, come in."

He leaned through and pulled the hat from his head. Lantern light revealed a purple haze around his left eye and scuff on his chin. Was that a cut on his lip? Her heart clenched and she reached toward him. "What happened to you?"

Pulling his hand from his side, he blocked her from

drawing near. He stepped closer to the fire, but without the loose ease he normally carried. "Sit down, Lola."

"You look like twenty miles of bad road. You sit, before you topple. My bag of medical supplies is—"

"I'm fine, Lola. Take a seat."

Her hands fluttered over her hair, smoothing loose strands. Confusion and alarm vied for her attention. "I didn't expect company," she said, her tongue caught in a stutter. "I was lost in a book and—"

"This isn't a social call. I probably should have gone to the mortuary." His brown eyes flickered a moment, and then the light blew out like a lantern before a storm. "I have business with you, Miss Martin."

She wrinkled her face. "'Miss Martin'? What's going on, Bridger? I should hope we were well beyond the formalities of—"

"I said, sit down!" His hand at her shoulder startled her and shoved her to the soft seat behind. "My boss sent me to clear up a matter of some money you owe."

Lola jerked, thankful for the chair under her. "Money? Your boss? You mean Ike? I don't owe him any money."

"Your father borrowed money before he died. You're required to pay the balance, or Mr. Tyler will own your business." His voice sounded wooden and stiff, but perhaps that quality came from her mind.

"But I live here!"

"Exactly. Your home and business both can be claimed."

Lola poised on the edge of the cushion. "My father ran a fine business in this town. He had no need of a loan. This is preposterous!"

Bridger withdrew a small book from inside his coat with stiff purpose. "He secured funds to send you to medical school, Lola."

"But how? Why? He had no notion I wanted to be a doctor!" She blinked hard to wash tears from her eyes.

Bridger faced her, his expression stone-hard. "Mr. Tyler says he wanted to have the finances before he told you, but he inquired back East about your acceptance into college." His shoulders twitched and his voice softened. "Your father knew you better than anyone, Lola. He knew, and he wanted to give you your heart's desire."

She flew to her feet, forcing Bridger back a step. Her clenched fingers shoved the book against his ribs and he grimaced. "Tell me what's going on here! What's happened to you? You're hurt. Let me—"

"No!" His voice rattled the windows. He grasped her wrist in his hot, calloused hands and pushed her away with firm pressure. "Look in this ledger and tell me this isn't your father's writing."

She stared at him, his eyes devoid of light, all tenderness vanished. Her gaze dropped to the book in his hand, and she took it from him. She opened the front cover.

The original sum on the front page staggered her. She fell back to the chair with a gasp. The figures were written in crisp, neat rows, carefully recorded. She couldn't deny her father's hand.

She shook her head, the numbers swirling as she studied the book through a veil of tears. She flipped over the next several pages, but the balance remained where it had upon Papa's death. Tallying the amount of seven months' payments in her mind brought a cold chill to the pit of her stomach. Maintaining the payment would be difficult enough without late payments to account for. Why would Papa make this kind of bargain? Her dreams weren't worth Papa's loss.

She wiped her hand across one eye, but not fast enough to catch tears falling from the other. "There's more going on here. How did Ike get this? Why didn't he come to me before?"

Bridger drew a shallow breath. "Mr. Tyler hoped you could arrive at another arrangement, but I understand that's no longer the case. As for the ledger, I found it among your father's things."

Lola's head throbbed. Something was missing. "You brought this to Ike's attention. Is that it?"

His lean frame grew rigid. He raised his chin and broke his gaze from her pained expression. "He was grateful for the reminder. We're splitting the profit from the interest."

Lola trembled, pulling to her feet. How could she have been so blind, so wrong about Bridger? Hadn't she learned anything from her broken engagement? She met his glassy stare. Why had she played the fool again? She'd been so sure Bridger Jamison was a far different sort of man.

She moved to the canister kept behind a loose brick in the fireplace. Her savings held nothing close to what she owed, but she could pay one month in good faith and discuss the matter with Ike. He had loved her once, of that she felt certain. Surely enough lingered to provide her some leeway. She bit her lip and thrust the bills under Bridger's nose. "This should tide you over until next month. I'm afraid it's all I have right now. You can tell *your boss* I'll stop by tomorrow to renegotiate my balance."

He took the bills, avoiding her fiery glare, and had the audacity to count them in front of her. "I appreciate your promptness in dealing with the matter, ma'am," he said. His lips mashed together, crumpling at the ends. He moved toward the door with an unsteady gait. "I'll see you next month."

Lola caught him at the door, muscles tense with desire to crush his lithe form in it. "Don't bother. I'll be dealing directly with Mr. Tyler and his other men." She drew herself up. "The snake that rattles at least provides a warning."

Chapter Twenty-Three

Bridger faced Lola as he stepped onto the porch. The broken trust in her glare staggered him. She looked slight and forlorn in the shadows, lips drawn tight with anger. Her long, pale fingers clung to the ledger. His heart jumped in his chest and he stretched an arm toward her. Her flinch cut him, and he knew he couldn't go through with this charade. There had to be another way. "Lola, I have to tell you—"

But her gaze focused beyond him. "What's that glow?" she asked.

He pivoted on his heel to follow her line of vision. Heavy fog reflected a red glow somewhere around the bend in the road, toward the middle of town. Fire!

"That's the hotel!" Lola picked up her skirts and dashed over the steps.

The stitch in his ribs stabbed him as he struggled to keep up. They joined the throng, the whole town racing. Some scrambled for buckets while others shuffled children away from the flames. Men closest to the hotel tossed water from nearby wooden troughs. Women joined in the battle, forming brigade lines. Jake Anderson ordered men into position, his commands all but drowned out by the roar and crackle of the blaze.

Bridger pushed through the crowd, guiding Lola from behind. They joined a second bucket line, and he grabbed the pump handle. The first tug burned along his ribs.

"You can't, Bridger." Lola thrust him away. "I'll do it."

"Faster together," he said. "Help me."

Together they locked hands along the red saloon pump. Bridger lost track of time as buckets, pots and wash bins of all shapes and sizes waited to capture the cool water they forced from the ground. Hot smoke blew toward him. He raised his bandanna to cover his nose, but Lola had no such protection. She coughed soot from her lungs, and her hair slipped from its knot. Ash-gray streaks clung to her cheeks. But she hung on and matched him pull for pull, with a stiff shake of her head in refusal of the neckerchief he offered.

"That hotel's a goner," one breathless voice said.

"Can't let it get to the mercantile," another added.

"Tyler won't be happy."

He couldn't bother to focus on anything except to keep the water flowing. If the fire spread, it endangered all of Quiver Creek.

Time lost meaning before the roar that filled the night around them dulled to a sharp crackle of embers. He continued to pump, determined not to fail Lola again.

Her soft touch at his shoulder grabbed his attention. "Bridger! It's enough. The fire's all but out now. You have to rest." She drew his clamped hands away and tugged the kerchief from his face. "We kept it from spreading. But the hotel is gone."

Bridger grabbed her roughened hand in his and dragged her toward the source of roiling smoke. The grand hotel Ike envisioned lay in a pile of glowing embers. Townspeople stood in quiet pods around the destruction, panting for lack of air and breath. He caught sight of Jake seated on the porch of the general store, where Grace wrapped a bandage around his upper arm.

Catching sight of Lola, she called out in a raspy voice for her friend. Lola grabbed his sleeve and dragged him behind. Maybe she would try to turn him in after all. The coward in him hoped she would.

"What happened?" she asked.

Jake shrugged. "Too soon to know."

Lola snapped her hands against her hips. "I mean to you!"

He glanced at the cloth Grace tied off. "Caught a burn, but it's not bad."

Bridger knew from his blanched face the instant Jake remembered what the fire fight had interrupted. "Listen, Lola," the marshal began, "we really need to talk about—"

Ike's voice boomed from the quiet of the crowd. "I found the rat that started this fire!" Toby and Jim broke through the cluster of folks gathered and shoved their captive to the ground. The huge man collapsed to his knees, bracing with his hands. When the fearful eyes rose to the people around him, Bridger leaped.

Frank!

He stormed ahead, shaking off Jake's hands to help his brother. "What's going on here?"

Ike smoothed his mustache, face pale and clean in the aftermath, as if he stepped fresh from the bathhouse. Far be it for the man to appear mussed and dirty in public, even if it meant saving his own business.

"I came out when I heard the commotion, saw the flames coming from the hotel. Fortunately, Toby and

Jim were surveying the town and saw this strange fellow throw a torch into the back of my hotel!"

Bridger stepped between his brother and Ike. "That's impossible!"

Toby shoved him back.

Ike's voice rose above the crowd. "Look at him! I knew the minute I saw him in this town that big freak would bring nothing but trouble!"

Bridger's chest grew tight. "He's my brother, and he hasn't done a thing wrong."

Ike smirked. "I trust my men. And I know what I've heard from folks in the towns you've passed through."

Bridger resisted the press of the crowd and leaned back to grab his brother's arm as murmurs grew louder.

"Awful big fella."

"Doesn't look right in the head, does he?"

"Probably don't even know what he's done. Ought to be locked up, man like that."

Bridger lunged at Ike. "Tell them the truth!"

The marshal stepped between, blocking him before he met his target. "Don't push this," Jake whispered.

Bridger coughed and grabbed his tight ribs. "I'm not going to let this mob get my brother," he ground out.

Jake stared at him, weighing the choice in the balance. Then he held his hands up, never breaking his gaze from Bridger's. "My name is Jake Anderson. I'm a U.S. marshal here to investigate the death of your sheriff. I'm taking this man into custody for questioning in regards to the fire until I can gather the information I need."

Bridger's heart plummeted at the sight of his brother's fearful face.

Jake grabbed Frank and hauled him toward the jail. "I'm declaring a curfew over Quiver Creek this evening, starting now. Mr. Tyler's men will continue to moni-

tor the fire and make sure it's completely out. Everyone
else, go home."

Marshal Anderson paused a moment as he trudged
past. "It's the best way to keep our cover at this point,"
he said, his voice a low rumble, no one close enough
to hear. "And the only way to keep Frank safe until we
straighten this out."

The crowd slipped off, voices hot and hard despite the
restored order. Lola wrapped her arms around Grace's
shoulders. Bridger watched them make their way toward
Lola's home, but she never glanced back. Toby and the
other men brushed by him to start the cleanup, raking
embers into piles.

Bridger glanced around in the darkness, standing
alone. Fire rose from deep inside his chest. *How much
am I to take, Lord? Please, don't let Frank pay for my
mistakes.*

Lola wrapped her dark shawl close and maneuvered
the quiet street, sticking to the shadows.

Sending Grace ahead to get comfortable, she returned
to the scattering crowd, darting behind Jake's determined
tread. He kept a strong, stiff arm on Frank's slumped
shoulder, pushing him toward the jail, while Bridger
hustled to follow. She determined to talk to Jake about
Frank. Grace had been none too pleased with the notion
of her defying the marshal's orders to sneak into town,
but how could she abandon Frank?

Surely Jake realized Frank Jamison could no more
endanger a person than she would. Despite the blood he
shared with Bridger.

No raucous laughter and plinking tunes wafted through
the swinging doors of the saloon. Ike's men raked remains

of the smoldering hotel, but even they worked without speaking.

Grit from the smoky air added to the bad taste in her mouth. She had been so sure Bridger matched a higher ideal. A reserved man, maybe, but strong and good—a model of Christ's love and protection for His followers. Why could she not see his true potential before this?

Yet something in his firm expression tonight felt stilted. Papa had taken the loan, impossible as it seemed. But laws existed about usury and public notice, did they not? Why would Bridger not come to her first? Her heart pleaded with her to play the fool again. Not that Bridger had asked for anything more than the money…of which he no doubt gained a healthy share.

Anger swirled with every other thought and emotion from the evening. She needed to focus and use her energies to gain Frank's release. The rest she could deal with tomorrow.

The jail, built behind the saloon facing the next street over, had sat empty since Pete's death, save the occasional drunk Ike's men guarded until he sobered. Lola slid along the alley, hesitating as the men banged into the sturdy office.

Rough voices rumbled through an open window before she reached the jail's front door. She slowed her steps.

"You can't lock my brother up. He didn't do anything!"

At least Bridger still had the decency to fight on his brother's behalf.

She heard boots pound on wood. "After I went along with your crazy plan, you—"

"That has nothing to do with this!" Jake's low voice belted.

The marshal knew about Bridger's visit? She covered her gasp and stooped closer.

"You're a bigger fool than I take you for if you think that fire isn't somehow connected."

"It's my job to find out," Jake said.

Spurs rang as boots scuffed the floor closer to the window. "It's a good thing for you my brother wasn't in that hotel when it went up in flames. We need to end this before Ike adds another notch to his tally."

Fear crawled up her legs and settled in the pit of her stomach. Would Ike have killed Frank? And why?

"Help me build the case, Jamison, and we will."

"I'll testify." Bridger's voice grew softer and she strained to hear. She clung to the rough planks and muffled a cough.

"I figured you would, but you only know about the extortion. I want him tried for murder!" Jake's normally calm tone broke with frustration.

"That's what I'm talking about," Bridger insisted.

Stillness reigned and Lola held her breath.

Then Jake's hushed voice whispered low. "What do you know?"

"Something Toby and Jim said while they were teaching me this little lesson," Bridger said. Lola recalled the bruises on his face and his stiff gait. "We have Mr. Anthony and Pete McKenna, but this goes back further. He had Lola's father killed, too."

A cold streak shot through her. Her feet blazed a path independent of thought, dragging her around the corner and through the front door. She slammed it shut and braced against it. Frank's head lifted from where he sat behind bars. The fire in her gut warred against the chill in her limbs. She fixed Bridger and Jake in her field of vision. "I want to know what's going on here." Her voice sounded ragged and weak to her own ears. "So one of you had best start talking—now."

Bridger froze. Lola stood heaving at the door, looking pale and fierce and as beautiful as he'd ever seen her. He picked up a chair to shift it closer.

"Don't!" she warned. "Talk!"

He returned the seat to the floor and slid it with his foot. "Please sit, Lola. It has to be a shock, hearing this way. Calm down and pull up a chair, and we'll explain everything." He glared at Jake. "Like we should have from the start."

She waited, gaze unblinking, before taking the seat. She wobbled and grabbed the edges, but her expression warned him not to offer aid.

He closed the window and shutters behind him, giving her a chance to catch her breath. "You'd best start talking, Marshal. Seems to me you have the most to say in the matter. It's about time we hear it all."

Jake's broad frame slumped to the dusty desk. "I told you I had come to investigate another matter in Quiver Creek when you wired the U.S. Marshals Department. I needed answers in the disappearance of a friend of mine, another federal marshal. Alex was looking into a racket being run by Ike Tyler, with several spokes to the machine—intimidation, vandalism toward businesses that refused to pay protection money and various other offenses."

"No marshal came through here," Lola said.

"He came in undercover, a drifter passing through. We discovered he hung for the murder of a local man, Mr. Roland Martin."

Lola gasped and tears filled her green eyes. She bit her lip, then took a deep, shuddering breath. Bridger slid closer, but she froze him with a glare to stop the heart of weaker men.

She crossed her arms. "Go on."

"Obviously, he didn't murder your father. I suspect Ike did but pinned it on my friend. He must've figured out what Alex was doing here, though I don't know how." He clenched his fists. Bridger felt his frustration as Jake returned his focus to Lola. "I do know Ike Tyler has hurt a lot of people, and I'm going to put him away if it's the last thing I do. What Bridger did tonight…he was only doing what I asked. It was a poor plan, but we didn't want to endanger you by divulging too much too soon."

Lola drew near with urgent steps. She grasped Jake's wrist, but Bridger warmed to see her eyes locked on his. He'd never witnessed the glow of faith restored in a woman's eyes before, and he longed to crush her in his arms.

"Let me help," she said. "I know Ike felt something for me once. I can get him to talk. I know it."

Fear clenched Bridger's gut. "No. The men all but said Ike was behind it all. I have enough information to confront him. I can play this part long enough to get his confession myself."

"I can help!" She gave Jake's arm an insistent shake.

"Not if I can prevent—"

Jake held up his hand, head shaking. "This is my case. I was foolish to involve ordinary citizens in the first place, and I won't make that mistake again."

Bridger rested his thumbs on his belt. "He'll never talk to you."

"Then we'll find another way," Jake said.

"What about Grace?" Lola asked.

Jake shook free from her grasp. "What about her?"

"She may have more information than she realizes."

"No, I read Pete's log. If he knew anything, he didn't write it there," Jake said.

Bridger wondered. "Lola didn't know anything, either, but her father kept notes hidden. What if Pete McKenna kept a separate log, waiting for something more concrete before he added it to his permanent files?"

Jake shrugged his shoulders. "That's a possibility, I guess." He slipped to his feet and leaned against the desk, arms crossed. "But Ike knows I'm a marshal now. If he sees me questioning Grace, it places her in greater danger."

Lola's skirt swayed as she stepped back. Her slender fingers clasped together like a woman in prayer, and her eyes gleamed. Her pink lips twisted in a determined grimace. "Let me talk with her. She has a lot on her mind, and the baby's to arrive within a few weeks. I won't upset her, and Ike won't suspect a thing, I promise."

Jake stared at his boots and Bridger knew the same sensation of gears whirring in his mind. What Lola said made perfect sense. Prying questions would be much easier to answer with another woman, especially as close as the two ladies were. Running every possible opportunity for danger scrambled his thoughts, but nothing reasonable came to mind. But his heart prevented rational thought and argued against any involvement from Lola.

Jake nudged his reaction with a nod. Bridger huffed, feeling the tug at his side. "When can you talk to her?"

"Tonight. She's staying at my place rather than ride home." Excitement filled Lola's breathless voice.

Bridger raked fingers through his hair and along his scruffy jaw. Rough whiskers bit raw against his palm, like the strain of the night on his mind. "I can't think of any reason for you not to ask Grace. But I still don't feel right about this. If Ike was willing to torch his own hotel, he suspects something. I think he's starting to unravel."

Jake interrupted. "You're absolutely certain Frank had nothing to do with the fire? More people than Ike suspect him, you know, and I have to give them something."

Bridger stomped forward, shoving the marshal and forcing his full attention. "How could you ask such a fool question after all this?"

Jake threw his hands up, backing toward the wall. But his tone remained adamant. "Even if it were an accident, the folks in town will expect some kind of answers. You'll never be able to stay in Quiver Creek when this is done if you can't lay those fears to rest."

Lola cleared her throat with a gentle cough. "He's afraid of fire. He won't even strike a match, isn't that right?"

Bridger stared at Lola. Her quiet strength gained the marshal's attention, too. Soft lantern light around the jail office gave her a warm glow, as pink returned to her face. "How did you—?"

Lola sent a wink toward Frank before she faced Jake. "I can testify to that, Marshal. Shouldn't that be enough for you?"

Jake wiped soot from his eyes and grinned. "Having the confidence of a fine, upstanding businesswoman such as you should go a long way to ease the public's fears."

Bridger stepped forward, grasping Lola's warm hands. This woman, who had been given so many reasons not to trust him—did. "Thank you, Lola. Just when I think I've tangled things up so bad even the Lord won't unwind it all, He reminds me what a little trust can do." He squeezed her fingers with gentle pressure, feeling their smoothness beneath his calluses. "We'll give you an hour to explain it all to Grace at your place, and then we'll have to bring you both here."

She leaned back but didn't pull her hands away. "The jail? Why?"

Jake stood tall, voice firm. "It's easier to guard you here. Once morning comes, we'll scout town, learn the lay of the land, so to speak, and then decide what to do next."

Bridger rubbed his neck and glanced at Frank, who waited in silence, hands grasping the bars with his broad face pressed between.

"What do you think, Frank?"

His brother grinned. "I think we're a scary-looking pair of fellas, Bridge. I'll back whatever you say."

Bridger crooked his lip, scar tugging his mouth. Tension stiffened his muscles, and uncertainty clawed at every sense, but calm peace flooded his mind. The Lord had more for them to do, but He promised to help them every step of the way. He'd sent unflappable faith through his brother and firm assurance from this beautiful lady to confirm that. "We'll see you again within the hour, Lola. This time, we're coming even if the whole town goes up in smoke."

Chapter Twenty-Four

The door creaked open with a careful push, and Lola glanced behind into the night before stepping through. Grace sat in the rocker, head leaned against the high rest, eyes closed. She rubbed a hand over her swollen middle with a firm press.

"Grace? Are you all right?"

Her friend blinked and coughed a rough bark. "Just tired. I swallowed a bit of smoke and this baby is giving me fits, that's all."

Lola rushed to her side, feeling for a pulse at her wrist and pressing her hand against the bulge of baby. "That's *all?* You should be resting!"

A wan smile crossed Grace's gentle face. "And so I was."

"I mean lying down," Lola said.

Grace sat upright. "Nonsense. This baby might as well know from the start I don't plan to be too indulgent with him. What did Jake say? Can he help?"

Lola looked at her friend and patted her hand. "There's more going on here than we knew."

She explained all she could in gentle tones but kept the details direct and light. Her words flew in a rush, a feeling of haste pressuring her heart. Bridger and Jake had created an environment of tense caution she carried home.

Grace's face paled, wrinkles creasing her forehead. Her eyes grew large with understanding. "So they think Pete was murdered?"

The tense quirk of her lips begged Lola to say she'd drawn the wrong conclusion. Lola believed that everything would have made more sense somehow had her papa died in an accident. Knowing hate had killed a man so full of love…was more difficult to understand.

She breathed deep and prayed for the right words to come. "Yes, Grace."

"But they said—" Her friend's coloring blanched further, lips a thin, bloodless line. "They said he fell from a horse, probably spooked by the cat he was chasing. You said—"

"I guessed, because he'd been called out to hunt. But the marks, Grace—something didn't look right." She knelt at the side of the rocker and smoothed her billowed skirt. "I think that's why I followed through and sent the wire to the federal marshal in the first place. Even more strange, I found some of the same marks on Cecil Anthony." Her mind flooded with memories of her father's death and she shuddered. Papa's neck had been broken, too.

She tugged on Grace's arm. "Think carefully. Did Pete mention anything he had been working on? Jake said he found nothing in his files at the office, but maybe he kept notes somewhere else."

Grace chewed her lip and rubbed her bleary eyes.

Lola settled closer. "Bridger found Papa's ledger in an old box of notes. Did Pete have any certain place where he kept important papers at home?"

Grace's eyes glazed. Then she rocked forward, face crumpled in pain. "In the buckboard! That box your father made us for our wedding present. Pete kept it locked under the seat, but I believe he kept a journal there. Sometimes if he was gone for a time, he'd share some of what he wrote with me when he returned. But he always placed it back in that box. Maybe—"

A sudden cry doubled Grace over.

"What's wrong?" Lola moved her hands across Grace's quivering midsection. She read the panic in her eyes in an instant and knew the truth. "Contractions?"

Grace nodded, tears escaping down her cheeks. "It's too early, Lola. The baby—he can't come now!"

"Shh, shh…" she soothed. "It's not much too early, and with all you've been through tonight alone, it's made him in a hurry to find what this big old world is all about." Her insides quaked. "There's plenty of time. I'll go back to the jail, and Jake can fetch Doc Kendall. They'll be here in plenty of time for that baby to come."

Grace's fingers dug into her arm, mouth parted in a silent cry. "Please, I can't lose the baby. He's all I have left of Pete!"

Lola helped her friend move to the stairway banister. "You go up and crawl in my bed." She grabbed her shawl from the hook by the door. "I'll be back in a jiffy and wait with you for the doctor. We'll pray together. You and this baby will both be fine, you hear me?"

Grace managed a tremulous smile and began her waddle up the steps. Lola gave a short wave and swung the door open, then jolted.

Ike blocked her at the door. "Now, now, my dear…"

The pulse in her neck jumped and hot dread sank to her toes. "What are you doing here?"

"The marshal wouldn't want you traipsing about, not

after he established a strict curfew." His cigar puffed in her face, adding to her irritation. "It's my role to support the law in Quiver Creek. You know that."

She glanced at Grace, who stood frozen at the bottom step. "We need the doctor. She's in labor."

Ike pushed his way past her, knocking Lola into the edge of the davenport. "I don't think there's any need for that yet," he said. "Though it does make the story all the more tragic." The gleam in his eyes did little to hide the black depths of his evil stare.

A dry throat choked off her strangled breath. "What are you saying?"

"Nothing, nothing," Ike said, swirling his cigar in the air. "It's just a greater shame that the good marshal will find not only our comely undertaker, but her dearest friend, as well."

Lola sensed his intent, but her voice slogged through the thickness in her throat to catch up. "Find us?"

"Oh, yes, he'll find you dead soon after Bridger Jamison arrives," Ike said. "Right on time to take the blame."

Stars provided the only light overhead and the mountains stood a shade darker against the night sky. The rush of wind blew loud with no sounds of the town to compete.

The horse tied in front of Lola's place caught Bridger's eye as soon as they rounded the bend. A glance at Jake's shadowed face told him he'd seen it, too.

"Looks a mite small to be your horse," Bridger said.

Jake nodded. "It is. I left mine at Grace's place. We drove to town in her wagon."

Bridger glanced at Frank, who straggled beside them. Maybe Jake should have won the argument to leave his brother behind at the jail.

Except he'd convinced Jake Ike's men wouldn't be

stopped by a few cell bars. Now he wasn't so sure Frank stayed any safer by trailing along.

Jake's pace never wavered. "Ike's?"

"Yep."

The marshal checked his pistol. "You wait outside."

Bridger grabbed his arm and spun him with surprise. "Let me try first. He'll know you're onto him the minute he spies you, and he could hurt those ladies. I have the money from Lola. If I convince him I'm looking for my cut, we have a chance to get them out first."

Jake pulled his hat brim low on his face. "That's a big 'if.'"

He threw Jake's earlier words back at him. "Where's your faith?"

A low huff of air whispered on the wind. "Back at the river, when we were talking about you."

Frank scratched his head and wobbled from foot to foot. "Don't seem like a good plan, Bridge."

He whipped his gaze to his brother and sensed Jake's attention shift, too. "It's the best we have. Besides, with you and Jake both out here praying for me, backing me up, how can it not work out?"

"I don't like it," Frank said.

"Listen to your brother," Jake added.

Bridger drew a deep breath. A sense of pervading peace filled him, but he supposed he might not feel the same if he waited on the outside while his friend or brother faced Ike alone, with the ladies between.

"I'm not going in by myself, you know. However this works out," he said, glancing at each of the men, then at Lola's dimly lit house across the street, "the Lord goes with me."

A pause filled with the sound of spring peepers wasted precious seconds, and Bridger's impatience grew. Every second they debated kept him from providing help for the women inside.

"I don't like it." Jake shook his head, stubble scratching against his fist like sandpaper. "But it might work. If he figures you're working against him, don't be brash. Do what he says, and try to get him outside without the women. Between us we'll even the odds a bit."

"Me, too," Frank protested.

"Oh, no." Bridger pressed against his brother's chest. "You're staying out of this altogether."

A low chuckle came from Jake. "Sounds to me like stubbornness is a family trait," he said. "We can't leave him here, Bridger. Besides, he could come in handy."

Frank's collarbone jumped beneath his fingers with his firm nod. "We're a scary-looking pair, remember? We got to stick together."

Moments ticked. "All right, we're wasting time. Frank, you stick with the marshal here like a burr on a horse's rump, you hear me? You do what he says and stay out of trouble. Keep your head down."

"I will, Bridge. It's easier to pray that way."

If everyone walked away from this, Frank might just be the hero of the night.

Chapter Twenty-Five

*B*ridger?

The knock at the door startled Lola as she and Grace quivered on the sofa. She glanced at Ike. His eyes gleamed over the gun barrel.

His patient wait felt days long, but the tick of the clock told her less than a quarter hour had passed. "Greet your guest, Lola," he said.

She shook her trembling fingers from Grace's grasp and eased toward the door. She prayed Bridger didn't wait on the other side, but hoped no one else became tangled in the scenario. Involving Grace was bad enough, even with the comfort she provided.

"Everything all right here, Miss Martin?" Bridger's greeting sounded stiff, but the lantern revealed a grim smile.

"Aren't you needed at the jail?" she asked.

Ike pulled the door from her hand and swung it open. His gun leveled at Bridger's chest over her shoulder. "Not so much as he's needed here, darling. Come inside, Mr. Jamison. I knew you couldn't stay away long with Lola involved."

Bridger slipped through the door without a glimpse

behind, and Lola's heart sank. Wouldn't he give a cue if Jake waited outside? Instead, he sent a sidelong glance her way and stood in the middle of the room. His narrow frame took new dimensions of strength in the light from lanterns turned low.

Ike cocked his head, and she returned to her seat next to Grace.

Bridger spoke to Ike but kept his warm brown eyes focused on her and Grace. He held out the envelope she'd given him earlier. "There's no need to hold these ladies, boss. Miss Martin paid for this month, and she's willing to work out a plan for—"

Ike shoved the barrel of his pistol deep into Bridger's side. The jab forced a gasp as he clutched his ribs. Ike snatched his weapon from the holster he wore. "That's no longer enough, Mr. Jamison. I've decided to collect payment in full…from all of you."

Bridger stood to full height, his movements slow and breath heavy.

"You can't kill us all, Ike," he said.

"Of course not," Ike said. "I'll see to it your dear brother gets credit for that. Poor boy, rage forced him to break out of jail, killing the fine marshal. Then he came after you." He clicked his tongue. "These poor women only happened to be in the wrong place at the wrong time. Fortunately, I'll wander in and bring him to justice before he can harm others."

Grace groaned as another contraction hit her.

"What did you do to her?" Bridger demanded.

"She claims her baby is on the way." Ike gave a disgusted sneer. "But that's of no consequence now. Pity, though."

Lola drew her friend close and wiped her brow. "She needs the doctor."

"I'm all right," Grace said.

Ike gestured the gun toward the two of them. "Get up."

Lola dug her fingers into Grace's arm. "Didn't you feel anything for me, Ike? Why would you do this?"

Ike's dark expression eased. "I felt everything for you, Lola. Everything I did was only to prove how much I cared. Your father thought me a slacker, I started a business. He didn't approve of saloon-keeping, I planned for a hotel. He found me weak, I proved myself by controlling this town and businesses throughout the territory, including his. It was never enough."

"So you killed him," Bridger said.

Tears filled her eyes and she rose to her feet. "I sent you away because you created a mockery of me with Mattie! Papa didn't need to say a thing."

"He would've forced your hand eventually. Don't you see? He was willing to take a loan from me—at prime interest—for the means to send you away. I wanted you to have the chance you desired, because you'd still come back to *me*. I'd have given you everything, but you threw it all away."

Lola struggled for breath in the suddenly heavy air. "I don't understand why Papa would come to you."

Ike laughed and she saw Bridger shift his stance. "You don't think a bank around here would grant a loan for a lady to become a doctor, do you?"

She shivered. Papa died trying to see the dream she hardly dared to speak come true. Anger poured out in tears across her face. Bridger's rough fingers grazed her hand.

Ike waved his gun. "Get away from her! A woman this fine shouldn't be sullied by the likes of you."

Grace bit back a gasp, breathing in ragged puffs.

Bridger glanced her way. "That's not what it will look

like when the town discovers she let me in this time of night."

Ike stroked his mustache, seeming to consider. "See, that's what I like about you, Bridger. Always thinking ahead. You could've gone far in my outfit."

He consulted his pocket watch. Lola flashed a glance to Bridger in time to catch a quick wink. *Thank You, Lord, for sending him. Whatever happens...*

Bridger lowered his head with a resigned slouch. His voice held a matching tone. "Take me to Martin's wood-shop. It wouldn't be unusual for me to work late there, especially when Lola has need of coffins."

Ike's eyes gleamed with madness. "That's good. That's very good."

He motioned Bridger ahead, pressing the smooth barrel tip into his shoulder. Ike swept his left hand with fake gentility. "If you'll allow me to escort you, ladies, I'll take care of Mr. Jamison first."

Grace began crying in earnest but managed to gain her feet when Lola tugged her arm.

"Now, now," Ike said, his voice eerily soothing, "business before pleasure, you understand. I promise we'll return here before your time comes, ma'am. That should be sufficient to protect your *stellar* reputations in this town."

Lola grabbed a lantern as they followed Bridger past the fireplace and rocker where she'd rested with such contentment only hours ago. She spared a look at the front door, gauging her chance at escape. But with Grace's contractions coming roughly ten minutes apart and a crazy man pointing a gun into Bridger's lean back, she couldn't risk it.

Prayers rolled from her tongue, more a pleading notion than organized thought, but she knew the Lord heard and understood all the same. Grace's soft additions gave consolation.

"Shut up!" Ike raised the gun to the base of Bridger's head. "You shut up right now or I'll not care what folks say about you and shoot him here."

Bridger froze, hand at the back door. "Maybe those prayers are for you, Ike. Looks to me like you could use some."

Ike cuffed the back of Bridger's head with a sharp crack of the pistol butt. Bridger wobbled but managed to brace against the doorjamb before reaching his knees.

Fury shook Ike's frame. "Shut up, I said! Praying for me would be completely insane."

Ike swung the gun toward Lola and she gasped, fingers cramping against Grace's tight hold. He nudged Bridger with an elbow at his back. "Bring the key."

Lola tugged it from the hook and wrapped her arm around Grace as they shuffled through the door, lantern glowing in her free hand.

The night sky held no moon, making it difficult to see Bridger beyond Ike's taller, broader shadow. He staggered a bit on the steps, and Lola realized what that knock to the head had cost him. But he managed a fairly steady gait across the narrow yard, damp with evening dew.

"Bridge!"

Frank's voice called from the darkness at the corner of her house. If he'd been released, wouldn't Jake be close by, as well?

She paused at the rail, pulling Grace tight to her side. Her heart pounded like thunder in her ears until she could barely decipher the voices around her.

Ike's mustache shimmered as he spoke in the dim lantern light. "Isn't this a perfect family reunion? You may be a dummy, Frank, but you have impeccable timing."

Ike swung the gun at Bridger with deadly intent. The glint of metal spurred a shriek, and she couldn't be sure if she or Grace were the source.

"Give it up, Tyler!" Jake's voice rang like church bells on Sunday. "You're under arrest."

The click of a hammer stopped her heart. Ike's voice took a shrill tone. "You're too late!"

A roar like a cyclone and heavy crash at her feet forced a scream. She raised the lantern to see Frank's broad back crushed over Ike. Her former fiancé kicked and squirmed, trying to bring his weapon to the proper angle to fire.

"No, Frank!" Bridger's fearful voice jolted her. "Jake, he has my gun. I can't—"

The shot came quiet and muffled, yet created a sudden echo against her chest. She dropped the lantern as the writhing battle at her feet ended with sickening speed.

The shot shattered the night, and Bridger fell to his knees, heart frozen in midbeat. "Frank!"

His vision wobbled between the darkness and blow to the head, but he managed to grasp his brother's broad shoulders and flip him over. Bridger wavered between drawing Frank in an embrace they hadn't shared since boyhood and shaking him in frustration. Why did Frank insist on throwing himself into trouble?

Blood streaked the front of his brother's shirt and Bridger jiggled his arm. "No!"

Wide blue eyes snapped open with confusion. Bridger crushed Frank's head to his chest. "Thank You, Lord!"

Frank struggled against him, forcing Bridger away with a sudden jolt. He blinked, eyebrows wrinkled in confusion as he patted his shirt. "I'm not hurt, Bridge. Stop smooshing me."

But the blood? Bridger glanced at the porch where the women huddled, arms supporting each other and tears mingling. Shuddering, but safe. His breath left him in a rush.

Jake kicked Ike's pistol away from his prone form and touched the man's neck. Bridger caught his eye as he shook his head, a look of disgust on his grim face. "He's gone."

Bridger slumped with relief but took no pride in Ike's death.

Frank trembled in his grasp. "I didn't mean it!"

He patted his brother's shoulder and pulled him upright on the cold ground. "We know, Frank. It was an accident. Ike did it himself. We all saw."

He sought Lola's face, her green eyes glistening with unshed tears, grief and shock. They looked large in her pale face, lit by the lantern's glow and contrasted against hair that reminded him of midnight sky. He admired her beauty, but the quiet strength of spirit forged by fire drew his heart.

A cry of sharp pain brought him to his feet. The motion drew Lola to attention, and she moved to comfort her friend. "Let's get you inside," he said.

Jake stood at the bottom step in two strides. "Grace? What's wrong?" Fear he hadn't heard in the marshal's voice before filled his tone.

"Get Doc Kendall!" Lola never turned from her friend. "The baby is on its way."

Jake became a statue, his broad frame silhouetted against the lingering fog of smoke. "Now?"

A slow smile tugged Bridger's lips. "Yes, now. You get the doc. Frank and I will take care of Tyler."

Like a bullet, Jake raced toward the front of the house. A loud whinny and the pound of shod hooves soon echoed in the night.

Bridger grasped Frank's fist in his hand and tugged his brother to his feet. "Come on, Frank. We'll need to wrap the body."

Lola turned at the back door. "Get a sheet from my front cupboard and wrap him, Frank, like we did before. Lay him on the table and I'll take care of him in the morning."

Bridger admired her no-nonsense tone but hated to think she'd be left to prepare the body of such a man for burial. Knowing what they had almost shared would cause pain; knowing what he'd become would bring regret. A woman of character as fine as Lola Martin shouldn't have to handle such matters. Ike had at least appreciated her quality.

"And you, Bridger," Lola continued. "Until the doctor arrives, you're with me."

Bridger gulped…and started praying for Jake's swift return.

Lola draped a blanket over her friend and rolled her sleeves back. She had helped Doc Kendall bring several babies into the world, but between events of the evening and thoughts of doing this alone, her heart tripped faster than a downhill train.

Bridger bumped the door and maneuvered his way through with two pails of steaming water.

She smiled at his pale face. But unless it held more confidence than she felt, he wouldn't gain much courage from her expression.

"Pour some in the basin," she said. He set one bucket

on the floor and hefted the other. Steam frosted the mirror, obscuring his firm jaw and scarred cheek.

The strike from Ike's gun handle had cut a gash along his neck, but the bleeding looked to have stopped. He should have ice to keep swelling at bay, and perhaps even a stitch or two.

Grace struggled on the bed. "Too soon, too soon," she moaned.

Bridger would have to wait.

She washed her arms to the elbows and dried them on a clean towel before moving to the end of the bed.

Bridger paced near the head, out of Grace's line of sight. "What do I do?"

She nodded to a bowl with a limp rag. "Keep her cool and calm."

He moved stiffly to the stand and wrung the cloth before placing it across her forehead at an awkward slant. He patted Grace's shoulder as she murmured, his Adam's apple bobbing in his throat. "You'll be fine, Miss Grace. Lola's here, and she's the next best thing to the doc, all right?"

Grace nodded, eyes squeezed tight.

"Soon you'll look back at this day and be plenty proud your baby was helped into this world by the first lady doctor in these parts." His gaze locked on Lola's, and he smiled.

Lola focused on the task at hand, but the notion filled her with warmth. Papa was gone, and Pete and Mr. Anthony. But the man responsible would find his eternal justice, even if he escaped a far more lenient one on earth. No one could hold her back. It was up to her to push forward and see where the Lord might lead.

The baby's head started to crown and she adjusted the sheets. "Get ready to push, Grace!"

A glance at Bridger found him gripping Grace's shoulder as tightly as he did the bedpost. "Miss Grace, if it's all right by you, this would be a fine time for us to pray."

Chapter Twenty-Six

Bridger slumped in Lola's rocker with an ice bag on his neck and watched sunrise glow through her window. Frank lay on the davenport, long legs sprawled to the floor in a position anything but comfortable. His soft snore testified to the fact it didn't prevent sleep.

Jake paced across the braided rug. Bridger had heard husbands describe the wait of childbirth, pacing outside a door and the long hours of uncertainty and helplessness. All that paled in comparison to the way he felt before Jake made it back with Doc Kendall in tow. He escaped just before the baby made its appearance.

The vision of Lola preparing to deliver a wee one left him with almost as much awe as the sight of Grace in labor. Birth may be a terrifying event to most men, but he counted it a mighty privilege to behold Lola's confidence.

Jake ran a hand through his hair, making it stand on end. "What's taking so long?"

Bridger rocked forward and removed the cold pack from his neck. "They said everything's fine. They'll call us soon as the baby's ready. Relax."

The creak of footsteps upstairs punctuated his words. Lola's skirts swished against the stair rails. She peeked around the bottom with a smile as wide as the Tetons. "Doc says you can come up for a quick hello if you stay quiet."

Frank roused, the quilt that covered him slipping to the floor. He rubbed his eyes. "All of us?"

Bridger caught her gaze, a thrum of excitement in his chest. She winked. "All of you."

They bounded up the stairway, Frank leading the way to the room where he paused to allow Lola's entrance. Bridger grabbed his sleeve at the last moment. "I think you may want the privilege of the first look, Jake," he said, nodding him through the door.

The marshal grinned like a boy with his first puppy and went in.

Silas Kendall washed strange-looking tools in the basin, then pushed his glasses along his nose and smiled when the troupe of them bounded in. "Looks like you all had quite a night."

Lola shushed him from the head of the bed, where she stood near Grace. She ran a tender finger over the baby's wealth of dark hair and along its unmarred cheek before she handed the bundle to his mother. Strange warmth tingled deep in Bridger's chest at the sight, bearing a dream of his own children...with this woman at his side to build a family and home.

Exhaustion lined Grace's face, and yet she held a new beauty as she took the tiny baby wrapped in a snug blue blanket. "Gentlemen," she said, her voice soft and raspy, "let me be the first to introduce you to my son, Peter Franklin Capland McKenna—Cap for short. I am certain he is pleased to make your acquaintance."

The baby's round face crumpled with a strong cry.

Jake slipped closer and chucked the baby's chin with

his thick, rough finger. Cap's tiny head turned and he settled to sleep.

A look Bridger recognized passed between Grace and the marshal. It made him smile.

Frank gripped his arm. "Hey, he's named after me!"

Bridger patted his brother on the back. "I reckon he is."

Grace tore her gaze from the baby long enough to glance at Frank. "If you hadn't acted with such bravery, my little boy might not have arrived into this world."

Silas spoke just behind his shoulder. "From what I hear," he said, "she had to narrow that name quite a bit from all those involved in last night's drama."

Lola's eyes clouded. "I've never been so terrified."

Bridger moved to her side and slid his hand over her sleek hair to rest on her shoulder. "I've never seen someone so strong."

Doc Kendall's eyes held pride. "I can tell you this—she did one fine job of getting that baby here."

Lola sent a sly glance his way before she spoke. "Thanks to you, Doc."

A laugh burst from Bridger. "Yes, I can honestly say, I've never been happier to see another human being than I was to see you at that moment, Doc." He slipped his hand to the small of Lola's back. It felt comfortable, warm, right. Her eyes lit.

"You did a fine job and would have seen it through if needed. You prayed when neither of us would've been able." The pride in Lola's smooth voice made him want to be a better man.

"I'm very happy to give the Lord full credit," he said.

"Me, too," Silas said. "I'm only a helping hand if He can use me."

Jake broke from his baby trance. "What about you, Lola? I've been thinking—"

"Thinking's good," Frank proclaimed, his attention focused fully on his namesake, as well.

Jake continued. "I've put your father's notes together with Sheriff McKenna's and some of my own digging. Your father kept track of other businesses being leaned on by Ike and his men, trying to gather enough to close them down. He made the initial contact with the marshal's office that brought Alex here. I think he may have talked to Ike about the loan in order to implicate him for usury and extortion, but somehow Tyler found him out. At any rate, the money sits in a Denver bank account, waiting your acceptance into medical school. Between that and the reward money on Ike and his men, of which you've earned a share, you ought to have enough to provide this town with a second doctor."

Her eyes grew wide. The dark fringe of lashes made their pale green color all the more mesmerizing. "We already have one doctor—"

Silas waved off her protest. "This is a growing town. I'd be obliged for the help."

"You'd be perfect for it," Grace added.

Lola clasped her hands together, long fingers steepled. "I don't know what to say."

The distance east to a women's medical college staggered Bridger, but she deserved every opportunity to help others the way the Lord saw fit. He shrugged. "Say you'll pray about it."

Lola waited as Bridger, Frank and Jake buried Ike's coffin along the far edge of the churchyard. Few had turned out for the service, though Pastor Evans delivered a fine sermon and did his best to portray Ike's wrong choices as a means the Lord might still use for good. She couldn't help but shed a few honest tears for the friendship they'd once shared. For a man who had served his life seeking approval from others—even if it were in all the wrong ways...such a lonely passage broke her heart.

Bridger brushed dust from his shirt and handed the shovel to Frank, who trailed after Jake to return them to the jail. Marshal Anderson would stay on to complete the investigation and provide primary law enforcement for Quiver Creek. Seeing Jake's pride for Grace and her son, it pleased Lola to know he'd be spending more time in town.

Bridger joined her. His brown plaid shirt held a vein of yellow that highlighted golden flecks in his eyes. His lithe frame moved with ease across the field, and she admired the warm strength he carried. Even the scar he believed marred his face only added to his handsome allure, and a flutter awakened in her chest each time she saw him. How could she think of going east to school?

Lost in thought, she was startled by his touch on her arm. "Are you finished? I thought we might take a walk along the river. I'd like to talk with you."

Warmth tingled through her, magnified by his gentle caress. He placed her hand in the crook of his arm and led her into the secluded stand of trees behind the church.

They walked in silence, his steps guiding her through flourishing bushes and trees bursting with thick leaves. They rustled in the breeze sweeping down from the mountains, but as the year turned toward summer, the air held no sting.

He stopped at the bend in the creek, where the water made its last swift turn out of town. A deep breath broadened his chest, and he stared into her eyes.

"I want you to go east, Lola."

She broke his gaze to look beyond the river, through the trees, along glorious mountain peaks, to the brilliant sky above. "How can I leave all this? How can I leave you?"

A laugh rippled from him and he rubbed his jagged scar, so much a part of the man he was. His voice dropped low with a mocking drawl. "I'm a scary-looking fella, ma'am. Ain't hardly fitting for a fine lady such as yourself to even be seen with a ruffian like me."

She swatted his chest, but he grabbed her hand and pulled her close. His gaze focused just below her eyes, and she drew her lips closed in anticipation. "You have all summer to figure that out," he said, his voice a whispery rasp. "But you've wanted this for too long not to take your chance. I won't let you give up your dream for the likes of me."

She pressed closer. His heart pounded beneath her fingers. "You're my dream."

His eyes searched her face, and he bent his head to capture her lips. The scent of warm mint and leather filled her senses as she lost her breath to his kiss.

He lifted his head but moved no farther. "I'm not going anywhere. I love you, Lola Martin. I want to spend my summer, your years of medical school, our children's lives and my old age all with you. But I'd leave it behind if it meant keeping you here without achieving the goal God has set before you."

She drew her hands along his arms, feeling their strength ripple beneath her fingertips. "I won't have that. I love you, Bridger, for now and always."

"Good," he said, dipping his head for another kiss.

She drew her hands behind his neck and through his silky hair. "But what will you do?"

He squeezed her shoulders, his excitement transferring to a shiver along her arms. "This is a growing town with plenty of opportunities. The new council members decided a fancy hotel is still a good idea, and I'm to over-see the construction. Grace has asked Frank to hire on when her folks leave, to help look after her stock. For a while, until we get our own place going on a sweet little parcel on the end of town, next to the new doc's place."

She felt his smile grow as he pressed his lips against her hair and pulled away. "Just like you have to follow your calling to be the woman God wants you to be, I need this time to stop and earn my way, to prove myself."

Lola pushed against his broad chest. "You've done that a thousand times over, Bridger Jamison."

He placed rough hands over hers and shook his head. "Not for this town, for myself. I've lived my whole life in the shadow of my father, trying to be everything he wasn't, trying to be everything I thought Frank needed. Somewhere along the way, I forgot about listening to what the Lord wanted *for* me. Already, He's brought me you. I need this time to become everything He expects of me. To build a strong foundation for our life together, if you'll have me." His eyes glittered with love and strength. "Besides," he whispered, "I've always had a hankering to find a wife to support me."

She gave him a playful swat, then grasped his face in her hands. She leaned away, yet unable to pull from his tender hold. The years of schooling loomed long, but their future would be bright in God's loving provision. "With comments like that, sir, I think you should be thankful the Lord provided you with a doctor to spend your life with."

How was it possible such a man would fall for her, the undertaker's daughter?

* * * * *

Dear Reader,

Spring carries a promise of renewal. I pray *Wyoming Promises* has refreshed your spirit with a reminder of God's love.

As Lola and Bridger have shown, we are shaped by our past and our choices, but in the Lord, we need not be bound by them. He always sees the promise in us and will draw it out if we seek to follow Him.

No one is more amazed than I am to see my second book in print. Praise the Lord for His continuing guidance!

I'd love to hear from you at *mountainwriter7@yahoo. com*.

In Christ,
Kerri Mountain

Questions for Discussion

1. Lola is put off by Bridger's rough appearance and the scar on his face. Is she right to be wary? How can "judging on the outward appearance" be helpful? How can it hurt us, and hurt others?

2. Bridger takes a job in a saloon, even though his morals don't agree with it. How does this compromise cause trouble for him?

3. Frank sees things in very simple terms. In what ways does this benefit Bridger? How does it frustrate him? How does God use simple teaching to deepen our relationship with Him?

4. Lola is confident in her abilities to do her job, but not so confident about handling herself in a predominantly male business world. How do traditional roles for men and women still affect us today? Is there a benefit to those roles? How should men and women of God handle business negotiations with the opposite sex?

5. In what ways do Lola and Grace support each other in grief? How does this strengthen their friendship?

6. Ike recognizes Bridger's drive to earn money and uses it for his own gain. What are some indications that the love of money has grown too strong in a person?

7. Mr. Anthony has an instant dislike for Bridger. Have you ever felt that reaction from someone you just met? How did you handle it?

8. How does Bridger's support of Lola's interest in medicine encourage her? Who has shown you that kind of support in seeking your dreams?

9. Ike arrives at Lola's doorstep when she's feeling particularly low. Why does she find it difficult to break all ties with Ike? How do you pull away from a relationship the Lord shows you is not good?

10. Compare Lola and Mattie. How could their similarities form a common bond? What approach could Lola take to win Mattie for the Lord?

11. "Forgive and forget" is a common phrase. Is this truly possible? Does the Lord intend for us to forget the transgressions of others completely? Do you agree with Grace, that our "God-given memory" is to help us stay wary in some cases? Why or why not?

12. Bridger and Frank have very different feelings about their childhood. How does Frank's attitude toward his injury differ from Bridger's? How has each brother been shaped by their father's treatment?

13. Lola's broken engagement to Ike makes her question her ability to discern her feelings for Bridger. Is this reasonable? How can we overcome the memory of a poor choice?

14. Bridger worries about his brother's safety. Is there ever a place for worry in the life of a believer?

15. Grace says, "There's no timeline on love and loss." Do you agree or disagree?

REQUEST YOUR FREE BOOKS!

2 FREE INSPIRATIONAL NOVELS
PLUS 2
FREE
MYSTERY GIFTS

Love Inspired.
HISTORICAL
INSPIRATIONAL HISTORICAL ROMANCE

YES! Please send me 2 FREE Love Inspired® Historical novels and my 2 FREE mystery gifts (gifts are worth about $10). After receiving them, if I don't wish to receive any more books, I can return the shipping statement marked "cancel." If I don't cancel, I will receive 4 brand-new novels every month and be billed just $4.74 per book in the U.S. or $5.24 per book in Canada. That's a saving of at least 21% off the cover price. It's quite a bargain! Shipping and handling is just 50¢ per book in the U.S. and 75¢ per book in Canada.* I understand that accepting the 2 free books and gifts places me under no obligation to buy anything. I can always return a shipment and cancel at any time. Even if I never buy another book, the two free books and gifts are mine to keep forever.

102/302 IDN F5CN

Name	(PLEASE PRINT)	

Address		Apt. #

City	State/Prov.	Zip/Postal Code

Signature (if under 18, a parent or guardian must sign)

Mail to the Harlequin® Reader Service:
IN U.S.A.: P.O. Box 1867, Buffalo, NY 14240-1867
IN CANADA: P.O. Box 609, Fort Erie, Ontario L2A 5X3

Want to try two free books from another series?
Call 1-800-873-8635 or visit www.ReaderService.com.

* Terms and prices subject to change without notice. Prices do not include applicable taxes. Sales tax applicable in N.Y. Canadian residents will be charged applicable taxes. Offer not valid in Quebec. This offer is limited to one order per household. Not valid for current subscribers to Love Inspired Historical books. All orders subject to credit approval. Credit or debit balances in a customer's account(s) may be offset by any other outstanding balance owed by or to the customer. Please allow 4 to 6 weeks for delivery. Offer available while quantities last.

Your Privacy—The Harlequin® Reader Service is committed to protecting your privacy. Our Privacy Policy is available online at www.ReaderService.com or upon request from the Harlequin Reader Service.

We make a portion of our mailing list available to reputable third parties that offer products we believe may interest you. If you prefer that we not exchange your name with third parties, or if you wish to clarify or modify your communication preferences, please visit us at www.ReaderService.com/consumerchoice or write to us at Harlequin Reader Service Preference Service, P.O. Box 9062, Buffalo, NY 14269. Include your complete name and address.

LIH13R